CALLED BY THE REDEEMED

WORLD BREACHER: BOOK 3

JALI HENRY

DIVERSE WORLDS PUBLICATIONS

Copyright © 2020 by Jali Henry

All rights reserved.

No part of this book may be reproduced in any form or by any electronic or mechanical means, including information storage and retrieval systems, without written permission from the author, except for the use of brief quotations in a book review.

❀ Created with Vellum

With thanks to my beta-reader-editor-Mum, Charlotte Mbali and my mother in law, Elizabeth Henry. You are both my biggest supporters on my author journey.

GLOSSARY

Sesotho (*Zulu) / English
Basotho/ An African tribe of people
Bongi/ Poet
Chakalaka/ Tomato-based sauce
Dineo/ Gift
Dintle/ Beauty
Dumela / Hello
Eish/ Expression of surprise
Haiybo/ Expression of surprise
Imphepho/ Ceremonial herb similar to sage
Ithwasa/ Physical and mental illness
Kabelo/ Inheritance
Kgosi/ Sir
Lerato/ Love
Molume/ Uncle
Monghadi/ Mr
Morogo/ Type of spinach
Motsumi/ Seeker
Muti/ Traditional medicine or magic potion
Naledi/ Star

Ngoana/ Child
Nkhono/ Grandmother
Ntate/ Father or Grandfather
Ntsiki*/Bless me
Palechee/ A staple maize meal carbohydrate
Puleng/ Rain
Pumla*/ Rest
Rondavel/ Round, earthen hut with thatched roof
Samp/ Type of carbohydrate
Sangoma/ Shaman
Sotho/ An African tribe of people
Tau/ Lion
Thato/ Will
Thando*/ Love

1
GIADA

W*hack!* Giada's face hit a puddle, splashing dirty rainwater all over her face and top, as she went crashing to the ground. She picked herself up, wiping her face with her hands, as she scowled at the girl who'd just tripped her up. Of all the things that Giada had been expecting from Heaven, being bullied by a bunch of 'mean girls' wasn't one of them. Her first two months had been perfect. She'd met her younger brother, Roberto, again. A smile crept onto her lips as she recalled their reunion. Little Roberto running across the lush grass field outside their house. His beaming face as she swept him up into her arms and nuzzled him with her nose. His look of adoration as he stretched up to put his fingers in her hair and giggled. Roberto had barely been able to believe that she was in Heaven. He'd waited so long for her to join him. He didn't seem to harbour any ill will towards her for not preventing his death. Her younger brother simply idolised her. How had she never noticed before how sweet he was? How much he loved her? Giada sighed.

So many wasted years.

She'd decided right then and there that she'd make up for it. She spent every spare waking moment after that with Roberto. They played together. They went for long walks and had long conversations. Giada felt they were finally having the relationship they should have had as children on Earth. They were not just siblings; they were best friends.

After those blissful first two months, she had to sign up for Redemption School, as all newly-redeemed souls had to. That's when her problems started.

She scowled and shook her head as she brought her thoughts back to the present. She owed it to Roberto to make it work here but it was almost like she was being pushed to fail. Hadn't she already suffered enough in Hell?

The mean girls had verbally attacked her on her very first day. Queen bee, Rika, was at the helm, followed by three other blonde-haired beauties. Giada had never been bullied at school and she'd always thought it was because she was attractive but in the presence of these supermodels, she felt like a frumpy librarian.

On her first day, archangel Gabriel had explained that one of the functions of Redemption School was to help them adjust to the radically different conditions of Heaven. The only thing Giada had adjusted to so far was being bullied for the first time in her life.

Giada dragged her feet along the white pebbled pathway as she headed towards the Redemption School hall. Up ahead groups of angels sat, talking, in the grass surrounding the school.

Giada looked at them with a pang of longing. She felt like the new kid at school, who had arrived mid-year, to find everyone else already in friendship groups. Giada would love to be an angel. They were the cool kids who everyone wanted to be. They got given a whole range of powers, flying, healing, manifestation, telepathy plus they got to fight demons! Even though Giada had been redeemed at the same time as plenty of other damned souls, there were few who were her age. Giada sighed. As a newly-redeemed soul, she had a long way to go before she'd even be considered for angelic promotion. She'd have to complete Redemption School first and the way things were going so far, she'd probably be here for a long time.

Arriving at the school, she looked up at its glittering crystal walls and dome-shaped roof. She walked up the grand steps and through the large, arched entrance into the assembly hall. The hall had a central lectern, surrounded by rows of ascending benches, all made of crystal. Giada slumped down on one of the benches. Rika's gang sat across the room, twittering and giggling as they gave her stink eye. Her heart sank at the prospect of another day dodging abuse from them. How was it even possible that such mean-spirited souls could get to Heaven anyway? Surely, they should still be in Hell?

"Look who it is: Italy's biggest loser," Rika called over at her. Giada felt her blood pressure rising.

Ignore her, ignore her.

She couldn't help herself though, "at least I don't need a group of lookalike fembots to back me up."

Rika's eyes narrowed, "what did you just say?"

"You heard..."

Rika stood up and clenched her fists as she glowered across the room. Giada's heart pounded as she readied herself for another beating.

But the fight never came. They were interrupted by archangel Gabriel, their teacher for the morning's lessons. She swept into the room in a shimmer of white floaty fabric, coppery skin and glittering afro hair tips. Her feline eyes danced with light and amusement. Her entrance was accompanied by angelic choral music which followed wherever she went.

Archangel Gabriel, or 'Gabi' as she liked to be called, carried a trumpet which she now blew into. The chatter in the room immediately went silent and all eyes turned to face her. "Good morning class."

There was a murmur of greeting in reply, the tone of which was less enthusiastic than her own. Her smile dropped, "you don't have to sound so disheartened about it. Today we have arranged a special tour. We are going to take you to the creation vault."

There was a chatter of excitement from the room. Giada felt her brow crease. What was the 'creation vault?' She turned to ask the person sitting next to her and did a double take, inhaling her breath sharply at the shock. He was the most beautiful boy she had ever seen. His high cheekbones descended into a strong jaw and full lips. Her gaze hovered over his lips for a moment. She watched as his tongue wet his lips enticingly. Forcing her gaze upwards, her heart skipped a beat as she met his large, soulful brown eyes. He looked at her quizzically, cocking his head to the side. His eyes displayed a sublime mixture of innocence and wisdom which made her feel almost dizzy. Flicking his floppy brown fringe out of his face, he half smiled at her. Giada felt her cheeks grow warm as she looked away. Her throat suddenly felt very dry and she coughed. She'd entirely forgotten what it was she wanted to ask him. Was he still looking at her? She daren't look back again so she forced her attention back onto Gabi.

"For those of you who don't know, the creation vault houses the spark of creation. An eternal source of power which has the ability to build or destroy worlds. The entirety of creation came from that spark and it continues to be an endless source of power which the Almighty uses according to his infinite grace." Gabi bowed her head and joined her hands together in a gesture of prayer. A few of the other students copied her. Giada shook her head slightly and smiled at the fakeness of these sycophants. A few weeks ago, they'd all been in Hell and now they were falling over themselves to act like the most saintly beings who'd ever existed.

Giada's eyes slid to the side. The boy lounged on the bench with his gangly legs askew. He looked about her age or a little older. His gaze was fixed on Gabi and he sat up, adjusting his jeans as he brought his hand up to clear his throat quietly. His movements had the grace and precision of a thoroughbred stallion.

Who is this boy and how have I never noticed him before?

Giada flicked her eyes back towards Gabi's introduction.

"Archangel Michael, who you've already met, is in charge of security. He will take you down to the vault. He will be here shortly but first I have another announcement to make." Gabi smiled as she looked around the room. "Over the next two weeks you will each be given your graduation mission. Indeed, some of you, those who have been here longer, have already been given a mission. This mission is unique to each person. Since your arrival, we have been watching you and assessing what your special talents are and this is the basis on which we will assign the missions. Completion of the mission means that you will graduate from Redemption School and will then be given your eternal assignment."

Gabi paused as if considering whether to add anything further. She opened her mouth then closed it again before looking at the ground, deep in thought. When she looked back up, she smiled brightly. "Does anyone have any questions?"

Giada's hand shot up. Gabi looked at her and nodded. All eyes turned to look at Giada and she gulped. "Erm, what happens if we fail to complete the mission?"

"You won't fail to complete it. We give missions based on what we know you are capable of achieving."

Giada wasn't at all satisfied with this response. "But, hypothetically, if someone did fail the mission… what would happen?" She had a mounting feeling of dread in her stomach as she anticipated Gabi's response. There was only one reason she could think of why Gabi had been reluctant to answer the first time. It was confirmed as the archangel replied simply.

"You would be sent back to Hell."

A gasp went up from the room followed by a low murmur as the students chattered amongst themselves.

Gabi patted her hands up and down as she tried to regain order. "Settle down, settle down. You have nothing to worry about. It is extremely rare that anyone fails."

Extremely rare but not unheard of.

This was just getting worse and worse.

A hand shot up from another corner of the room. Gabi nodded towards the bald, pot-bellied man who wanted to speak.

"If we get sent back to Hell, would it be eternal damnation?"

Gabi nodded, "you only get one chance to redeem yourselves. If you blow that chance, it doesn't come again."

The room erupted in chatter once more. Giada felt her eyes blur with tears. She turned to look at the boy next to her. He seemed unfazed by the announcement. Almost as if it didn't concern him. Giada couldn't prevent her brow from furrowing briefly in confusion at the boy's lack of anxiety. Maybe he'd already been given his mission and it was dead easy?

She turned back to the front. Gabi was taking more questions from others, but Giada struggled to listen. Her thoughts rushed from one scenario to the next. She could be back in Hell and this time with no way out. At least before, she'd had an unproven and shaky belief that redemption might one day happen. If she returned, all hope would be gone. Memories of the torture rooms flashed into her mind. The agony. The smell of blood sweat and fear. She'd witnessed, and been victim, to the kind of sick depravity that would haunt her for the rest of eternity. She shuddered as she thought about the absence of sunlight. Her nose wrinkled at the memory of the constant smell of sulphur. She could almost smell it now and she gagged. She couldn't go back; she'd do anything to escape that fate. Whatever her mission was, she'd make damn sure she completed it.

2

NALEDI

"Why did you go with them, if you knew what they were going to do?" Naledi asked Thato, her student. Thato sat in the armchair opposite, chewing on her nails as a blush of shame blossomed on her cheeks.

"I like their company, they're good fun," she replied.

"They're dangerous. Especially for you. You know how risky it is to be around drug-takers. If you get high and then engage in spiritual practices ..." Naledi shook her head and pursed her lips, "... you could get possessed by a dark spirit - even a demon."

"But I didn't smoke with them. I never have."

"I'm glad to hear it but you still have to stay away from them." Naledi sensed that she wasn't getting through to Thato, so she leaned forward, making eye contact.

"Look Thato, I know it probably feels flattering to have the attention of these older boys, but they are not good for you."

Thato's eyes widened and she ran a hand over her close-cropped hair. "But they're my only friends."

"Find new friends," Naledi snapped. Then she softened her voice as she saw Thato flinch. The girl was even more vulnerable than Naledi had been when she'd started her training with Motsumi.

Thato had an air of innocence which was enhanced by her sweet features. A gap between her two front teeth and very large eyes which got larger with each scolding.

"I'm just trying to protect you Thato. This is not a game. I am teaching you advanced spiritual practices here. We're getting in touch with other dimensions of reality. There are all sorts of beings floating around in those dimensions, many of which are hostile, and you're not yet equipped to deal with them. The consequences of acquiring a dark spirit could stretch beyond this lifetime. I don't want the stain of your karma on my conscience. You're far too valuable to lose."

Thato bit her lip as she smiled shyly. Naledi knew that her student responded well to praise but these weren't idle words. Thato was indeed talented, and it would be a shame to waste that talent on teenage curiosity and a careless quest for excitement.

Naledi continued, "you have to decide for yourself what you want the most. Think about how you longed to train as a sangoma and ask yourself if you're willing to risk throwing it all away for the company of these so-called friends. Do you understand what I'm saying?"

Thato looked down at her lap as she nodded. "Yes, teacher."

Naledi's lips twitched as she suppressed a smile. She'd told Thato again and again that she could just call her 'Naledi', but her student still sometimes fell into the schoolgirl habit of calling her 'teacher'. She supposed it was a good sign. It showed that Thato respected her.

Another thought came to Naledi and she addressed it immediately. "None of them have touched you, have they?"

"Touched me?" Thato's face, at first, scrunched up with confusion, then settled into understanding. "No, not in that way. I'm still a virgin."

Naledi exhaled, "good. That's another reason why it's best to stay away from them. I don't mind you hanging out with well-behaved boys from good, Christian families. Boys who will respect your virtue and understand the reasons for it."

"You mean boys like Tau and Kabelo?"

"Exactly." Naledi felt a smile creep to her lips as it always did whenever she thought of Tau. An image of her handsome boyfriend smiling at her flashed into her head. She shook the thought from her head and looked at Thato. "Go on, go and join the others. You can probably still catch up with them. But remember what I've said, won't you?"

"Yes teacher...I mean, Naledi. Thank you." Thato stood up and rushed out of the front door. The poor girl was likely relieved that the grilling was over.

Naledi walked over to the window and watched her running over the grassy hills to catch up with her classmates. Naledi had sent her students out to collect wild herbs to make smudging sticks with. The sticks had various uses depending on which herbs were collected. Some herbs purified the workspace of any dark or malevolent energy. Other herbs invited the ancestors to join them in spirit. Whilst others helped to induce trance states of mind necessary for visionary journeying. Naledi pulled her blanket around her shoulders. She'd definitely felt the arrival of cooler weather as they were now approaching winter. Thato joined the other girls and Naledi watched them walk over the hill and disappear into the valley on the other side. She felt her body relax as Thato was now in the safe hands of her peers.

Naledi sat back down to finish her tea and reflect on the conversation she'd had with her student. When she'd decided to accept Thato as her first student, she'd had no idea what a challenge it would be. There was no denying the girl was gifted. She already communicated with the dead as easily as if they were still living. Spirits flocked to her and she was so open and trusting that she simply let them close. Indeed, she showed signs of becoming a trance medium one day. This would make her a powerful and much sought-after sangoma. She would have to first learn how to close herself off from dark spirits but the potential for greatness was there. However, Thato was also impressionable and immature. Naledi wondered if she'd made a mistake by accepting her as a student when she was only twelve years old. But it was not Naledi's place to decide if Thato was ready or not: the ancestors had decided, and their will must be obeyed. The ancestors had called Thato and if she'd ignored their call, she would've eventually gone mad.

After Naledi had accepted Thato, word had quickly spread. Before long another girl, Ntsiki, had turned up on her doorstep, requesting training. Then after that Thando and Pumla had arrived. Naledi now had four students and it was getting close to the point where she would have to start turning people away. She couldn't manage more than five. After all, she still had Dineo and Puleng to take care of. Looking after her younger sisters would always be her first priority. Plus, lessons had to be conducted at weekends and in the evening, after the school day had finished. This meant that they had very little time and the more students who joined, the less time they had.

Naledi found that training her initiates was a role that was part teacher, part counsellor and part mother. It was the 'mother' bit that was hard. Naledi wasn't a mother - she was barely out of childhood herself having just turned fifteen. Adults who didn't know her had recently started addressing her as 'sis' which denoted an equal instead of 'ngoana' which meant 'child'. The first time it had happened Naledi had blushed and opened her mouth to correct the stranger but then closed it again.

THE GIRLS WERE STILL out collecting herbs and Naledi had just finished cleaning the kitchen when she heard a knock on the door. She shouted out, "coming!" Drying her hands on a tea towel, she went to answer it.

In the door stood a nicely plump girl with a round face and eyes that invited a smile as they twinkled and shone. She wore a head scarf and simple cotton dress. Naledi noted that her shoes were in good condition - a sign that she wasn't destitute or from a family trapped in extreme poverty.

Naledi's eyebrows rose, "yes, can I help you?"

The girl's smile widened, exposing a row of perfect white teeth. Giving Naledi the impression that she was brimming with an abundance of good health.

"I'm Bongi," the girl extended her hand and Naledi took it.

"Naledi," she replied. Bongi had a very strong grip and shook Naledi's hand vigorously.

"I've come to train with you."

Naledi's eyebrows rose, "have you indeed?"

Bongi's eyes shifted from side to side, apparently realising the error of her presumption. She backtracked quickly. "I've heard that you are still accepting students. I have been training with another sangoma for some time so my ithwasa symptoms have already subsided."

Bongi's expression darkened. "My teacher's health has declined, and she's had to let me go. She can no longer train me. Perhaps you have heard of her? Ma' Lebone?"

Naledi shook her head, "I'm not well known in sangoma circles…"

"Oh, but you are. I've heard so much about you. I'm very excited to finally meet the girl behind the legend."

Naledi blushed and smiled shyly. "You're just trying to flatter me."

"No really. People talk about you all over Lesotho. I travelled for two days to get here."

"Where are you staying?"

"At Ma' Ruthe's"

Of course. Where else would she be staying? Ma' Ruthe's was the only place that had rooms for travellers to rent. It meant that Bongi didn't have any relatives nearby. It also meant she was wealthy enough to afford the rent. Naledi wondered what the source of her wealth could be. It was rude to ask though. If she decided to take her on as a student, she'd find out sooner or later. She'd have to test Bongi first though. So far, each student who'd arrived at Naledi's door had been genuine, but she had to eliminate the possibility that the girl was either a wannabe time-waster or simply delusional.

"Please come in." Naledi held the door open and gestured for Bongi to take a seat on the sofa.

"Can I get you something to drink?"

"Yes please, a glass of water."

Naledi went to the kitchen to get a glass of ice-cold water. Walking back to the sitting room she mused that life had certainly got better for her since inheriting Motsumi's money and house. Such previously unimaginable luxuries as a fridge were now commonplace for her. She handed the water to Bongi then sat down in the armchair opposite. Meeting Bongi's eyes, she asked, "tell me a bit more about yourself."

Bongi explained that she had grown up in a large family in a small town on the other side of Maseru. She was the middle child of six and had three older sisters and two younger brothers. At sixteen, she was older than Naledi and she had been afflicted with ithwasa at the age of fourteen. She'd started training with Ma' Lebone soon after and had progressed to the point that she was able to start accepting clients. Establishing a small healing practice, she'd had a steady flow of clients. The money she'd saved had allowed her to travel to Marula in search of Naledi.

"It sounds like you're already doing well for yourself. Why do you want to train further with me?" Naledi asked

"I haven't mastered all of the disciplines yet. I'm a good healer and I can also journey and connect with spirits but there's still so much more I want to learn. My ultimate goal is manifestation."

Ah yes, manifestation. The highest and most sought-after of the sangoma powers.

Naledi cast her mind back to how she had felt the first time she'd acquired the skill of manifestation. The power of being able to call into being whatever she needed at any one time. It was a godlike feeling and for that reason, Naledi used it seldom. She didn't want to offend God by competing with his majesty. Fortunately, manifestation, for her at least, had an in-built limitation: if she attempted it more than twice a day, she'd begin to experience ithwasa symptoms. And if she ignored this warning, she'd reach full-blown psychosis. This had only happened once since coming fully into her powers, but it had been enough to stop her from ever attempting it again. Dineo and Puleng needed her too much.

Naledi studied Bongi for any signs of deception. She had an

honest face and Naledi liked her already. "You understand that I will have to test your skills?"

"I would expect nothing less," Bongi replied.

"Okay then. I have four other students. They are out collecting herbs, but they should be back any minute. I will accept you on a trial basis. I'll spend the first session getting to know you and seeing what you can do. If I decide to accept you, we will perform the binding ceremony. How does that sound?"

Bongi gulped down a big swig of water. "It sounds good."

"Has your old teacher released you from bondage?"

"Yes, Naledi."

Naledi bristled slightly, raising her eyebrows. Bongi realised her error.

"Yes, teacher."

Naledi smiled and said, "it's okay, you can call me Naledi." She didn't mind her students calling her Naledi and in fact invited each of them to do so. But Bongi had gone straight to using her name before any such invitation and this gave Naledi a slight red flag. Naledi pushed the thought to one side. Bongi had an easy way about her; an affability. Perhaps it was just her personality? Naledi hoped she hadn't taken on another student who would give her as many headaches as Thato.

3
GIADA

Giada was still reeling from archangel Gabriel's announcement when archangel Michael arrived. Walking into the room, his stern expression, issued from skin the colour of jet stones, was in stark contrast to Gabi's infectious smile. Michael had the kind of presence whereby he didn't have to say a word to get people's attention. As he entered, the entire room went silent and all eyes were on him. He wore his 'sword of righteousness' in a scabbard, slung diagonally, across his robes. Giada had learnt that all archangels had a magical tool which complemented their eternal assignment. Gabi was God's messenger and so she had the 'trumpet of truth' which, when blown, could be heard anywhere in the universe that she wanted. Michael's sword could slay the immortal forces of evil: demons, dark entities and other malevolent supernatural creatures.

Michael stood next to Gabi and greeted the room. The lacklustre response would've deterred even the most boisterous entertainer. Michael raised his eyebrows but nevertheless ploughed on.

"As Gabi has already explained, I am here to take you down to the creation vault. We will now proceed to the Hall of Creation. The entrance down to the vaults is narrow so we will go in small groups of four at a time. I will take each group down whilst the rest of you stay in the hall with Gabi." Michael smiled, "are there any questions?"

Rika's hand shot up, "can we choose our own groups?"

Michael nodded, "You may. We'll leave you to divide yourselves into groups for a few minutes."

Rika mouthed, 'yes' and shook her fist in celebration. Her three friends beamed and high-fived each other.

Giada rolled her eyes. It was like watching a group of frat boy 'bros'.

Inside her chest she felt a flutter of fear
What if nobody picks me?

The room was now filled with chatter as people busied themselves with finding a group. Giada casually looked around, feigning indifference. She made a conscious effort not to look at the boy. She turned to the person sitting the other side of her. It was an old woman who Giada hadn't met before. The woman smiled at her,

"Would you like to go with me? I'm Irene. What's your name, dear?"

Giada smiled back, relieved that Irene had made the first move, "Giada."

"Do you mind if I join you?" a deep voice on her right said.
It's him.

Giada turned to see that the boy had stood up and was leaning forward slightly. He was very tall and broad shouldered. An intoxicating smell of maple syrup and musk wafted across her nose as he moved. Giada had never smelt anything more enticing.

"I'm Luke," he stuck out his hand. Giada looked at it, noticing how the veins of his forearms stood out against his muscle. She scrambled to her feet and took his hand. The minute his hand touched hers, an electrical charge ran down her entire body. Giada's breath caught in her throat and she shivered. She felt the hairs on her arms stand up. Looking into his eyes, Giada hoped to God she wasn't blushing as obviously as she felt she was. The buzz of noise from the rest of the room melted away and it was just the two of them: standing in dead silence.

Am I still breathing? Breathe, Giada, breathe!

Giada blinked as she struggled to keep her mind on the simple task of introducing herself.

"I'm Giada."

"So, how long have you been here, Giada?"

"Just over two months."

"Oh, you've just arrived. I remember my first few months…" his eyes assumed a faraway expression and a slight smile before his smile disappeared abruptly. He raised one eyebrow. "It's not all that easy at the start, is it?"

Giada's brow furrowed before she smiled and relaxed her shoulders. This was the first time she'd heard anyone say anything even slightly negative about Heaven and it made Luke even more intriguing to her. "You're right, it's not," she replied.

Luke held her gaze for a moment longer before apparently remembering Irene. He looked over Giada's head at the old woman still sitting behind. "How about you, Irene, are you a newbie too?"

"Not really dear. I've been here three months. I've already been given my mission."

Luke's eyes widened and he grinned. "Really? Me too."

Giada's head whipped from Irene to Luke. "How long have you been here?"

"Four months."

Giada's mouth dropped open, but she closed it again quickly.

Impossible! How has he been here this entire time and I've never noticed him?

She carefully worded her next question, calming her expression, in an effort to obscure the fact that she was already obsessed with him. "What are you still doing in Redemption School? I thought you would've graduated by now?"

Luke shrugged and flicked his hair out of his dreamy eyes again, making Giada feel slightly dizzy. "Everyone graduates at different rates. It depends what assignment you're up for. If I complete my mission, I'll be part of Michael's elite team."

Irene and Giada exchanged a look. Michael's elite team was the heavenly equivalent of the military special forces. They were the angels sent in as spies or specialised soldiers against the forces of Hell. Giada reflected that the angels which had taken out Sehloho in the failed resurrection would have been Michael's elite team.

Irene smiled warmly as she addressed Luke, "very impressive, young man." She looked around the room, "we need one more person. I'll go and see who still needs a group." Irene walked off leaving Giada and Luke alone.

Giada felt unbearably awkward. She was never lost for words, but Luke's heartbreaking looks were like kryptonite to her superman charisma.

Luke looked at her, "I'm glad she's gone. To tell you the truth, I've been looking for an opportunity to meet you."

Giada was flabbergasted, "you have?"

"Yes. I wanted to meet and congratulate the girl who helped to take out the Countess. That's a big deal you know. Michael's team has been trying to get to her for years."

Giada smiled at the compliment, "well, it was mainly Naledi, the human breacher, I just happened to be there."

"Come on, you're being modest. I heard you had a hand in Sehloho's death too."

"Not exactly a hand, well sort of... Wait - how do you know all this about me?"

"Michael's team makes regular trips to the Akashic realm. He knows everything about everyone."

"Yes... I see... Makes sense," Giada mumbled, hating herself. Her normal wit, charm and eloquence had completely deserted her.

Pull yourself together, Giada

Thankfully Irene reappeared with another woman. A middle-aged, honey-complexioned woman, wearing a headscarf. The woman introduced herself as Aisha. She was another relative newcomer, having been redeemed at about the same time as Giada.

"This is exciting, isn't it!" Aisha's long-lashed, dark brown eyes twinkled.

Giada nodded and smiled but inside she was thinking that she would have felt a lot more excited without the cloud of eternal damnation hanging over her head.

The sound of Gabi's horn drew silence from the room. Michael clapped his hands together. "Right, let's go."

THE HALL of Creation was a good walk from the Redemption School. Giada would have said it was about half an hour, but it was impossible to say for sure since time operated differently in Heaven. Time didn't exist in the same linear, measurable fashion and Roberto had told her that after a while she would start forgetting about it. On the way, Luke walked next to Giada whilst Irene and Aisha walked behind chatting.

"Do you have any family here, Giada?"

"Yes, my younger brother, Roberto and my Mama. I've also met a lot of aunts and uncles and ancestors but it's like they're strangers. How about you?"

Luke chuckled, "I know, right. All those dead ancestors who turn up in Heaven and want to get to know you.... I suppose it'll be like that for us one day. I don't have any close family here though. They're all still alive - well, all except my twin brother. He's in Hell, he hasn't been redeemed yet."

Giada didn't know what to say. "I... I'm sorry. That must be hard for you."

Luke sighed. "It is but you know the system. Everyone has to get here by themselves. I wish I could help him but ..." His voice trailed off.

Giada wanted to ask how they'd both died but she didn't want to keep the conversation on a topic that was likely very painful for him.

"It's okay. I tell myself that I'm making it easier for him when he arrives. He won't have to struggle to make friends and fit in like I did."

He struggled to make friends and fit in?!

Giada kept it casual, "it sure seems like everyone is already in a friendship group." She added a little laugh at the end for good measure.

Luke stopped walking and turned to face her. He touched her arm lightly, causing her stomach to dissolve into her pelvis. She looked up at him.

"Giada, I've seen Rika and her friends being mean to you. You should ignore them. They're just jealous because they've heard about your reputation. It might feel like you're all alone right now but you're not." He ran his fingers through his hair. Giada looked at his hair and wondered what it would feel like to run her fingers through it. It looked so soft and bouncy. It probably smelled as good as he did. An image of her putting one hand through his hair and clenching her fingers as she pulled his lips towards hers flashed into her mind. She shook the thought away as Luke continued.

"What I'm saying is, don't waste your time worrying about a bunch of bullies. Once you get given your mission, concentrate on completing it and before you know it, you'll realise you fit in just fine here."

Giada was stunned. Was she that easy to read? He had articulated everything that she'd been thinking and feeling so precisely that it was like he was reading her thoughts. She knew that angels *could* actually read thoughts but only on Earth. Plus, Luke wasn't an angel yet. He would be when he completed his mission and joined Michael's elite team but right now, he was still just a redeemed soul.

"Thanks," Giada managed to whisper as she looked into his eyes.

Irene and Aisha bustled past them. "Come on, we'll get left behind." Aisha said as she shooed them along with her hands.

Ahead of them, Giada saw the Hall of Creation. It was a vast, donut-shaped building made entirely of crystal. Out of the central hole, bright white light shone towards the blue sky. Giada lifted her hand to shield her eyes. As she squinted, she saw the vaguest outline of iridescent fractal crystals, bouncing against each other as they moved in and out of the light.

"It's beautiful, isn't it?" Luke murmured.

"Why does it have a hole in the middle like that?" Giada asked.

"It represents eternity."

Giada and her group joined the rest of her class inside the hall. At the centre of the room, a couple of tall angels stood on either side of an open trapdoor. Steps led down from the trapdoor and Michael was nowhere to be seen. When she asked, a nearby student told her that he'd already taken the first group down. After a while Michael reappeared and took the next group down. Eventually it was time for Giada's group to go and Michael led them down the narrow steps. What struck Giada immediately was that although they were descending, it wasn't getting any darker. In fact, it was just the opposite. The further down they walked the lighter it became. It was an unnatural brightness which almost hurt Giada's retinas. She squinted and carried on walking. Behind her, she felt Luke's warm breath on the back of her neck as he leant closer to her. "You'll get used to the light".

Had Luke been here before? What was the deal with him? Why did he know so much? And if he was so knowledgeable, why was he in Redemption School?

Luke was right. Before long Giada's eyes settled down and she felt energised and excited. Were these feelings real, or the rejuvenating effects of being near the centre of creation, she wondered? The scent of jasmine hung in the air. It instantly transported Giada back to a road she used to walk along on the way to school in Rome. Jasmine plants hung over a wall there and it fragranced the entire street.

They reached the bottom of the stairs and Michael gestured for them to gather around a circular glass tube with railings around the outside. Inside the tube a shining crystal of light floated in the air. It turned around, beaming rainbow shards of light all across the room.

Michael cleared his throat. "Here we are. This is the spark of creation."

Irene asked, "I was expecting it to be a lot smaller. The size of a spark of fire maybe."

"Your response is very perceptive," Michael replied. "'Spark' is somewhat of a misnomer. There are billions of atoms inside that crystal. Each atom is powerful enough to create entire universes."

"Wow!" Giada moved closer to the glass tube. "Can I touch the tube?"

"Go ahead," Michael replied.

She put her hand to the tube and felt a warm, rhythmic vibration. It felt almost like putting a hand on an animal's chest - as if the crystal was alive. She looked at Michael and he anticipated her reaction.

"That's life itself that you're feeling. The rhythm of life which exists in all of us and all of creation."

"Why is it inside the tube?" Aisha asked.

"It's too powerful to be held by anyone except the Almighty. If any lesser beings tried to touch it, they would be obliterated immediately."

Irene asked the question that they were all thinking. "Is it safe down here? That seems like a lot of power to be contained in one place."

"Why should we worry?" Michael replied. "Access to Heaven is tightly controlled. Only the most worthy souls make it here. Besides, like I said, nobody except God can touch it and live."

"In that case, why do you have the guards outside?" Aisha asked.

Michael's lips twitched slightly. "It's an extra precaution but it's not really necessary. We've never had any trouble before. Plus, this entire room is wired up to alarms. If even a single atom gets disturbed, it goes off and summons me and my entire team. We've had a couple of false alarms over the millennia but nothing more than that."

This seemed to satisfy Aisha and the others, but Giada still wasn't convinced. If there was one thing her time in Hell had taught her, it was to always be prepared for the unexpected. Or to put it another way: shit happens.

4
GIADA

After visiting the Hall of Creation, they had an angel skills class. Not all of them would become angels but they nonetheless all had to learn the skills. This was so that the archangels could observe which of them was particularly gifted and grant wings to those who showed merit. Today's angel skills lesson was levitation. Giada was excited as it was their first lesson on a skill which she had been looking forward to learning. Archangel Gabriel was leading the lesson. The class sat in the assembly hall listening to her explain that most of the skills angels have are actually innate in humans too, but they've simply allowed them to become dormant. She then explained the technique which involved quietening the mind and having absolute faith that levitation would happen.

Giada had learnt a good technique for quietening the mind when she was in Hell although she still wasn't great at it. Her friend Aaron had taught her the method as a way of distracting her mind from pain whilst being tortured by demons. After Gabi completed her instruction, she told the class to separate into the same groups as before so that they could practice. Giada felt a frisson of excitement at getting the opportunity to spend more time with Luke.

"Right, shall we just get straight into it? We just all try it and then discuss afterwards, once Gabi sounds the trumpet?" Aisha suggested.

Giada shrugged, "I guess so."

The others all agreed, and Giada settled into the bench and began relaxing her body with her eyes closed. She did a basic body scan, focusing on each part of her body and relaxing that part before moving onto the next. Once she'd finished scanning her body she focused on her breath. She counted her breaths up to ten and then started again. The first couple of rounds went fine but by round three her mind began to wander. The room was quiet, but Giada's mind still found a way of latching onto the smallest noises. In the corner a man kept coughing - what was wrong with him? Couldn't he go and cough outside?

That's not fair, he can't help it if he coughs. Oh no! Now I'm thinking again. Back to the breath...

Giada realised she was allowing herself to get irritated each time her mind wandered.

Don't get irritated.

Then she realised she was getting irritated *about* getting irritated.

Don't get irritated. Stay calm.

Now somebody else was fidgeting and wearing clothes which rustled. What kind of clothes rustled anyway?

Oh, this is impossible!

Giada opened her eyes a crack to see how the others were doing. They all seemed to be deep in meditation. Luke's eyes were closed, allowing her to study his beautiful face undetected. She drank in his long eyelashes, lightly closed; the curve of his jaw; the movement of his Adam's apple, as he swallowed; his broad chest, as it rose and fell. He really was breathtaking. She brought her eyes back up to his face and froze as his eyelids fluttered open. His eyes twinkled with a mischievous smile, knowing that he'd caught her staring at him. Her eyes widened slightly in shock before she jammed them shut again. It felt like she was tensing her eye muscles in an effort to keep them tightly closed. She willed her face to relax but were her shoulders tensing now? They were! Her heart was also thumping way too much to reach a meditative state.

Oh balls!

She'd completely messed this up. Now Luke would think she was a weirdo. She took a deep breath, trying her best to calm her breathing. Was he still looking at her? Should she open her eyes to check? She was desperate to open her eyes and check. No! Then if he *was* still looking at her, she'd look like even more of a weirdo. She tried to calm her mind, but her thoughts returned to her embarrassment again and again and eventually she admitted defeat and opened her eyes with a sigh of exasperation.

When Giada opened her eyes, she was amazed to see about half of the room levitating, including both Aisha and Irene! How had they all managed to do it so quickly? And on the very first attempt?! Giada was not having this. She tried again. But she just couldn't. She wasn't even able to clear her mind, let alone trust in her ability to levitate. It seemed like the harder she tried, the more it slipped away from her. Giada opened her eyes once more and her jaw dropped open: Rika and her friends were all levitating too! She gritted her teeth and forced her eyes closed but it was too late.

Gabi sounded the trumpet announcing the end of the session.

"Start to wiggles your fingers and toes. Allow yourself to come back to the room slowly." Gabi's voice echoed around the room.

'Come back to the room?' I never went anywhere. Giada thought bitterly.

All around her, Giada heard the sounds of excited students gushing about their success. She heard laughter and even clapping from some groups. Reaching both hands up, she rubbed her forehead. Turning to Irene, Giada plastered a bright smile on her face.

"How did you get on?" She knew full well how Irene had got on but, if her enquiry deflected attention from her own failure, and her embarrassing crush on Luke, it was welcome.

Irene clapped her hands together as her face cracked open in a huge grin. "It was wonderful. All of a sudden, I just started floating. It was the best feeling ever and so easy. Much easier than I was expecting, don't you agree?"

Giada felt herself blush, "well, erm, actually..."

Luke interrupted, "I found it very hard. I wasn't successful at all." He looked down then peeked discreetly at Giada from under his long lashes and gave her a slight smile before looking back at Irene.

"Well, I'm sure you'll manage next time, dear. How about you Aisha?"

Giada was no longer listening. Luke had just rescued her from embarrassment. That either meant he was a really nice guy who wanted to help her or maybe, just maybe, he liked her too. Butterflies burst free inside her stomach and her chest tingled. She realised she was smiling like a simpleton and forced her mind back onto the conversation. But inside she was still bubbling over.

She had a chance with the boy of her dreams.

AFTER THE SESSION Rika and her friends made a beeline for Giada. Rika's white gold hair and sinewy frame were in stark contrast to her own curvy body and mousy brown hair. Giada's heart sank as she imagined Luke comparing her unfavourably to Rika and her supermodel friends.

"What do you want, Rika?" Giada's voice came out weary and defeated.

"We just wanted to know how you got on with the levitation. Oh, that's right - you failed!" Rika cackled along with her friends.

"How would you even know that if you had your eyes closed?" Giada spat, more venomously than she had intended.

"I got so good at it towards the end of the session that I did it with my eyes open - like a real angel."

Giada clenched her fists and glowered at her. She'd love to punch Rika in the face right about now. Would that get her sent back to Hell? It might even be worth it just to wipe that smug smile off her face.

Irene shuffled over and tapped Giada on the hand. "Don't worry, lots of other people didn't get it today. I'm sure you'll do it next time."

"Come on let's go." Rika motioned for her groupies to join her and they sashayed out of the room. As they walked past her, one of them said 'loser' in a not-so-quiet whisper. Hatred bubbled in Giada's veins.

She looked at the sunlight reflecting off Rika's perfect golden skin. She actually did look like an angel. It was just a pity her soul was as nasty and dark as a demon's.

She waited until they'd passed before hurrying out. She wanted to put as much distance between her and the source of her shame as was possible. Why had everyone else found it so easy? Was there something wrong with her? She'd meditated before and had found it much easier than today.

It was Luke.

His handsome presence had completely disarmed her. She cursed herself. It wasn't like her to get so giddy over a boy. She must sit well away from him next time or at this rate she'd never graduate from Redemption School.

Giada was so deep in thought that she didn't notice Luke jogging to catch up with her. When he appeared at her side she was surprised and delighted, but still embarrassed. She looked into the middle distance, fixing her eyes on anything that would scramble her thoughts less than his divine face.

"I was thinking..." he started, "...as we both found levitation hard, perhaps we could practice together before the next session?"

Giada could hardly believe her ears. He wanted to practice *together*... with *her*?

She tried to keep it cool. She turned to him and stopped walking. "Erm, sure, that sounds like a good idea."

Luke smiled, "How about we meet at the fountain of eternity at sundown today?"

Giada gulped and nodded, momentarily losing the power of speech as she got lost in his brown eyes.

Say something... Anything... Speak Giada, for the love of God!

"Sure, I'll see you there" she eventually forced out, in a voice that sounded way more squeaky than it normally did.

"Great, I'll see you later." Luke jogged off. She watched his body moving up and down rhythmically with the ease and grace of an elite athlete. Giada frowned, immediately regretting her acceptance. How was she going to practice levitation with Luke when she could barely function properly around him?

5
GIADA

After Redemption School, Giada walked home. She lived with her mother and brother in a modest townhouse in the suburbs of Celestial West. Outside the house was a garden filled with strawberries which her mother tended to during the day. Giada opened the white picket fence and stroked their cat, Oscar, who always came and greeted her by rubbing along her legs and purring. He was the neediest cat she had ever come across. Roberto ran outside and made eye contact with Oscar. An unspoken communication passed between him and the cat. Oscar snarled at Roberto as if he was offended then padded off.

"What did you say to him?" Giada asked. She found Roberto's ability, to telepathically communicate with animals, fascinating. It was a by-product of his eternal assignment on the animal husbandry team. Just like her mother's ability to communicate with plants was part of her eternal assignment as a strawberry grower.

"I just teased him about his crush on you." Roberto answered.

Giada laughed, "No wonder he looked so pissed off."

Roberto walked up the path and hugged her. Warmth spread throughout her chest and she ruffled his hair.

"How was your day, Squirt?"

"Amazing! Pin Pin gave birth to a new litter today. They are so cute; you should come and have a look tomorrow." Roberto's face lit up as it always did when he talked about the bunny rabbits he looked after.

"Yeah, maybe." Giada's smile faded from her face as her thoughts did a quick recap of her day.

Roberto frowned. "What's wrong?"

She breathed in deeply and painted her smile back on. "Nothing, I was just thinking."

"Thinking about what?"

Giada gazed over the top of Roberto's head as she tried to formulate her thoughts in a way that would make sense to him. "Did you struggle with fitting in when you first arrived here?"

Roberto scratched his head. "Not really. All the other kids in Heaven are super excited to be here and just want to play and be friends with everyone."

Giada felt a stab of jealousy. "Well it's not like that for older kids, I can tell you."

Roberto's little face crumpled with anguish. "Aren't you happy here?"

"I'm not unhappy," Giada hastily replied. "I love it here. I'm just finding Redemption School really challenging. The tasks are tough and not everyone is as friendly as... as you say the younger children are."

Roberto's shoulders relaxed and he looked towards the sky. When he spoke again, his voice sounded much older. "People don't always know who they really are. Some people here are still trapped in the same thought patterns they had when they were in Hell - or on Earth."

Giada looked at him. "But why would they get redeemed if they still have lessons to learn?"

"We all have lessons to learn, even in Heaven. Redemption is about more than the person being redeemed. It's also about soul connections. Some are here solely to test others and such souls don't even know that is their purpose. We are all unwitting participants in the eternal wheel of karma." He looked deeply into her eyes as he said the last two sentences in a way that made her feel he was no longer talking just about heavenly redemption.

Giada felt her breathing increase as her pulse quickened. Since she'd been redeemed, she hadn't yet talked to Roberto about his final moments on Earth. Giada had told herself they didn't have to. He'd obviously forgiven her, so what was the point of dredging through the muck of the past? She realised now though that they did need to discuss it. Not because Roberto expected it, but because she needed it. She had to know if he forgave her, and not just in some assumed way. She had to actually hear him say the words. If she didn't, there would always be an unspoken chasm that existed between them. Giada had been lying to herself. The real reason why she hadn't brought up her past sin was that she was scared. Their relationship was so good now; she was so happy; she didn't want to rock the boat. But focusing on the calm waters around her, while closing her eyes to the storm clouds overhead was lunacy. The time had come to talk to him.

"Roberto..." she began, then stopped. It felt like the words had literally closed her throat. She coughed as beads of sweat rolled down the side of her face.

He looked at her and furrowed his brow. "Are you alright? You've gone pale."

She nodded then took a deep breath and tried again. Looking him dead in the eyes she said. "I'm sorry Roberto. I'm sorry I let you die. I'm sorry I treated you so meanly when you were alive." Tears prickled at her eyes and she sniffed but she had to continue. If she didn't get this all out now, she never would. "I'm sorry.... I'm so sorry". The tears cascaded over her eyes and down her cheeks, splashing onto her top as she looked down. Waves of pain radiated throughout her body and once again, she wished she could take back what she'd done.

Roberto spoke quietly. "It's okay Giada, it's..."

She interrupted him. "No, please. Let me finish." She took a few loud, deep breaths and looked towards the sky. "When I was little,

Mama and Papa doted on me, but after you were born things changed. I felt like they loved you more than me and I hated you for it. I wished you would die." Giada's voice came out as a whisper, "I even prayed for it." She shook her head as if trying to exorcise the memories and her dark deeds. "When I saw you, with your neck caught in the curtain chord, I... I dunno, I guess I didn't think it through fully. If I had, I never would've done what I did but when I saw you there, a voice inside me said *this is my chance to be loved. This is my chance to be the favourite child again* and I listened to that voice... so help me I listened." A strangulated yelp of pain came unbidden from Giada's lips as she melted to the floor in a puddle of shame and salty tears.

Roberto knelt down next to her and enclosed her in a hug, his small hands rubbing her back and shoulders. For a few moments they didn't speak. They just sat there, with Roberto comforting her. This made Giada feel even more ashamed. She was the one who had wronged him and yet here he was comforting her. Giada didn't mention that she now knew the Countess had sin-baited her into doing what she did. She didn't want Roberto to think she was trying to dodge the blame. After all, she was still accountable. The Countess may have nudged her, but Giada had still had free will. She could've ignored that voice. If only she'd ignored that voice.

As these thoughts raged through Giada's mind, Roberto pulled back from her and lifted her chin with his little index finger. He looked deep into her eyes. "I forgive you Giada, but you have to forgive yourself. You were a child."

"So were you!"

"I know but we both had our parts to play in our own destinies. Part of my destiny was to die in front of you. Part of your destiny was to learn from it. You've done a lot of work to get here. You've suffered enough. Now it's time for you to let it go."

Giada let his words wash over her like a cleansing balm. In Heaven, people's bodies maintained the same physical age they'd had on Earth. Although Roberto still looked like a six-year-old boy, he was so much wiser. The more Giada got to know him, the more she realised that he had been the best teacher she ever could've had on Earth and he was still teaching her now. She wasn't surprised her parents had loved him so much: Roberto was one of the most amazing human beings Giada had ever met.

She nodded and dried her tears and he brought her in close for another hug.

"Now, tell me more about your struggle to fit in. I sense there's more to this than you're telling me."

Giada smiled and nodded as she closed her eyes in relief. It felt like a weight had lifted off her shoulders. She'd broached the topic she'd most feared with him and he still loved her anyway. She didn't deserve him, but she was so glad that he didn't feel the same way. Giada started again, from the beginning, telling Roberto more about her lack of friends and her worries over not achieving levitation. She even told him about Luke. They talked like soulmates until the shadows were long and the honey golden rays of dusk sun danced over their skin.

6

THATO

Thato collapsed onto her back, laughing as she looked up at the cyan African sky. White clouds drifted slowly by and she watched the 'V' of a flock of geese making its way through the air. She turned her head to look at Menzi who'd passed out next to her. An empty bottle of beer rested in his half open hand. He was already drunk, and it was just past lunchtime. The others were standing around chatting about something that didn't invite her attention as much as the warm soft ground. If she stood up her head spun unpleasantly but when she lay down, she felt like she was in Heaven. Her entire body was floating, all alone, in the cosmos. She felt held and protected like she never had before. Thato didn't even care about the ants which crawled over her ankles with free abandon. They were probably biting her, but she was so comfortable, she didn't want to move. She wanted to lie there forever, watching the fluffy clouds make their slow pilgrimage through the sky.

"Hey, Thato, do you want a pull of this?" Amose called out to her. He staggered over, tripping on a tuft of rough, yellow grass as he bent down to hand her the rolled up joint.

Thato reluctantly hoisted herself up to sitting and reached forwards, "sure". She took the joint and drew in a long, slow inhale.

Drawing the pungent smoke deep into her lungs. Then she coughed and spluttered as she exhaled. The smoke stung her eyes and she squinted and waved her hand in front of her face as she passed the joint back to Amose.

"Still too strong for you, huh?" he laughed and went back to the other boys. "You'll get used to it," he called over his shoulder.

Thato sank back to the floor. She was having so much fun. She loved spending time with Amose and the others. Thato had never really got on well with girls. She'd always felt out of place around them. They talked about things she found boring or just confusing. She didn't care about the latest fashion in shoes and felt awkward discussing her emotions or boys or any of the other things girls liked talking about. She felt exposed around girls, as if she'd be found out some day as not being like them. Boys were so easy to be around. Their conversations lacked emotional intensity in a way that made her feel included. She didn't have to pretend to be something she wasn't. She enjoyed talking about football. She enjoyed the humour and light banter. She even enjoyed talking about girls. Boys got her and she got them.

Secretly, she wished she could've been born a boy. Life would've been so much easier if she had been.

Plus, her grandmother wouldn't have been on her case so much. Her grandmother's voice rang out in her head.

Thato, put on a dress. Smooth your hair down. Why do you always want to wear trousers? You'll never find a nice man to marry, when you're older, if this is how you go around.

Thato shook her head in an attempt to dislodge the words from her mind. Everything had been fine up until her breasts had started to grow and that's when everyone had started with that nonsense. All that talk of husbands and acting like a lady and wearing dresses - nobody ever treated boys like that.

When she hung out with Amose and the other boys, they didn't treat her like that. They treated her like she was one of them because they understood that she *was* one of them. Thato's lips curled up into a smile as she thought of Naledi asking her if any of the boys had touched her. The thought was absurd. Her friends would be just as likely to make out with another boy as they would be to touch her in that way.

"Hey Thato, stop gazing at the sky and come and get some beer." Amose called out to her.

Thato took a deep breath and forced herself to her feet. She looked at Amose. He'd separated from the other boys and was walking towards her. She rubbed her eyes, clearing her blurred vision as she struggled to focus on him. He held a large bottle of lager in his hands and waved it in her direction. She put one shaky foot in front of the other and made it to his hand, grasping the bottle and taking a few deep glugs before handing it back. She let out a burp as she looked at Amose then they both descended into a fit of giggles.

"You'll pass out soon - like Menzi."

"Let's hope so" Thato replied and they both bent over with laughter once more.

Amose clapped his hand on Thato's back. "Tell me Thato. How many beauties have turned up at your teacher's house this week?"

"We did get a new student join us this week. Bongi"

Amose's eyes lit up, "and?"

"She's... pretty I suppose. She has a pudding face."

"'A pudding face'. What's that supposed to mean?"

"Kind of like a round bun. She's got lovely eyes though. Plus, plenty to hold onto." Thato stretched out her hands towards her own tiny breasts, a lascivious smile on her face.

"Sounds right up my street. When do I get to meet her?"

Thato's mouth dropped open, aghast. "I'm not introducing her to you. Then Naledi will know I'm still hanging out with you."

Amose clicked his tongue against his cheek in an expression of annoyance. "What's her problem anyway? We're just friends."

"That's her problem - the fact that we're friends. She knows your reputation."

"Reputation? We're just young people, having fun. What's wrong with that?"

Thato sighed, "I just need to keep it from her, that's all. I don't want to be kicked out of the group."

Amose apparently wasn't willing to give up on the promise of Bongi just yet. "What good is it having you as a friend if you won't introduce us to any of the honeys you have access to?"

Thato grabbed him by the scruff of his shirt whilst forming her other hand into a fist, aimed at his nose. "Haiybo! Are you saying that you only want to be friends with me for the girls I bring you, eh?"

Amose squirmed out of her grasp and shrugged his shoulders. "Well..." then he started laughing and slapped her on the back. "I'm just kidding. You know you're one of us." Amose handed Thato his beer again and offered her another sip. She took it.

Daniel, one of the other boys, wandered over. "Hey Thato, didn't you say you had to be back by two for another lesson?"

"Why? What's the time?" Thato asked, taking another sip of beer.

"Two."

Beer sprayed out of Thato's mouth as she handed the bottle swiftly back to Amose. "Two?! I'm late. Omigod! I've got to go." She stumbled backwards over the grass. "I'll see you tomorrow. Bye."

Thato turned and ran across the valley. Wind whistled past her ears as her feet pounded the hard earth. She'd never been late back before. She'd known she was taking a risk by drinking and smoking before a session. Would Naledi smell it on her? Unlikely. The girl was older than her but somehow still so innocent. Thato was certain she'd never drank or smoked, and she was surprised that she had a boyfriend. She was obviously still a virgin. How could Tau stand waiting for her like that? His right hand must be permanently cramped from overuse.

THATO MADE it to Naledi's house within a few minutes. She didn't knock, knowing that they would likely already be in meditation. Instead she crept inside. The other girls were all seated on the floor in a circle with their eyes closed. Thato tiptoed over to sit next to the new girl, Bongi. A window was open blowing the smell of grass and wood smoke inside, as well as the cool autumn air. She sat down as quietly as possible, studying Naledi for any signs of anger. Her teacher's face remained impassive; her eyes lightly closed.

Good, she's deep in meditation.

Naledi would know that Thato had got there late but hopefully she wouldn't detect any smell. By the time the meditation finished, it would've worn off. She was relieved that the window was always kept open during the sessions. Something about allowing positive energy to circulate.

Thato closed her eyes, taking a few deep breaths. Her heart was still beating fast from the run to get here. As her breathing slowed and her heart rate finally settled, she realised that her head was still spinning from the beer and weed. A small voice of doubt entered Thato's mind. Maybe she shouldn't participate in the session today? She could just go home and tell Naledi later that she'd felt unwell. But if she did that, Naledi would be sure to hear later that she'd been seen with her friends and she'd know that she'd gotten high. Her teacher would kick her out of the group for sure.

Thato felt so conflicted. She knew she should stop hanging out with Amose and the others and start taking her sangoma training seriously but she just hadn't managed to cut them loose yet. She needed them. They were the only ones who truly understood her. But she also needed her training: without it she would go mad. She sighed. She'd have to stay and complete the session. She'd just keep her eyes closed and pretend to do it, that way she wouldn't risk opening herself up to dark forces, as Naledi had warned would happen.

Thato closed her eyes and simply sat. She didn't try to clear her thoughts or get into a meditative state yet somehow, the fact that she wasn't trying, made her sink deeper than she ever had done before. She was surprised yet delighted to find that she was soon floating just above her body. She looked down at her sitting form and flew to have a closer look.

I'm actually astral travelling!

This was the coolest thing ever! If she'd known that getting high, before a session, made it easier to accomplish astral travel, she would've done it long ago. She looked at her hands, they were translucent but otherwise looked exactly the same as her physical hands. It was uncanny. She spun around, giggling with delight. Nobody else could hear her. She could do whatever she liked in this state!

Just as Thato was planning what cool thing she'd do next; she saw something flit at the corners of her vision. It looked like a dark person-sized shape, similar to a shadow. She whirled towards what she'd seen but there was nothing there. Had she imagined it? Perhaps a hallucination brought on by the smoking? However, a feeling of dread crept across her belly. In spite of her intoxication there was still a part of her which knew truth from delusion and this part now told her that something was horribly wrong.

Something else was in the room and whatever it was, it had evil intentions. The minute this thought crossed her mind, she realised that her body was completely open. She had to get back inside, right now. She dove towards her body, but the dark shadow beat her to it. She tried to fight it off, swatting her hands in the air as she tried to pull it out, but it was no use. The dark being was as insubstantial as her own astral hands were. She was powerless to stop it and watched in mute horror as the dark shape sank into her own body, trapping her outside.

Thato started to scream but nobody could hear her. Her body sat, looking exactly the same but Thato couldn't get back inside.

What have I done? ...

7
NALEDI

Naledi decided that the best way to test Bongi's healing skill was with a real client. One of her schoolteachers, Mrs. Gumede, had made an appointment to treat recurrent migraines. Mrs. Gumede agreed with Naledi at the time of booking that she consented to having Bongi perform the healing with Naledi sitting and observing. If Naledi disagreed with the way Bongi was performing the healing session, she would step in and take over. Naledi had already tested Bongi's journeying and it had been outstanding. This was the final test and if Bongi passed, Naledi would perform the binding ceremony to fully accept Bongi into the group of initiates.

Naledi anticipated that Bongi would pass the test so she sent the other students out to collect firewood in preparation for the binding ceremony. This also meant that they had the house to themselves for the healing session. Although Naledi lived in Motsumi's old house, she'd kept her previous family home as a base from which to run her practice and her school. She'd felt it was better to have some separation and it meant that Lerato could look after Dineo and Puleng at Motsumi's old house whilst Naledi worked.

Bongi sat opposite Naledi. She tapped her heel up and down in a manner suggesting she was nervous although Naledi couldn't understand why this would be. Surely she'd treated lots of clients before. She shrugged the thought away, reasoning that some people just didn't like being observed.

"Have you treated Mrs. Gumede before?" Bongi asked

"No, but I know her. She's a teacher at my school. I was quite surprised when she booked the session. She strikes me as a very private person so she must trust that I won't talk about it at school."

Bongi's eyes narrowed, "You won't, will you?"

"No of course not and I'm sure you won't talk about it outside of these walls either. A sangoma's business success is based on confidentiality and trust."

Bongi smiled and nodded. She stared at Naledi, as if considering what to say next. Although she'd originally come across as confident, there was something about her that seemed hesitant. It was as if she was constantly planning what to say or do next to make the best impression on people but especially on Naledi. It was probably just the nerves of a newcomer, trying to fit in and be accepted. Naledi could understand that.

There was a knock at the door and Bongi's shoulders collapsed with relief.

"I'll get it!" she sprang out of her chair

Does she find me that intimidating?

Bongi and Naledi welcomed Mrs. Gumede into the treatment room and, as agreed, Naledi sat to the side, watching Bongi perform the session. Bongi's treatment style was precise and structured, Naledi reflected that her teacher must have been very strict. It was different from her own, relaxed, conversational style but Naledi couldn't fault her method. Bongi performed the session perfectly and at the end Mrs. Gumede seemed delighted with the results.

"Come back again for a free session if the migraines reoccur within the next two weeks, won't you?"

"Yes, Naledi, thank you. And thank you Bongi." Mrs. Gumede handed Naledi her payment as she was leaving. "This problem has been so persistent. It's a big relief to have a healing session. I feel much better."

Mrs. Gumede headed for the door but just as she was leaving she hesitated. Naledi held her breath

Oh no! Is she going to complain about the treatment?

"It's a terrible business what happened to Esther Mothopeng, isn't it?"

Naledi had no idea what she was talking about. "Why? What's happened?"

"You mean you haven't heard? She went out to fetch water and never came home. Her poor grandmother is distraught. She's been gone for two days."

"She was fetching water from the village tap?"

"Yes. How someone can disappear from right under our noses like that is beyond me. A few people saw her at the tap, but nobody saw what happened to her after that. It's like she vanished into thin air."

Naledi pursed her lips. "I wish her grandmother had come to me."

"Why? Are you able to locate missing children?"

Naledi scratched her head. "I can try."

Bongi chimed in, "you could try to read one of her objects... or..." her voice trailed off as she noticed Naledi's stern expression of warning. It wasn't correct to discuss methods in front of clients.

"I'll go and visit her and reassure her."

"You're very kind Naledi - you know her circumstances. She won't be able to pay you."

Naledi nodded, "I'll help as best I can anyway."

"Thank you." Mrs. Gumede dipped her head slightly and clapped both her hands twice before shaking Naledi's hand with both of her hands. This traditional way of saying thanks was particularly respectful and Naledi blushed, feeling honoured that one of her teachers would show her such deference. Mrs. Gumede smiled and headed out of the door.

Naledi shut the door and turned around. Bongi stood behind her smiling expectantly.

"Well?" she asked.

Naledi nodded, "you have passed the test. Congratulations!"

"Yes!" Bongi shook her fist, a look of triumph on her face. She then dropped it quickly, "erm, I mean. Thank you, Naledi."

"That's okay, you have every right to celebrate."

Naledi heard voices outside the door: her other students had returned with the firewood. Thato was first through the door. It seemed the girl had really taken Naledi's warning to heart. She was focusing more on her studies. She had stopped hanging around with the boys Naledi had warned her about. Indeed, Naledi had been surprised but pleased to see Thato blanking Amose entirely when he'd walked past and greeted her the day before. She'd acted as if she didn't know him at all. The boy had looked hurt and confused but he'd get over it. It was for the best. It seemed that Bongi was a good influence on Thato. They had already become firm friends and spent every spare moment together. This was a relationship that Naledi was happy to encourage. Thato would only grow stronger with the influence of a more experienced, older girl to guide her.

"Dumela, Bongi" Thato greeted her friend. "How did it go? Did you pass the test?"

Naledi reflected that even Thato's voice seemed a bit deeper. She was growing up.

"Yes, I passed!" Bongi gushed. She rushed over to Thato and held both her hands in excitement.

Naledi watched them as they made eye contact. Thato's eyes flashed with glee. She seemed genuinely happy for her friend. As Naledi watched, Thato's gaze flicked briefly to her. Her eyes narrowed slightly, and her lip curled in an expression of contempt but just as quickly it was gone.

What was that about?

Naledi instantly dismissed her suspicion. She must have imagined it. Thato harboured no ill will towards her and indeed the girl was so fragile she seemed incapable of such thoughts.

Naledi instructed her students to start building the fire and preparing the outside area for the binding ceremony. After tonight,

Bongi would be a fully accepted initiate. And just like Naledi's other students, Bongi would be tied to Naledi until she graduated or died or until Naledi released her from her bondage. Naledi thought back to her own binding ceremony with Motsumi. It had been such a life changing experience for her. She wondered if it was as intense for everyone else or if she was particularly sensitive.

    Standing at the window, watching her students make the preparations outside, Naledi's thoughts turned to the disappearance of Esther Mothopeng. She knew the girl well, as she did with everyone in the village. Esther was ten years old and about to start confirmation classes at church. What could have happened to her? Naledi couldn't stop her mind from rushing to the worst possible conclusion. Could she have been abducted? And if she had been, for what terrible purpose had she been taken? She shuddered as she remembered the sacrifice room, she'd seen in Hell containing children's body parts. Could Esther have been snatched by demon worshippers? Naledi shook the thought from her head. It was far more likely, if she had been snatched, that it had been by regular men. The things men would use her for would be almost as bad and in some cases worse than demon worshippers' actions.

    Naledi pulled her Sotho blanket up around her shoulders as she felt a sudden chill. She didn't know if she could locate the girl. She could try a location spell and reading an object, as Bongi had suggested and also astral travelling to connect with the girl's spirit. Even if she tried all those things, she still might not find Esther. A feeling of nausea rose in the pit of Naledi's stomach. In this part of the world, women and girls had to fend for themselves. Most able-bodied men had died of the epidemic. The police either didn't care or only came to the aid of those who were willing and able to grease their palms with cash. Naledi balked at the idea of bribing them to do a job which they were already paid to do.

The sun was starting to set by the time all the preparations had been made for the binding ceremony. Naledi's students were inside the house helping Bongi to put on ceremonial attire and wash her body before the ritual. This wasn't necessary, but it was something that initiates often wanted to do. Naledi gave the outside area one more sweep, removing any twigs and bits of dried grass from around the fire. They would dance and celebrate after the ritual. She didn't want anyone tripping over things if they went into a trance state. This often happened, especially for Thato and one or two of the other more sensitive girls. Tomorrow was Saturday and Naledi was looking forward to having a full day at home with her sisters. She'd worked late with her students every day this week and she hadn't spent enough time with Dineo and Puleng. She also missed Lerato. Her best friend's lively, humorous presence was like a balm to her serious soul.

Hearing footsteps pounding the earth, Naledi looked up to see a dark figure, wearing a woollen hat, running towards her. She assumed a fighting stance. Brandishing her broom in front of her, her muscles tensed, in readiness for an attack.

"Who's there?" She barked.

As the person came closer, she saw that it was Amose - Thato's friend. He was panting and his eyes were wild.

"Amose," Naledi relaxed and dropped her broom to rest on the end. "If you're looking for Thato…"

He interrupted, "No. I came to speak to you. I need your help."

"Oh?"

"It's grandma. She's gone missing. She went to use the latrine earlier today and she never returned. It's only a few metres away from our house. I've looked everywhere. At first, I thought she might have fallen but there are no potholes, nowhere for her to fall." The words had all come out in one long, unbroken torrent but now he looked at Naledi. His eyes were dark with worry and he wrung his hands. "It's like she just disappeared."

"Is she confused? Could she have wandered off somewhere?" Naledi tried but she knew the answer before Amose replied.

"No." He was emphatic. "She may be old, but her mind is sharper than mine. She was feeling perfectly well when she went to the toilet. I think there's only one explanation: someone has taken her."

Naledi looked at him, her brows furrowing. What could have happened to the old woman? Esther's disappearance was something that made a sick sort of sense: a ten-year-old could be valuable for all sorts of reasons and sadly, abductions were not unheard of - but an old woman? There were now two villagers missing. Was it related or just a terrible coincidence?

Amose continued, "And I'm sure you've heard about Esther too... I'm worried that... my grandmother, she's all I've got and..." his features twisted with the effort of keeping tears springing to his face. He covered his face with his hands. Naledi rushed over and put her hand on his shoulder, patting it in what she hoped was a comforting manner.

"Don't worry Amose, I'll help you. We'll find her."

He uncovered his face, peering at her hopefully. "Are you really able to do that? Do your powers extend to finding missing people?"

Naledi nodded. "Sort of, but it depends on if magic has been used to cover up the crime. I can't break through shrouding spells."

In spite of Naledi's caveat, Amose's body instantly relaxed with reassurance. "Thank you." He turned his head to wipe his runny nose in the crook of his arm.

Naledi blinked away from the disgusting habit. "Please can you go home and come back with an item of hers so I can do a reading to see if I can locate her?"

"Yes of course. Anything in particular?"

"It doesn't matter, just make sure it's something that only she uses - so as not to confuse her energy with that of another person."

"I understand. Thank you Naledi. Thank you." He put both his hands together and bowed slightly whilst walking backwards, almost tripping over a stone in the process.

"Don't mention it. I'm very happy to help." She replied.

"I'll be right back." Amose sprinted up the path to get the object.

Naledi watched him run, feeling a glow in her heart. A smile played on her lips. Using her powers to help her neighbours gave her such joy. Since word had spread about Naledi, the other villagers trusted her powers implicitly. Indeed, they believed she could do anything. Her smile faded. Had she given him false hope? If his grandmother had been abducted, then it was highly likely that a shrouding spell had been used.

If so, Naledi would be powerless to find the old woman.

8

GIADA

Giada walked along the gleaming quartz path which led to the fountain of eternity. The sun was starting to set, and the sky was streaked with jagged pinks, purples and oranges in a manner reminiscent of a modern art painting. Sunset in Heaven was a particularly idyllic time. Groups of angels lounged in the soft green grass on either side of the path, singing and playing music together. One or two angels got up and started spontaneously dancing. Giada predicted that by the time she was on her way home, the entire grassy area would look like an ultra-sober music festival. It was the same every night. Angels were the cool kids in Heaven and most regular souls either aspired to be them or were actively working towards it. She reflected once more on Gabi's announcement. When would she get her mission? What would it be? And most crucially of all: would she succeed?

Giada turned her attention back to the present. She would try and forget her worries for tonight and just enjoy her date with Luke.

Date? Is this a date?

Was she getting ahead of herself? He'd given her no suggestion that this was anything more than a study session. But she couldn't lie to herself. She hoped it was a date. She'd picked out her most alluring outfit just in case. A figure-hugging, red skater-style dress with gold hoop earrings. She'd applied light make up so as not to make it too obvious that she'd made an effort. She was hedging her bets so as to not lose face, in case it wasn't a date.

Nearing the fountain, she spotted Luke standing with his back to her. He wore fitted jeans and a white t-shirt which complemented his tan superbly. A fine mist of moisture cloaked her bare arms as the wind blew water spray from the fountain in her direction. Luke must've heard her footsteps approach as he turned around, flicking his hair as he did so in an action that made Giada catch her breath. He gave her a devastating smile and she stumbled slightly, inwardly cursing her decision to wear heels.

I should've just gone with flats.

Fortunately, Luke didn't seem to notice. "Hi Giada, how's it going?"

"I'm good thanks, how about you?"

"Same. Did you get a nap this afternoon?"

Giada smiled and nodded. All residents of Heaven slept at night and then had at least one nap per day - normally in the afternoon. Some residents also had a mid-morning nap. People could basically do whatever made them happy and most people, when given the choice, wanted as much sleep as possible.

Luke looked her up and down, smiling slightly. She thought he was about to complement her appearance but then it seemed that he thought better of it. Giada's heart sank as he got straight to business. "I was thinking that we could go to the Amphitheatre practice rooms. Nobody uses them after hours, so we'll have enough privacy to concentrate on our levitation. What do you think?"

Giada would've agreed with almost anything he said. "Sure," she replied.

It was quite a walk to the Amphitheatre and Giada was relieved when Luke immediately broke the ice by asking her about her life back on Earth. She told him about her home in Rome and her family. Then she asked him about his background. He was from Ohio. He seemed reticent to talk more about his family and Giada wondered if the relationship had been a complicated one, as it had been for her and her family. Giada wanted to ask him more about his brother but understood it was likely a tender subject. She was still ruminating on it when he turned the conversation to her time in Hell.

"How long were you there for?"

"Only a few months but it felt much longer." Giada blew air out of her mouth.

"Yeah, I know how that is. The time that I spent there felt like an eternity."

Giada looked at him with curiosity. How had he survived in Hell? What depravity had he witnessed? She asked in the politest way she could think of. "What was it like in your part of Hell? Did you have to sin-bait to survive?"

Luke replied matter-of-factly. "We had to if we wanted to progress up the hierarchy. I was a full demon by the end."

Giada's eyes popped out. "What?! And you still got redeemed?"

Luke stopped walking and turned to her. He stared into space; his eyes dark with a haunted look on his face. "I was never happy there. Not for one single minute. Even when I was getting high off causing pain. I had this deep void in my heart that no amount of torturing could fill. Eventually I realised the only way to become happy was to change my ways. I led a rebellion against the ruling demon prince. I was in the second circle, so it was Satan's son, Jethniah. I was killed in the battle but when I died, instead of being reborn in Hell, I was reborn here."

Giada exhaled, "I didn't even know that was possible."

Luke nodded, "it's very rare for demons to get redeemed. Normally demons stay put and reap the benefits of their high status in Hell. I realised that all the status in the world couldn't create happiness where there was none to be had." His brown eyes turned to meet hers and she trembled at the intensity of his expression.

Giada gulped. Her own redemption story seemed pale in comparison.

"What about you? How did your redemption come about?"

Giada giggled nervously. "Oh, it seems a bit...I dunno. A bit silly after yours."

He broke into a grin. "No, go on, tell me"

"Well, to cut a long story short. I learnt to be grateful for my damnation because it made me realise that my mama loved me, and it brought me closer to her. It was as simple as that. Nothing dramatic, more of a personal epiphany."

Luke looked at her solemnly, "that sounds really profound. I don't know why you're embarrassed about it. It's a sweet story." He held his gaze and cocked his head to one side. His face was framed by the golden light of the retreating sun. Giada blushed. Although he wasn't an angel yet, he sure looked like one.

Luke started walking again. "Anyway, that's why Michael is keen to have me on his team. Having the intel of a former demon on your side is a powerful advantage."

"I'm sure." Giada nodded.

"That's why it's so important that I master all of the skills. I can't fail. If I go back, I'll be tortured for information for sure."

Giada's heart sank. So that was why he wanted to practice with her. He was desperate to succeed. It was business. Nothing more than that. She put her disappointment to one side and tried her best to ignore his heartbreaking good looks.

THEY ARRIVED at the Amphitheatre just as it got dark. The new moon and a full blanket of stars illuminated the night sky, casting glittery light on the circular, white, quartz stage.

Giada sat on the first row of seats and Luke perched on the edge of the stage, facing her. "What did you find challenging about the levitation?" he asked.

Your distractingly handsome presence.

"I think it was the meditation. I found it hard to sink into stillness."

Luke's eyes lit up. "Same as me! There were a lot of distractions in that room."

Giada giggled.

"What's so funny?"

"Nothing, it's just... I was thinking the same thing. It's like you read my mind."

Luke smiled mischievously. His eyes glittered in a way that was almost flirtatious. He had to know how beautiful he was, surely? Was he toying with her?

"But you know that telepathy isn't possible between souls in Heaven," he replied.

Thank God for that.

"I know telepathy isn't possible..." her voice trailed off as his gaze became serious. Why was he looking at her like that? Was it her imagination?

"Giada?"

"Yes?" she stood up a little too quickly then cursed her eagerness. Why couldn't she play it cool around him?

"Do you ever feel like nobody understands you here? Like everyone else fits in fine but you.... Never mind, forget it...."

Giada interrupted him. "Yes. Yes, I feel like that all the time." She laughed with relief as her shoulders relaxed. "I thought I was the only one."

"Me too!" Luke laughed.

"I thought it would get easier. You're up for angel promotion, surely you feel like you fit in by now?"

"Sometimes I do. But sometimes I wonder... if God made a mistake by redeeming me."

Giada's eyes opened wide. "No Luke, why would you say something like that? You're..."

"What?"

Giada had been about to say he was more angelic than anyone else she'd met in Heaven, but she stopped herself just in time. She felt herself blushing and looked down, hoping he hadn't noticed. "I don't think God makes mistakes," she quietly replied.

The silence suddenly seemed deafening. It was broken by the

faraway singing of angels - a sporadic melody that chimed throughout heaven day and night. Slowly she raised her chin to meet Luke's eyes. His expression softened and his eyes roamed around her features. She knew she was now blushing furiously, but she no longer cared. She could hardly breathe as he took a step closer and lifted her chin a bit more. "You're a very kind person, you know that?"

Giada blinked. "That's not how I would describe myself"

She felt him unearthing every secret she'd ever kept locked inside of her with his penetrating brown gaze. "How would you describe yourself?" he whispered.

Melting, at the sound of his soft, rich, deep voice, she replied. "I dunno.... I guess I'm just someone who's still trying to figure it all out."

"Aren't we all." Luke said, still staring at her. His chest rose and fell, and she thought she could hear him breathing but it was hard to hear it over the thud of her own heartbeat. It was a perfect moment and Giada felt more seen than she ever had before. Then all at once it was over. Luke seemed to shake himself out of his reverie as he clapped his hands together. "Right, let's get on with this or we'll never make any progress."

Giada nodded, swallowing her disappointment.

I thought he was going to kiss me.

He was right though. They'd come here to practice not to chat and stare into each other's eyes. Had she imagined the connection between them? Did he feel anything at all for her?

Luke was an enigma. A mysterious package that she longed to unwrap.

AFTER THEIR SESSION, Giada walked back home alone. Her thoughts were filled with visions of Luke. His mischievous smile, his soulful brown eyes, his broad chest. She knew she was falling for him badly - had already fallen for him, if she was honest with herself, but she didn't care. She deserved this. She'd never really had a serious crush whilst she was alive. Well, there had been a few boys, but none that made her feel the way she felt when she was with him. Luke was handsome, sure, but it was more than that. When he spoke to her, it was like he was speaking to the depths of her soul. He got her, more than anyone ever had and being with him felt intoxicating. She couldn't wait to see him again. Even if he didn't share her feelings, and she wasn't sure that he did, just being in his presence made her feel more... alive!

Giada was so deep in thought that she barely noticed the journey home. Looking up, she suddenly found herself standing outside her house. She opened the front door - nobody locked their door in Heaven. Roberto and Mama must have already gone to bed, as it was quiet and dark inside. She walked into the living room and flipped the light switch on then froze as she saw archangel Michael and archangel Gabriel sitting waiting for her. Gabi stood up; her face more serious than Giada had ever seen.

"Giada - we have come to give you your mission."

Michael looked at her, his face suddenly looking weary. "Some time ago, we detected demonic activity in a village called, Marula, in the African country of Lesotho. I sent a member of my team - Domenico, an experienced archangel, to investigate. He never returned."

Gabi chimed in. "We've also heard prayers of humans in the village. A couple of the villagers have gone missing. We believe this is linked to the demonic activity. We want you to investigate and see what happened to Domenico and the villagers."

Giada's body went rigid. She'd been hoping for an easy mission, something that carried no risk of failure. Gabi had even promised that the missions would be achievable. This didn't sound achievable: this sounded difficult and dangerous. She knew that she had no choice though. If she wanted to stay in Heaven, if she wanted to stay with Luke, she had to complete the mission and find out what had happened to the villagers and Domenico.

9
NALEDI

Naledi's students had finished getting ready and were now lighting the fire. Amose returned after a few minutes clutching a pair of reading glasses. As he walked past Thato, he flicked his eyes towards her but again she blanked him. Naledi brushed away the guilt she felt at seeing his hurt expression: this was for the best.

Amose shook his head slightly, as if to dislodge the thoughts, then he looked at Naledi. "Will these do?"

"Yes, they are perfect. Please, come inside."

Amose followed Naledi into the house and shut the door behind him.

"Please take a seat. Can I get you a glass of water?"

"No. Nothing thank you." Amose was clearly in a rush to get started so Naledi settled herself down in the seat opposite him. She placed the glasses on her lap and closed her eyes to begin the practice. Naledi emptied her mind, in the same way as she'd done countless times before. Once her mind was clear, she brushed her fingers over the glasses and gently picked them up. She waited for images, thoughts and feelings to flash into her mind.

Naledi frowned. She sensed information, but a dense fog surrounded it. As she tried harder, beads of sweat broke out on her forehead. Her breathing increased and she clenched her jaw, trying with all her might. But it was no use: the fog persisted. She'd been right. A shrouding spell had been used. She wasn't yet ready to give up though. She put the glasses back down and took a few deep breaths, clearing her mind, before she picked them up again. This time she travelled further back in time, in her mind's eye. She smiled as she saw the familiar old woman going about her day. Amose's grandmother was baking steamed bread and singing as she cleaned her kitchen. Then she walked out of the back door of her house, passing Amose on the way. Naledi sat up slightly, guessing that she could be on her way to use the toilet. As the old woman walked through the tall grass, Naledi sensed her emotions. She was calm and happy.

Then all at once it changed. There was a violent jolting sensation and Naledi gasped. Feelings of fear and confusion took hold of her body. A brief image flashed through her mind. It was a violent struggle. Arms thrashed; nails scratched. She saw a hand being clamped over a mouth, cutting off the yelp that she'd briefly heard. The images were so fleeting, she couldn't see any faces. However, Naledi saw a flash of red eyes. A deep, menacing voice said, "Naledi." She gasped, emitting a short, sharp cry, before the fog descended and she was once more locked out of the vision.

Naledi opened her eyes, coming back to the room abruptly. Her face was bathed in perspiration and she wiped it with her hands.

Amose looked at her with wild eyes. "Are you okay? You were thrashing about a bit. Then you called out."

"Yes, I'm fine. That sometimes happens when the images are very intense." She decided against telling him that she'd heard someone calling her name.

"And?" He inched forward in his seat.

Naledi bit her lip. "It's not good news I'm afraid. You are right. Your grandmother has been abducted."

Amose stood up and put his hands to both sides of his head. "Oh my God!" He dropped his hands and looked at her. "Who? Who has taken her?"

"I'm afraid I couldn't see. It's as I suspected. Whoever has taken her has used a shrouding spell. I only got flashes but what I did see…" Her voice trailed off. How could she tell him that his beloved grandmother had been abducted by demons? It didn't even make sense. Demons couldn't come to Earth, in physical form, without a human host. Amose pulled her thoughts back to the room as he asked. "What? What were you going to say?" His expression was full of worry.

Naledi couldn't keep the truth from him. There was no easy way to say it, so she just told him bluntly. "I saw demons in my vision."

"Demons?! From Hell you mean? Actual demons?"

"Yes. I know it sounds crazy but believe me, I know what I'm talking about. Your grandmother has been abducted by demons."

"Why? Why would they want her?"

Naledi sighed and rubbed her temples. Attempting to break through the shrouding spell had taken a lot out of her and she now had a headache. "Demons have all sorts of sick reasons for wanting humans. I can't say for sure what they could be using her for, but it will be something depraved. We have to get her back as soon as possible."

"Yes. I agree. Let's leave tonight. Can we use your truck?"

Naledi patted her hands up and down, encouraging him to calm down. "Hold on, we don't even know where they're holding her."

"Why don't we just try all the places rumoured to have demon worshippers? We could start with Joang. That place is a hotbed of devil worshipping or so I've heard."

Naledi looked at him sympathetically. "We could do that, but we risk wasting a lot of time chasing our tails. I think we need to investigate further to get concrete leads first."

Amose took a deep breath. "You're right. What do you want me to do?"

Naledi gulped. "Nothing - I mean, not nothing. Keep your ears open and if you hear anything let me know, but I don't want you involved other than that."

Amose looked crestfallen. "Why not?"

"I'm sorry Amose. I know your grandmother is important to you but you're too close to this. Investigating demons is dangerous. I have powers that I can use to fight any we encounter. If you're there, you'll only get in the way and make me weaker. Sorry, I don't mean to offend you. But you're a normal human and you're vulnerable. Does that make sense?" She looked at him with kindness in her eyes.

"I guess so... If you think it's better that way."

"I also can't do much tonight. I have an important ceremony to perform with my students. But I promise I'll get straight onto it first thing tomorrow morning."

Amose's head whipped up. "She could be dead by then!"

"If the demons wanted to kill her, she'd be dead already. If she's still alive today, she'll still be alive tomorrow."

He sighed. "I suppose you're right."

Amose looked down, fidgeting slightly as he looked from left to right. Then he looked back up again and scratched behind his neck. "Erm, I can't pay you. You know that, right?"

Naledi smiled. "Don't worry. I'm happy to help out with something as important as this."

"Thank you Naledi. Thank you so much. I owe you one. I'm so worried."

Naledi reached forward and held his hands as she looked into his eyes. "I promise you; I'll do everything in my power to get her back safely to you."

Now that she knew demons were involved, seeing the missing ten-year old, Esther Mothopeng's grandmother had just become more urgent. The two cases had to be linked. Leaving out the specifics of what was going on, she told her students the binding ceremony would start a little later as she had to make a house call first. Her students didn't need to know the details. Client confidentiality should be maintained until she knew more.

Naledi walked up the hill, along the pebbly pathway, towards Esther Mothopeng's house. The girl lived with her grandmother in a rondavel on the west side of the village. The last of the sun was disappearing behind the mountains and a few bats flitted across the skyline.

Reaching the rondavel, Naledi knocked on the front door. Esther's grandmother answered. The buxom old lady wore a Sotho blanket around her lower half and a t-shirt on the top half through which Naledi saw the bulge of a handkerchief stuffed into her bra. Ma Mothopeng's eyes were red and her face was drawn. She looked exhausted.

The poor woman probably hasn't slept a wink since Esther disappeared.

"Naledi. Thank you for coming. Ma Gumede told me I should expect you." A weak smile appeared on her worry-lined face. "Please come in."

She gestured for Naledi to sit on one of the wooden chairs inside the living room. The room was heavily cloaked in smoke and Naledi coughed. She'd forgotten what it was like to live without electricity.

"I'll just get you some tea."

Naledi waved her hands in front of her face. "No thanks, I've just had some." She knew this refusal would be brushed away. Basothos of Ma Mothopeng's generation were very proud and never allowed visitors into their home without giving them some refreshments.

Just as Naledi had expected, the old woman replied. "Please, I insist." Before shuffling towards the back of the room. Naledi saw an iron kettle on top of the fire which was underneath a chimney. The chimney did little to disburse the smoke which tickled Naledi's nose and stung her eyes.

At least she has a chimney. Some houses don't even have that.

She smiled at the implied compliment to her status. The kettle had probably been on that hearth at all times since Mrs. Gumede had told Ma Mothopeng that Naledi would be visiting.

Naledi sat listening to the soothing sound of water hitting the cup as the old woman poured the tea.

"Sugar?" she asked

Wow! She really is pulling all the stops out. Offering me sugar as well! I'll be respectful and accept.

"Yes, two please. Thank you."

Ma Mothopeng handed Naledi the cup and then sat down.

"Can you tell me everything that happened, in your own words?" Naledi asked.

The old woman stared at the wall behind Naledi as she started talking. "It was mid-afternoon, the day before yesterday. It had been a normal day. Esther helped me with cleaning the house in the morning. Then after lunch I sent her to refill the water barrel at the tap in the centre of the village."

"Did anybody see her there?"

"Yes, lots of people did. She filled the water barrel and then she put it on her head and walked towards home. Somewhere between the water tap and home, she disappeared. Nobody saw what happened to her or who took her."

"Why are you so sure she was taken?"

"What other explanation can there be? It's a short walk from the tap to here. It's impossible that she could've got lost. She must have been kidnapped."

Naledi took a sip of tea as she thought how best to phrase her next question. "May I ask, how is your relationship with Esther?"

"It's good. Since my daughter died of the epidemic... well," Ma Mothopeng's eyes grew misty with the painful memories and she sniffed. She fished the handkerchief out of her bra and blew her nose loudly.

"I'm sorry. As I was saying. Since the death of my daughter, Esther has become like a daughter to me. She's only ten years old. A good girl, bright - she does well at school." Her eyes shone with pride and she smiled slightly but then her smile dropped as she fought back tears. "She's my whole world." Ma Mothopeng's voice cracked and she could no longer keep the tears from running down her face. "Excuse me," she said as she wiped the tears away and blew her nose loudly once more.

Naledi felt a rush of sympathy and pity towards the old woman. She knew what it was like to lose family members. The old woman looked her in the eyes and Naledi felt the shared understanding of deep and intimate grief pass between them. Ma Mothopeng loved Esther. Of that, there could be no doubt, and this meant there was no possibility the girl had run away or that Ma Mothopeng was somehow involved in her disappearance. It was clear to Naledi that here sat a woman who was desperate to get her granddaughter back.

Naledi leant forwards and took the old woman's hand in hers. "Ma, please don't feel you need to hide your distress from me. I understand your pain. I'm sorry that I have to put you through these questions. I'm just trying to help bring Esther back home to you."

Ma Mothopeng nodded and took a deep breath, as she wiped the last of her tears from her face with the, now sodden, handkerchief.

"Just one more question. Is there anywhere in the village that Esther likes to play. Or any friends she may have decided to go and visit on the way home?"

"She does like to play by the rocks - the same as your sisters do. But we've checked around there thoroughly. Plus, why would she go there on the way home with a heavy barrel of water on her head? She wouldn't. She would come home and leave the water here first. The same with visiting her friends. We've asked around at each of her friends' houses and they haven't seen her but even so she would have come here to drop off the water first."

"So, you never did get that water?"

"No. She disappeared with the barrel." The old woman's face sagged, adding years to her already wrinkled face.

Naledi set her lips in an expression of determination before adding. "I will do whatever it takes to find Esther and bring her home to you."

"Thank you Naledi... I'm... I'm afraid I can't pay you anything."

Naledi shook her hands vigorously, "That's okay. I don't expect any money at all. It's an honour for me to help you."

Ma Mothopeng took Naledi's hands in her own. "God bless you Naledi. May God shine his abundance down on you and your family. May the ancestors protect you. You have a kind heart. I am so very grateful."

Naledi felt herself blush. "Thank you, Ma, and may God bless you too. Do you have any objects belonging to Esther that I could read please?"

Ma Mothopeng gave Naledi a schoolbook and Naledi performed the same process that she had done earlier on the glasses. She saw even less than before. Once again, a shrouding spell had been used. She did get a sense of evil though, and a slight smell of sulphur. It was fleeting but it was enough to confirm her suspicion that the cases were linked. Esther had almost certainly been abducted by the same demons. She tried to get more information, but she was too tired from the earlier reading that she had done. It would be no use to try and astral travel to their location. If a shrouding spell was in place, it would be used to conceal their whereabouts. She'd only get over tired, leaving herself vulnerable to an attack of ithwasa. She told Ma Mothopeng as much as she could, whilst being as tactful as she could. The old woman was a devout Christian, like herself, and worrying her would accomplish nothing.

Saying goodbye to Ma Mothopeng, she reassured her one final time before leaving the rondavel. As she waved goodbye Naledi smiled brightly, but inside she was gripped by worry. She'd fought demons before and had won but each time it had nearly killed her. It seemed that no matter how much she wanted a quiet life, as a breacher, she was destined to constantly be battling evil.

10

GIADA

Giada looked at Michael. "Wouldn't it make more sense to give this to a more experienced angel - an archangel even? I'm just a trainee."

Michael smiled, "We've been watching you for some time, Giada. You are uniquely placed to handle a mission of this magnitude."

Giada blinked at him, "I am?"

Michael chuckled, "Don't be so modest. We know that you were involved in an espionage mission in Hell. This mission ultimately led to the destruction of the Countess and her plans to allow demons to go to earth in physical form. We also know that you were instrumental in sabotaging Sehloho's resurrection."

Giada shrugged. "I was just in the right place at the right time."

"No. In each of these cases, you chose to do the right thing, at great personal risk to yourself. You have the right blend of strong morals and creative thinking which we need for a mission like this. Plus, you are friends with the human breacher, Naledi. She has already begun investigating the villagers' disappearance. You should work in partnership with her."

A thought struck Giada. "If you've sensed demonic activity in Marula, why don't you just swoop in and kill all the demons?"

"If we do that we may never find out where Domenico and the missing villagers are. Plus, my team is too busy working on another resurrection attempt in Asia. We don't have the resources to work this case too. You'll have to do it alone."

Gabi added. "If you get into serious trouble once you've found the villagers - if there are too many demons for you to take on alone, then you can call on us at that point."

"But I don't know how to fight demons. I've had no training; I don't even have any weapons."

Michael waved his hands in the air and a golden bow and arrow appeared. He stepped forward and gave the weapon to Giada.

Giada raised a sceptical eyebrow. "A bow and arrow. Seriously?"

Michael smiled. "This is no ordinary bow and arrow. It works with your intention and cannot miss. If you intend to hit a target, and you have that target in your sight, you will hit it, no matter how bad your archery skills are."

"Good because I've never used a bow and arrow before in my life."

Michael continued. "Also, it's a kill-on-contact weapon for any demon or dark entity. Regardless of where you hit them, they will be instantly annihilated."

Giada felt more confident now that she had the bow and arrow, but she still wasn't sure. Michael saw her hesitation. His deep-set eyes blazed with authority out of his dark-skinned face. "I'm going to be honest with you. We can't discount the possibility that Domenico has defected to the other side."

Giada's eyes popped out. "What?! Does that happen often?"

Gabi looked slightly uncomfortable. "No, but it does happen. Demons can be very seductive - as you know."

Giada cast her mind back to when the Countess had almost managed to persuade Naledi to join the forces of darkness and she nodded in agreement.

Michael looked at her. "We need you, Giada." He implored her with his eyes. "No one else can do this. You haven't been drawn into any of the gossipy angelic cliques yet, so we can count on your discretion."

Giada's body went tense at the thought that they'd been watching her and had noticed her lack of friends. Was it obvious to everyone? Had Luke noticed? Is that why he was hanging out with her - because he felt sorry for her? A cold feeling of disappointment and failure cloaked her body like mud and she suddenly felt like the biggest loser in the universe.

Rika and her friends are right. I am a loser.

She was relieved that Michael and Gabi couldn't read her thoughts.

Giada collapsed on the sofa, putting her head in her hands. She had to admit, he made a compelling argument. Something about this just didn't feel right though. She held back from accepting, she felt like she needed time to think.

"Time is of the essence," Michael continued. "If Domenico and these villagers have been abducted by demons, they could be being tortured in some Earth twilight region as we speak."

Giada had learnt in Redemption School that demons used powerful shrouding spells to hide their activities from angels. If demons did have Domenico and the villagers, they wouldn't be easy to find.

"Do I have a choice in this? Could I request to be given another mission?" Giada looked at Gabi as she said this, and the archangel shifted nervously from one foot to the other. As God's messenger, Giada knew that archangel Gabriel couldn't lie.

"You do have a choice. But if you request another mission, you won't become an angel." Gabi said.

Michael delivered the final nail in the coffin of Giada's resistance. "If you complete this mission, not only will you become a fully qualified angel. But you'll also have a place on my team. You'll be on a path leading to archangel status one day. If you fail... well..." His voice trailed off. He didn't have to complete the sentence. She knew that her place in Heaven was at stake. Giada couldn't go back to Hell, she just couldn't. She'd worked so hard to get here. She'd do anything to stay. Plus, a place on Michael's team meant working with Luke, every day.

"I'll do it."

Gabi smiled. "Good. we knew you'd see sense."

"Now," Michael stated, briskly moving through the order of business. "You cannot discuss this mission with anyone at all. You can tell people you've been given your mission but not what it is. If you tell anyone, it will count as an instant fail and you'll go straight back to Hell."

Giada gulped and nodded, "I understand. I won't tell anyone."

Michael continued. "Come to the Hall of Creation tomorrow morning before Redemption School. We will brief you further." He started moving towards the door with Gabi beside him. "We'll see you tomorrow. Goodnight."

"Goodnight," Giada murmured, and she went to bed.

EARLY THE NEXT MORNING, Giada went to the Hall of Creation as instructed. It was locked. Two tall angels, with long dark hair, who were close enough in resemblance to be brothers, stood guard at the door. One of them opened the door. The other, told Giada to go straight down the stairs and press the buzzer at the end of the passageway. Giada thanked them and went inside. She descended the stone steps, the temperature dropping as she went deeper underground. The air smelt slightly damp and musty. Goosebumps broke out on her skin. She wasn't used to feeling cold anymore and she shivered, folding her arms.

At the end of the passageway, the corridor was flooded with a kaleidoscope of different coloured lights, which bounced off the walls. Giada gasped as she realised that 'glass door' had been an understatement. It was a beautiful stained-glass door containing intricate patterns of winding vines and trees on whose branches perched birds and butterflies. She looked around the corridor in search of the source of light and realised that it must be coming from the other side of the door. Walking forward, she pressed the buzzer and waited. A voice she didn't recognise crackled from the intercom requesting her name.

"It's Giada Cantinelli. I have an appointment with Michael."

The door buzzed and she pushed it open.

Giada walked into a circular room. As she'd suspected, it was flooded with sunlight. As she looked up, she saw that the skylight of the donut-shaped building's central hole, descended all the way to the basement level. The circular room was split into two levels. A lower level which had a large table and various electronic devices. And an upper level featuring swivel chairs and large monitors. In front of each monitor sat an angel working. Giada watched in awe as they moved their hands around and muttered softly under their breaths.

Michael came over to greet her with a welcoming smile. "Good morning, Giada"

"Morning Michael." Giada still stared at the angels working and Michael followed her gaze.

"They're guardian archangels. They protect whole regions, major cities typically or war zones. Their work also involves gathering intelligence on the plans of the other side. This information is stored in the celestial database."

"Why are they muttering?"

"They're communicating with sometimes, hundreds of people at the same time. It's an advanced telepathic technique. Hopefully one day you might learn it."

Giada laughed nervously. "Hopefully".

I doubt it

Michael looked around the room, "I'll introduce you to a few of our operatives first and then take you to the briefing room."

Giada's heart skipped a beat as Michael gestured towards a floppy-haired boy with his back to her. She'd recognise those broad shoulders anywhere.

"I believe you've already met Luke," Michael said.

Luke turned around and flashed her a heart-stopping smile as he waved. Then he turned back to his monitor leaving Giada to scoop up her insides from where they'd melted onto the floor. Michael shepherded Giada around, introducing her to more of his team. There was a dizzying number of names and faces to remember. Michael must have noticed her worried expression as he reassured her. "Don't worry, we don't expect you to remember everyone on the first day. I'm introducing you more for their benefit. If your mission goes as well as expected, you will be joining our team as a permanent member."

He beamed at Giada and she smiled back, weakly, feeling more uncertain of her abilities than ever before.

Michael ushered her through to the briefing room. It was a medium-sized windowless room with a whiteboard at the front and a large oval-shaped glass table around which were twelve chairs. Giada was surprised that they were alone.

My mission must be secret from everyone except Gabi

"Gabi was going to join us, but she had some unexpected business to attend to. We don't really need her here anyway." Michael waved his sword in the air and images started to appear in mid-air. It was like a movie screen.

"This is Domenico," he began. An image of a fresh-faced teenage boy with almond eyes, rosy cheeks and dark curly hair appeared.

Giada's eyes widened. "He's young," she commented. She had been expecting someone either middle-aged or even older.

"He's not as young as he looks. He's been here thousands of years." Michael explained.

"First some background information." Images appeared of Domenico walking towards an apartment building, "that's where he lives. It's close to you in Celestial West".

"Yes, I recognise the building," Giada murmured. "Just out of interest, how did you collect these images? Do you have surveillance cameras installed?"

Michael laughed. "Of a type. We call it the 'Celestial All-Seeing Eye' or 'CASE' for short. It records all events that take place within the Heavenly Gates. We don't check the footage all the time, only when something goes wrong."

"Do you have any evidence Domenico defected to the other side?" Giada asked.

"He had expressed some dissatisfaction to some of the other archangels before he disappeared but that doesn't mean he's definitely defected. It could be why he was targeted by demons. Because he looks like a good candidate for defection. Therefore, his possible defection makes the investigation harder as we have multiple avenues to pursue."

Giada put her head in her hands and rubbed her temples. This was going to be hard.

Michael slid a file across the desk to Giada. "We prepared this for you, so you'd be able to work on it at home. It includes stills of all the recordings of his movements just before he disappeared."

Giada chewed on her lip as she leafed through the stack of photos. "When was he last seen?"

"I sent him to Marula a week ago and we lost contact with him as soon as he was on Earth. This points to some kind of shrouding spell."

Giada nodded pensively. "Okay, thank you Michael. I'll go off and give this some thought and then come back to ask you more questions if I have any."

Michael looked her in the eye. "No - thank *you* Giada. We're lucky to have you on our side."

AFTER THE MEETING, Giada went to Redemption School. She hadn't seen Luke when she left her meeting with Michael and she'd assumed that he'd be at school. She looked but couldn't see him. Perhaps he was working on his mission today? She remembered him telling Irene that he'd already been given it. When she was sure her eyes had scanned the entire hall, she hung her head and brooded. She had no right to feel disappointed. They were barely even friends. Acquaintances: that's what they were. As she looked down at the floor, she suddenly became aware of someone sitting down next to her. She turned her head slightly and saw a pair of small-sized feet. Lifting her head up Giada's eyes met the sparkliest smile she had ever seen. A girl who looked about her age, with auburn hair, had sat next to her and was now holding her hand out.

"Hi, I'm Bronwen. Pleased to meet you."

Bronwen had an American accent which was softer than Aaron's. Perhaps she was from the mid-west? Her eyes had an unusual dark ring around the brilliant blue iris. This, coupled with her shiny white teeth and chipmunk cheeks, gave her a particularly intense expression which bordered on manic.

"I'm Giada," Giada took Bronwen's hand and noticed how firm her grip was. Bronwen shook her hand several times.

"I've just arrived - newly-redeemed. How about you?"

"I've been here a couple of months."

Bronwen's eyes opened wider, "So you're quite new too? I don't find folks around here are all that friendly. What do you think?"

Giada smiled, "You're right, they're not."

Bronwen's face relaxed and she smiled at the solidarity.

The directness of Bronwen's next question caught Giada completely off guard. "What were you in Hell for?"

This girl has no filter at all

Giada blinked at her. "I watched as my younger brother accidentally strangled himself to death and I didn't save him."

"Whoa! That is some evil shit!"

Giada studied her closely, waiting for more judgmental comments. She was surprised when Bronwen moved the conversation straight along, barely batting an eye at Giada's confession.

"Me, I was soul-snatched. It was about fifty years ago. Worst thing that ever happened to me."

Giada raised her eyebrows, "You're not kidding."

"It's much better here though... well, except for the unfriendly people."

Giada looked at Bronwen and decided she liked her. She seemed guileless and wore her emotions all over her face. Giada made a snap decision. "Don't worry about them. We can be friends."

Bronwen's eyes opened wide. "You and me? Really?"

Giada smiled and nodded. Bronwen was like a small child. Giada briefly wondered if she suffered from some kind of mental deficiency or was perhaps on the spectrum.

"Awesome! You can show me all the coolest spots and… ooh, we can pair up whenever there are partner exercises at school. I've seen you hanging around with that good-looking dark-haired boy. Is he your boyfriend?"

Giada felt herself blush furiously. "No, he's just a friend."

"But you like him, right?"

Giada's head whipped towards Bronwen. "Is it obvious? Oh no, please don't tell me I look like a lovesick teenager."

Bronwen giggled, "But you *are* a lovesick teenager."

"I don't want him to know that, do I? I want to look cool and sophisticated. I want to play hard to get."

"What's the point of that?"

"To make him like me."

"Why don't you just tell him you like him?"

"What?! That'll never work."

Honestly, Bronwen has no game whatsoever.

Bronwen shrugged, "It's always worked for me."

"Who've you been trying to get? The village idiot?"

Bronwen's face fell, "That was way harsh."

Giada immediately felt guilty. "Sorry Bronwen, I didn't mean… my sense of humour can be a little biting sometimes. I didn't mean to upset you. I'm sure the boys you've been out with have been very nice."

Bronwen's shoulders sagged. "The truth is… there weren't many boys before I…y'know." Her voice trailed off and her eyes got a little misty before she continued. "I died so young; I didn't really get a chance to date."

"I know what you mean. It was the same for me."

They looked at each other in silence. The unspoken trauma of an imagined life, never lived, passing between them.

"Just means we have a lot of catching up to do here, ey?" Bronwen winked and elbowed Giada in the ribs suggestively causing Giada to hoot with laughter.

As their conversation lapsed into a natural silence, Giada caught a snippet of hushed talking behind her. The girls were speaking in a loud whisper and Giada's ears pricked up as she caught the tail-end of what they were saying.

"They're trying to keep it quiet, but you mark my words, he's fallen. I wouldn't be surprised if we find out he's a senior demon in Satan's army soon."

"Keep your voice down, someone will hear you." The girl whispered but Giada could still just about hear.

"I'm sure he'll turn up soon. He's a senior archangel. There has to be another explanation."

"What other possible explanation could there be? I'm telling you, whenever an angel goes missing, they've defected to the other side."

"He could've been killed on Earth."

"Yes, but that's less likely."

Maddeningly, their conversation was cut short by Gabi entering and blowing her trumpet to signal the start of class. Giada wouldn't get to hear the rest of what they were saying. Gabi started explaining the morning's activity, but Giada was only half-listening. Her thoughts returned again and again to what she'd overheard. Whoever was talking knew too much. This was supposed to be a secret mission. Casually turning, she flicked a glance at the angels behind her. She was shocked to see that they were two of Rika's lackeys. What were they doing sitting behind her and why wasn't Rika with them? Now Giada was suspicious. Did they know about her mission? Were they trying to lead her astray with false information? She shook the thought from her head. How could they know? Her mission was confidential. Besides, that seemed more like something a demon would do. Giada had to stop thinking that every angel was out to get her. At the very least, it seemed these two had access to some quality intel that could be essential to solving this crime. She decided she would spy on them. She would get to the bottom of this and if she found out that Rika was involved, it would make her victory so much sweeter.

11

NALEDI

"What you are telling us is very troubling." Kabelo rubbed his chin as he looked at Naledi. He, Naledi, Tau and Lerato were all sat at Tau's house, discussing the problem of the missing villagers.

"Yeah, I thought demons couldn't exist on Earth in physical form?" Lerato asked.

Kabelo looked at her. "They can't normally. But if a human agrees to host a demon, it breaks down the etheric barrier between Hell and Earth, allowing demons to come here."

Tau looked pensive. "Could that have happened - without us knowing, I mean? Perhaps someone has agreed to host a demon?"

Kabelo shook his head. "If that were the case, demons would be pouring onto Earth, like they did when Sehloho briefly resurrected. It would be a major celestial war between both sides and impossible to miss." He looked up at the ceiling. "There has to be another explanation."

Naledi's blood suddenly ran cold. She remembered the device the Countess had been conspiring with Vassago and Ratu to create. She felt blood rise to her face at the memory that she'd almost defected onto their side. Thank God she'd seen sense in the end. She had to share her thoughts with the others. "There is another possibility. When I was in Hell, there was a demon by the name of Ratu, who was developing a technology that would allow demons to come to Earth in physical form."

Kabelo sat up. "Why haven't you mentioned this before?"

Naledi blinked at him. "It wasn't important before now. I watched Ratu get torn apart by hell hounds which I'd summoned. And my minion friend, Giada, destroyed the blueprints for the device."

"But you know he will have reincarnated in another part of Hell, don't you?"

"Yes, but surely he can't have already recreated his technology within a few months. He told me it had taken him years to build it in the first place."

Tau and Kabelo exchanged glances. "Anything's possible where demons are concerned."

"I think we have to follow this lead - it's the only one we have right now."

Naledi frowned. "Are you suggesting what I think you're suggesting? That I go back to Hell?"

Kabelo looked sheepish. "Yes. If you don't mind."

"I do mind!" Naledi put her hands on her hips. "You guys seem to forget how dangerous Hell is."

"But you're a powerful sangoma. You've survived there before; you can do it again."

"I've barely survived, each time I've been there. It's not a risk I take lightly. I have Dineo and Puleng to think about you know." She flung her hand towards the window, outside which her sisters could be heard giggling and chatting as they played.

"You're right, I'm sorry." He looked around and rubbed his forehead. "Let's explore other avenues of investigation first and only consider that as a last resort. Have you prayed to the angels yet? They might have gathered some information on the other side which we're not aware of."

Naledi blinked at him. "Haven't you heard anything?"

"No." Kabelo replied. "But Heaven has lots of different intelligence teams. I think you should try asking."

Naledi nodded. "You're right. I'll go home and connect with them. See what I can find out..." Naledi's voice trailed off. For some reason she was hesitant to share everything she'd seen and heard when reading the missing villagers' objects.

This wasn't lost on Lerato who furrowed her brow. "What is it?"

Naledi pursed her lips. "There's something else. When I read Amose's grandmother's glasses, I heard a deep voice saying my name."

Tau looked doubtful. "Could you have imagined it?"

"No. It was very clear and sounded malicious - like a demon's voice." She bit her lip. "Do you think these demons could be after me?"

Lerato cocked her head in Naledi's direction. "Girl, I bet Hell is full of Naledi haters after all the shit you've caused for them."

"Not helping, Lerato!" Kabelo spoke through clenched teeth.

"Sorry."

He looked back at Naledi. "If the demons are after you, why have they abducted random villagers instead of attacking you directly?"

"Maybe they think I'm too powerful?"

Kabelo chuckled, his eyes twinkling. "I've never known demons to back away from a fight. They're so arrogant. They always think they'll win. It's part and parcel of their demonic nature."

Tau chimed in. "You're overthinking this, Naledi. Maybe you did hear your name being called, but it could be that some nearby demon sensed you and called your name. I don't think you should worry about it too much."

"I suppose you're right." Naledi still felt anxious though.

She stood up. "Come on, Lerato, we better get going. I want some time to pray alone."

~

NALEDI AND LERATO walked home with Dineo and Puleng, happily skipping behind them. Naledi went straight to her room and sat on her bed, closing her eyes in prayer.

Gabi? ... Michael? Are you there, I need help?

Naledi was surprised to hear, not Gabi or Michael's voice responding to her, but Giada's.

Naledi! How are you?

Giada? How can you hear me?

I'm in heaven. I achieved redemption. Can you believe it?!

Oh Giada! That's fantastic! How is it there?

I'm in training to become an angel. I've been tasked with helping you find the missing villagers. Is that why you're calling for me?

Yes. Two villagers have gone missing so far. A young girl, Esther. She's ten years old and an old woman, of about eighty.

Giada replied. *It's unlikely to be human trafficking with such an old woman also taken.*

That's what I thought so I did a reading on a couple of their personal objects.

And?

They've been taken by demons.

Oh no! We suspected as much but didn't know for sure - they must be using a shrouding spell. We detected demonic activity in Marula. That's why I was assigned to the case. Apparently, I now have a reputation in Heaven as some kind of demon spy-slash-assassin.

Join the club Naledi laughed. Then she shuddered and scrunched up her face in disgust and anguish. *You know what I'm most worried about, don't you? I keep thinking of the sacrifice room inside that other hell dimension.*

Giada replied *I know, me too.... Let's not think the worst.* She paused. *I'm thinking.... I overheard stories about a group of demons worshippers clustered around a twilight region at Joang. Perhaps we should start there?*

Naledi wasn't convinced. *I heard the same rumours, but it's a long car journey - at least a day, more if the roads are bad. If it's a dead end, we'll have wasted a lot of time. Don't you have anything more concrete.*

I'm afraid not. I haven't been on this investigation for long.

Naledi sighed. *Well, if that's all we've got, I guess we better start there. It's not ideal but we can't very well sit here waiting for the right information to fall into our laps. People here are depending on me to sort this out.*

Naledi felt the enormity of what she'd just prayed: she had become the unofficial guardian of the residents of Marula.

Don't go alone, will you? I know you have advanced sangoma powers, but a group of demons might be too much, even for you.

Naledi agreed. *I'll take Lerato, Tau and Kabelo with me. Can you come too?*

There was a slight pause. *I can meet you there, but I can't come all the way with you. As you know, angels can't exist on Earth for long periods of time, unless it's in a twilight region. Joang is a twilight region.*

But what about Kabelo? Naledi asked

Who?

Kabelo. He's an angel but he's on assignment here in Marula. He's been here for months.

Is he inside a human body? Does he look like a normal human?

He does. For ages I had no idea he was an angel.

Then he must've incarnated into the body of a human.

How does that work?

It was probably a devout servant of God, who agreed to give up his body in return for eternal salvation.

Did the boy who gave up his body...die?

His soul went straight to Heaven, yes. Then Kabelo's spirit entered it.

Wow, that's quite a sacrifice.

It might appear that way, but we don't know all the details. There are more people than you realise who would gladly surrender their life for an immediate place in Heaven.

Naledi made a mental note to ask Kabelo more about this at an appropriate time in the future.

Have you made many friends in Heaven?

Not really. Heaven is not as welcoming as I'd been expecting.

Really? What do you mean?

Well... it's quite cliquey. Everyone seems to have their friendship groups already figured out and I don't feel like I fit in anywhere. I'm a bit lonely to tell you the truth.

Oh Giada, that's terrible. Perhaps I should introduce you to Kabelo. I know he's not in Heaven right now but he's really nice and well-connected. I'm sure he could help you to meet people.

Thanks, I'd like that. But enough about me. How are you getting on in life generally?

I'm doing great, thanks. I'm doing well at school and in the evenings, I'm training a small group of girls to become sangomas. I train them in my old house - we don't live there anymore. We moved into Motsumi's house because it's bigger and more comfortable.

Giada joked. It sounds like you've gone from badass sangoma to badass sangoma teacher.

I think I'm badass both Naledi giggled and she heard Giada's laughter inside her head.

What are your students like?

An image of Bongi, Thato and a couple of her other students came unbidden into Naledi's mind and Giada instantly saw them.

All girls then?

Yes, actually, I don't accept boys - it creates problems.

You can say that again. Naledi got the feeling Giada was speaking from personal experience.

Which is your best student?

Probably Bongi. She's my newest and she's incredibly gifted. She's already been practicing for some time, but she wants to deepen her skills. She's also a good influence on Thato, one of my more challenging students.

Images of Bongi and Thato flashed through Naledi's mind as she transmitted these thoughts.

They look like lovely girls, Giada commented.

As they chatted, Naledi found herself relaxing. Giada's presence reassured her and made her feel like everything would be okay. That was the thing about angels, they had a way of doing that and it seemed Giada had already mastered the skill.

12

NALEDI

Suddenly, Lerato emitted a blood-curdling scream from the living room. Naledi sat bolt upright. Her stomach leapt into her throat. It was a scream of pure terror. She raced out of her bedroom, totally forgetting about Giada. Naledi reached the living room in what felt like a split second. Lerato stood, holding Dineo and Puleng against her skirt. In front of them, with his back to Naledi, stood a tall, muscular white man. He had dirty blonde, buzz cut hair and wore a shirt with sleeves rolled up to expose tattoos covering both forearms. He turned to look at Naledi and grinned at her. Sounds became muted and Naledi's perception of reality shifted as she met his eyes. They were deep, pure red and full of malice.

A demon! How is he here? On Earth?

Marula wasn't a twilight region. It didn't make any sense but Naledi couldn't concentrate on that now. She gulped down her fear, reminding herself that she'd taken on worse than him before. Looking him dead in the eyes, she steadied her voice, trying to ignore her thumping heart. "If it's me you want, let the others go."

"Why would I do that when I can have all four of you?"

These words acted like an atomic bomb on Naledi's interior. He could try whatever he wanted with her, but how dare he threaten her sisters! Summoning her powers, she rose up into the air, growing in size as she called upon the elements. "You'll have to come through me first." She shouted, hurling a lightning bolt at his head. With super-fast, demon speed, he ducked and glared at her. Naledi felt herself grow faint.

The demon death stare!

She cried out and looked away. It was only a millisecond, but it was enough for him to leap towards Lerato and grab her. Dineo and Puleng scrambled around and through his massive legs.

"Run to Tau's house - tell him what's going on. Run!" Naledi shouted at the twins. She had to get them out of the house. They made it to the door and bolted out, screaming hysterically as they went. Naledi turned back to the demon. He held Lerato by her hair and licked the side of her face. Lerato grimaced and started whimpering.

"Let her go or she'll be the last thing you ever hold." Naledi growled.

The demon laughed manically and shook his head. "You have no idea who or what you're dealing with, do you? You can't threaten me." His eyes widened as he goaded her. "Go on, try your best to kill me - I dare you."

"Oh, believe me, it'll be my pleasure." Naledi called upon her deadliest power: manifestation. A blazing sword appeared in her hands. The blade was white hot, but the handle was rubberised and easy to hold. She flew towards the demon, swinging the sword at his head, like a samurai warrior. He ducked and let go of Lerato. She scurried to relative safety behind the sofa.

This was just what Naledi had been waiting for. Now that Lerato was out of his filthy clutches, she'd tear him limb from limb. She pounced on him, muttering incantations to protect herself from his demonic death sting and death stare. The minute Naledi made contact with his body, a slurry of images flashed through her mind. She saw a mining town which she half recognised. There was an abandoned prison on the outskirts of the town. The image flitted to a cell, containing a dirty human girl in a heap on the floor. Lifting her head, the girl stared at Naledi with terrified eyes. She gasped as she recognised Esther Mothopeng. Naledi let go of the demon in shock.

It was a mistake that she would relive in her mind again and again.

The demon lunged at Lerato.

"Noooo!" Naledi screamed as she catapulted herself at him. But it was too late. She watched in mute horror as he scooped Lerato up and sprinted out of the door. Naledi flew after him but when she got outside, Lerato and the demon had vanished. They'd disappeared into thin air: just like the other two villagers. Naledi had failed to protect one of the people she loved the most.

Exhausted after the fight, she sank down towards the floor and felt the first flickers of ithwasa curling the corners of her vision like warped film footage.

NALEDI WAS STILL KNEELING on the ground in shock when she heard heavy footsteps running towards her. Pushing her ithwasa symptoms back down through sheer force of will, she looked up. Tau and Kabelo were sprinting in her direction. Tau crouched down, hugging her from the side. As he did this, tears sprang to Naledi's eyes.

"Dineo and Puleng told us what was going on. What happened? Has the demon gone?"

Naledi looked up, her lip wobbling as tears flowed down her face. "Yes, but he's taken Lerato with him. I couldn't stop him. I tried. I used all my powers, but I failed. I failed." Her voice cracked and she covered her face with her hands.

"Hey, hey, don't cry. You did your best." He rubbed her shoulders soothingly.

Naledi looked up at him. "Where are Dineo and Puleng?"

"At Ma Mothopeng's house."

"How are they?" Naledi started to get to her feet. "I have to go to them. See how they're doing."

Kabelo stopped her, putting a hand lightly on her shoulder. "I'd advise against it. The state you're in, you'll scare them further."

"Besides," Tau added, "Esther's grandmother will look after them for as long as we need. She's eager to help."

Naledi nodded and started ambling back into the house as if in a daze. In truth, she was relieved that Kabelo had stopped her. Her thoughts were fragmented and buzzed around her mind like wasps around a spoon of honey. She felt as if she'd just done ten rounds with a boxing heavyweight champion.

The boys followed her inside where she collapsed onto the sofa. Tau and Kabelo sat down opposite and waited for her to speak. She stared into space. Numb.

Kabelo broke the silence. "What I'm wondering is, how did this demon get here? Marula is not a twilight region, so he shouldn't even be able to exist here in physical form."

"That's what I was wondering." Naledi replied. She still couldn't believe she'd failed. With all her powers, the demon had gotten the better of her.

Tau sat up slightly. "Could Marula have suddenly become a twilight region? How do they get created?"

"Normally it's when dark magic has been practiced at a specific location. Or a history of physical demonic presence. For example, in Uhuru, there was a demon resurrection, which weakened the etheric boundary between the realms." Kabelo explained.

Tau sat back again. "Nothing like that has happened in Marula. It must be something else."

Naledi was only half listening, still ruminating on her failure. Then a lightbulb went off in her mind. She sat straighter, holding up her finger with excitement. "I know what I'll do. I'll just go back in time and stop it from happening. In fact, I can go back in time and stop each of the villagers from being abducted."

"Absolutely not." Kabelo was emphatic. "You know how risky it is to go back in time and interfere with events affecting humans. Look what happened the last time you did that. It created Motsumi!"

Naledi sank back into the sofa. But her mind kept whirring and she suddenly remembered the vision. "I know where they are! Well, at least, I saw it. When I was fighting the demon, I had a vision when I touched him. I saw a mining town. I kind of recognised it, but I'm not sure I can name it. It has an old abandoned prison on the outskirts."

"And you say you saw this when you touched the demon?" Kabelo asked.

"Yes. It happens to me sometimes. It's like my skill with reading objects except I read people."

Kabelo nodded, raising his eyebrows. "Very useful."

Tau rubbed his chin. "I don't know the place you describe."

Kabelo chimed in. "I have an old roadmap of Lesotho. It includes landmarks and might give us an indication of where it could be. I'll go and get it."

Kabelo left to go to his house. He returned moments later with the map and a marker pen. He spread it out on the floor and the three of them knelt in a circle, peering over it.

"These are the mining towns." He pointed at various points on the map with his pen. "But only these two have prisons. I'm not sure if either of these prisons are abandoned or still operational." He circled both of the towns.

Naledi perked up when she read the name of one. "Wait, one of the towns is Joang? Amose and Giada both mentioned that town. There are rumours of demon worshipping going on there and it's a twilight region."

"Then I suggest we start there." Kabelo folded up the map and put it in his back pocket.

Naledi rubbed her forehead, scrunching her eyes shut a few times to wake herself up. "If I rest for a bit, I can breach a portal to Joang. We'll get there in minutes."

Kabelo shook his head. "If you do that, you'll have to go with Tau alone. The human body I reside in would not survive a trip through a portal."

Naledi and Tau looked at each other. Could they leave Kabelo behind? He had just as much reason to want Lerato back safely as any of them but if his presence slowed them down, was it worth it? Could Naledi defeat a bunch of demons with only her and Tau? She didn't even know how many demons were there. It could be a whole army, and if it was, Kabelo's telepathic abilities might be useful.

"No, we need you with us. We'll take the truck."

Tau nodded and stood up, setting his lips. "That's settled then. I'll drive. Kabelo, you go and explain to Ma Mothopeng that she'll need to look after the girls a little longer. Naledi you rest. I'll pack some provisions and call you when we're ready to go."

Naledi gazed at Tau adoringly. He was taking charge at the moment she most needed him to. It reminded her why she loved him so much. She nodded gratefully and staggered to bed to rest.

After a little nap, Naledi felt a bit better. She wasn't back up to full strength yet. This meant there would be no option to use her powers if they got attacked but they all agreed that this couldn't wait. The journey to Joang would take a day by car and she could rest more en route. Tau had recently turned sixteen and had been learning how to drive. He didn't have his license yet, and in fact it wasn't even legal for him to be learning until he was seventeen. Nonetheless, they all decided it was best for him to drive Motsumi's old truck. There was always a risk of getting stopped by the cops but if that happened, Naledi should have replenished her reserves enough to perform a memory wiping spell. In addition to provisions, they packed as many weapons as they had. Tau packed his knives and Naledi took her fighting staff. At the last minute she packed Lerato's sling shot - it would come in handy if they found her and needed to fight their way out of wherever she was being held.

13

NALEDI

On the way to Joang, they stopped at a petrol station. It was hot inside the truck and Naledi and Kabelo got out to stretch their legs and get some fresh air while Tau went to pay. Naledi stretched her arms wide, looking up at the blue sky. She sighed, savouring the breeze that blew over the mountains, caressing her bare arms. The call of a warbler bird punctuated the quiet of the sleepy rural station. Another truck pulled up to the station and it was one that she recognised. The owner, Zeke Moshoeshoe, stepped out, giving her a broad grin.

"Dumela Naledi Makwetla. Long time no see!"

"Dumela Zeke. Indeed! Why have you been neglecting our village?"

Zeke looked sheepish. "Well, I always enjoy visiting Marula, but I don't make much money there. A man has got to eat you know."

Naledi nodded with understanding. The products that Zeke sold, hair oils, toothpaste, Vaseline and other sundry items, were of the type which people always wanted but would bypass if they were poor. And everybody in Marula was poor - except for her, now.

"Where are you off to on this fine sunny morning?" Zeke asked

"We're on our way to Joang."

"So far away? What are you going there for?"

Naledi thought quickly. She couldn't very well tell him that they were going to rescue her friend from a demon kidnapping. She reminded herself, as Motsumi had taught her, that the best lie was one that stuck closest to the truth. "It's not a happy trip. Three villagers have gone missing from Marula. We think they may have been abducted. We've heard there may be a possible lead in Joang."

"Abducted! Haiybo! Who is missing?"

Naledi's face crumpled, "one of them is my friend Lerato."

"Oh no, not Lerato!"

"Yes, and also Esther Mothopeng and old Ma Mutsi"

Zeke put his thumb and forefinger to his chin as his eyes rolled skyward. "That's a strange mixture of people, isn't it? All female but why would anyone take such an old woman?"

Naledi nodded, "That's what I thought."

Zeke looked into the middle distance. Naledi could almost see the cogs of his mind working. "This has all the hallmarks of a sacrificial abduction. It's muti murder or devil worship. It has to be."

Naledi was relieved that he'd come to that conclusion by himself. "Do you think so?" She feigned ignorance, opening her eyes wide. "What do you think such people would do with them?"

Zeke looked from side to side then lowered his voice. She didn't know why. Kabelo was wandering around near the shop so he wouldn't have heard them anyway. "I don't want to cause more worry but if it is a sacrificial abduction, you have to get them back quickly. Their bodies could be carved up and used for dark magic or muti."

Although Naledi already knew this, she couldn't help feeling a knot of anguish grip her stomach. Zeke noticed her discomfort and shook his head, clicking his tongue in an expression of sympathy.

Kabelo walked over and greeted Zeke. "Hey, Uncle. What's up?"

Zeke shook his hand and grinned. "Nothing much my brother. I'm sorry to hear about the purpose of your journey. I will pray for a speedy return for all three villagers but especially Lerato, who I know is dear to you."

Kabelo's smile dropped slightly and he dipped his head. "Thank you, that's very kind of you to include us in your prayers."

Zeke continued. "I may be able to help you. I hear a lot on my travels, and I've heard rumours that a village near to here is engaging in demonic worship. The village is called Lehlaka and it's on the way to Joang. Why don't you drive through there and see what you can find out?"

This was indeed valuable information. There was no guarantee that Lerato was at Joang, even if Naledi had seen Esther there in her vision. And if Lehlaka was on the way then it made sense to investigate there first.

"Can you explain clearly how we get there?" Naledi asked.

"Here, show us on this map." Kabelo withdrew the map from his back pocket.

Kabelo spread the map out on the bonnet of the truck and they all bent over it. Zeke pointed to which main roads they needed to travel by and then which smaller roads they should turn at.

"What are the people like there? Are they welcoming to strangers? Should we hide the fact that we're from Marula?" Naledi didn't need to explain this further to Zeke. It was common knowledge for miles around that Marula's population had been devastated by AIDS. Ignorance and stigma, over the disease, were still common and some villagers wouldn't want them to visit, fearing that they may be carriers.

"No, they are friendly, lovely people. I was actually so shocked when I first heard the rumours about them. But I find normally there's no smoke without fire."

Naledi looked towards the shop and saw that Tau was just finishing up. She looked back at Zeke. "Actually, as you're here, let me get some stuff off you. How much for a large tub of Vaseline and that hair oil you sold me the last time? African pride?"

Zeke's body sprang to attention with the excitement of a sale and he walked briskly to his truck and started rooting through boxes. He produced the Vaseline and hair oil.

"That'll be fifty-five loti please."

Naledi raised her eyebrows at him and half smiled. She knew he was ripping her off, but she liked him and was grateful for the information he'd given them. She paid him without complaint, and he bid them goodbye. He waved out of the window one last time as he drove off.

Tau was walking back to the truck. "He left before I got a chance to buy something! I wanted some razors."

"Why didn't you shout out to us?" Kabelo said.

"I didn't know he was going to drive off so quickly." Tau sighed, "I guess I'll just have to stop at the next shop we see. They're all out of razors in the shop here."

"I don't mind a bit of stubble anyway." Naledi affectionately rubbed her hand over his chin and then bent forward to give him a kiss.

"Well in that case maybe I should just give up shaving for good." Tau smiled and pulled her closer to him, planting kisses up and down her neck whilst simultaneously squeezing the flesh around her ribs. Naledi giggled and half batted him away.

"Hey, hey, hey. Break it up you two, we have some people to rescue" Kabelo swatted his hands around, but his tone was playful. Plus, he was right. They all got back in the truck and ate the lunch they'd packed, then drove off, following the map to Lehlaka.

THE ROUTE to Lehlaka was somewhat treacherous. The main roads had been fine but once they got onto the smaller roads, without tarmac, they found them in dire need of regrading.

"Slow down, Tau." Naledi warned after he swerved to avoid a pothole and narrowly missed careering down a steep drop. Tau slowed right down. While this gave them the chance to enjoy the majestic mountain vistas, Naledi felt anxious. "Do you think we'll make it before night fall at this pace?"

Tau failed to keep the exasperation out of his voice. "Decide which you want Naledi - to get there before nightfall or to get there in one piece."

"I want both!"

"That's not possible," Tau replied quietly.

Kabelo chimed in, "We might still make it. If the road improves.

Naledi felt doubtful. "Perhaps we should forget about the detour to Lehlaka. These roads are slowing us down too much. I'm not sure we can afford a diversion that might prove to be a waste of time."

"Why don't we wait and see if the road improves before making a decision?" Kabelo suggested. "Then we can pick up the pace again."

Naledi thought for a moment, "Okay, let's do that. We're on the way anyway."

Just then there was a loud bang and the nerve-tingling sound of metal scraping stone as the bottom of the truck grazed the dirt road. The truck started swerving wildly from one side of the road to the other and Tau fought to control the steering wheel. But this only resulted in him hitting a pothole on the other side of the road. He gave up the fight and stopped the truck to look at the damage. Getting out of the truck, he bent down to look at one side. He exhaled loudly, whilst wiping one hand over his sweat-beaded face.

"Great! Just perfect! Now we have a blow-out."

Tau walked around the truck to inspect the other tyres. "On both sides! Two blow outs!" He slapped his hand to his face and exhaled loudly.

Kabelo got out and inspected the tyres. "We hit that pothole back there. That caused the first one. Then when you swerved and hit the other pothole, it blew the other tyre too."

Tau shook his head and scowled. "I shouldn't have taken my eyes off the road for even one second."

"Don't blame yourself, Tau." Naledi said. "These roads are so bad; it could've happened whether or not you were looking."

Tau smiled at her gratefully, but she could tell he was still angry at himself.

Kabelo spoke. "Let's not stand around feeling sorry for ourselves. Naledi, do you have a spare in the boot?"

"One, maybe, but not two." Naledi actually wasn't sure she even had one. It had been Motsumi's truck and she hadn't thought to check. She opened the storage compartment in the centre of the truck and was relieved to see a new spare tyre shining in the sun.

Good old Motsumi!

"That solves one tyre. I think I've revived enough to do a manifestation spell to get another one."

Tau frowned. "But won't that mean you'll be too tired to fight any demons we find at Lehlaka - if there are any?"

"I'll be too tired to do any more manifestation spells, but I can still do other magic to fight demons. We have no other options anyway."

Naledi closed her eyes and wished for a new tyre to appear. It instantly materialised in the grass next to the truck.

Kabelo and Tau got to work on changing the tyres. Naledi sat on a nearby boulder and waited.

Thankfully, Kabelo and Tau changed the tyres quite quickly and they got back on the road again. But the damage had been done. It wouldn't be possible to reach Joang that day, they'd have to find somewhere to stay and resume their journey in the morning.

By the time they reached Lehlaka, the shadows were long, and they were tired and hungry. Approaching the village, they saw what looked like a celebration going on. There was a large fire in front of some kind of community building with people moving around inside. Villagers sat around on chairs, chatting and drinking beer. A small band was playing music. A man strummed a lovely line of rhythm on a guitar. He was accompanied by another man on tin drums and another who had a penny whistle. Children danced around the band, kicking up sandy dirt as they stamped their feet in joy. The smell of roasting meat filled the air and Naledi put a hand to her stomach as it rumbled in complaint.

"I wonder what's going on here?" Naledi asked

"Let's find out," Tau said, parking the truck by the side of the road.

They walked up to an old man and woman who were having an animated conversation. The conversation came to an abrupt halt as both the man and woman stared at them approaching.

"Dumela Ntate, Dumela Ma" Tau began.

"Dumela son" the old man replied.

"I wonder if you can help us please? We are travellers, on our way to Joang and we had car troubles which delayed our journey. Now we need food and a place to sleep for the night before we continue on our way tomorrow."

The old man nodded in understanding. It wasn't advisable to travel at night around that area. The roads weren't good enough and there were the added dangers of drunkards and animals wandering into the road. Also, the possibility of being ambushed by bandits was greater at night.

The old man replied. "You're welcome to join our festivities. My granddaughter, Dintle and her partner got married today. There will be enough food for you. I will ask around to see who has space to offer you a bed for the night."

Tau bowed slightly and clapped his hands together twice. "That is very kind of you Ntate, thank you so much."

The old woman next to him stuck out her hand, "I am the mother of the bride. You can call me Ma Futsana, and this is my father, Ntate Dino." She put her hands on both of his shoulders and he smiled up at her. His hair and beard were flecked with white, but his face was otherwise quite young and healthy looking. Looking around, Naledi saw plenty of adults here. She wondered if the epidemic had touched this village at all. It didn't look like it. Perhaps most of these people were guests who had travelled here for the wedding.

"Please, go and help yourself to some food and drink." Ma Futsana gestured to the community building behind her.

"Thank you," Naledi dipped her head, as did Tau and Kabelo and they all trailed off towards the hall. Naledi was certain the boys would be just as tired and famished as she was, but she mustn't forget why they'd come here. As soon as people had eaten and started drinking beer, their lips would loosen then she would start discreetly asking questions.

14

GIADA

Giada was hiding behind some reeds listening to Rika and her friends chatting by the side of the celestial river. She'd been perched in this spot for the last hour or so, hoping to get more nuggets of information about the missing archangel. So far, she'd learnt that Rika's best clothing colours were sky blue and peach; that Annabel's date with Stuart had gone very well; and that Safi dreamt of birds again last night. In short, their conversation was not only inane, but also completely useless. If they did know anything more about Domenico's disappearance, they weren't talking about it today. Giada sighed, deciding to abandon her espionage. She'd try again later.

She crept off, keeping hidden behind the reeds until she was at a safe distance before she straightened herself up and walked casually away. She hadn't gone far when Bronwen spotted her and rushed over.

"Hey Giada. I was hoping I'd run into you. Are you going to the newly-redeemed welcoming party on Wednesday night?"

Ah yes, the party. It happened every week to welcome new arrivals. Giada hadn't been to one yet. When she'd first arrived, she'd been so overwhelmed with bliss at being in Heaven and reunited with her brother again that she hadn't felt like going. She'd wanted to spend all her time with her family. Then the weeks drifted by and after a while she stopped thinking about it. She probably should've gone. Maybe then she would've made friends and not felt like such an outcast. "Um, I hadn't really thought about it. Why? Are you going?"

Bronwen's eyes widened and her mouth formed an 'O'. "Does the devil wear red socks? Spoiler alert: he does. Of course, I'm going! Why wouldn't I? Come with me Giada, it'll be fun."

"Erm… I'm not sure. I'll think about it."

"What's there to think about?"

What to wear for a start but that was the least of her concerns. She couldn't afford to waste time partying the night away when she had her mission to work on.

Bronwen wasn't giving up easily. She fluttered her eyelashes, cocking her head to the side. "You could invite Luke you know."

Giada looked at her aghast. "Absolutely no way! In any case, he's been here a while. I'm sure he's already fed up of those parties."

"Oh, come on Giada. If you don't come, I'll have no one to talk to. Pleeease!"

Giada sighed. She could always use it as another chance to eavesdrop on Rika's gang. They were sure to be there, being the attention junkies that they were. At any rate, Bronwen was not going to drop it so she may as well make life easy on herself and just say 'yes'.

"Alright, I'll come."

Bronwen looked quizzically at Giada's clothing. Giada realised that one or two dried reeds were stuck to her dress and she brushed them off quickly.

"What were you doing over here anyway?" Bronwen asked.

Giada thought quickly. She couldn't tell Bronwen that she was spying as part of her mission. She sensed that her new friend was not one for secrets. Either keeping them or being kept from them. If she knew Giada was on a secret mission, she'd go out of her way to find out what it was. Giada settled on, "I was just… having a nap." She had learnt that naps were always an acceptable excuse in Heaven, no matter the time of day nor who was asking.

Bronwen nodded and linked her arm through Giada's. "Man, I will never get over how lucky we are to be able to nap whenever and wherever we feel like it. It's a dream come true!"

"I know what you mean."

"So anyway, back to the party."

Bronwen babbled away, dissecting her wardrobe and the merits of each outfit as Giada listened. Giada felt grateful to have someone so nice who wanted to be friends with her. Bronwen had even seemed grateful when she'd proposed it.

It had been a long time since Giada had had someone she could talk to. She'd had friends in Rome when she'd been much younger but after the death of her brother and her mother's descent into addiction, Giada became withdrawn and stopped hanging out with her friends. At first, they'd tried to get her to open up about her feelings. They'd done their best to keep the friendship going but one by one Giada had pushed them away with her frequent angry outbursts and seething bitterness. Eventually it had been better for everyone that she be left alone. Then after a while, she'd gotten so used to her own company that she forgot how to be social.

Bronwen was like a breath of fresh air. She didn't expect anything from Giada except for light conversation and the camaraderie of simply hanging out. She didn't have complex boy issues or emotional baggage and Giada found this unusual especially considering she'd just come from Hell. But then, maybe she'd worked through all her issues in damnation, much like Giada had? Their friendship hadn't yet matured to the point where Giada felt comfortable asking these deeper questions and she was not sure she ever would. She liked the lack of emotional intensity to their interactions. She found it cleansing and easy. It suited her, just as, she suspected, it suited Bronwen.

The girls neared the fountain of eternity and at a distance Giada spotted what looked like Luke's frame, sitting at the edge of the fountain, outlined by rays of sunshine. She didn't take her eyes off him but felt Bronwen's gaze turn to her and study her expression. Giada half smiled.

"I think that's Luke over there y'know," Bronwen said.

"It looks like it." Giada's smile deepened.

"Go and talk to him."

"No."

"Why not? He's by himself, it's the perfect opportunity."

"The perfect opportunity for me to make a fool of myself?"

"No. The perfect opportunity for you to ask him to the party on Wednesday night."

"I am *not* doing that. If he wants to go, he can go, and I might see him there."

Bronwen rolled her eyes, "I bet he wants you to ask him."

"No boy ever wants a girl to ask him out."

"Who said that?"

"I did, just now."

"Well, you're full of shit. He'll be flattered. It's every guy's dream to be asked out by a girl like you."

"You're just saying that."

"I'm not! Giada, you've got the goods, trust me. You're beautiful, funny, smart. The fact that you act kind of aloof makes you even hotter to guys."

"I do not act *kind of* aloof around *him*. I act like *kind of* a nervous wreck. It's embarrassing. He makes my brain turn to mush."

Bronwen raised her eyebrows. "I'm sure that's not true. If he doesn't want to go out with you, he's an idiot."

"Maybe I'm not his type?"

"And maybe you're just making excuses."

Giada slapped her hands to her cheeks and pulled them down her face as she exhaled loudly. "This is all wrong. He should be asking *me* out, not the other way around."

Bronwen stopped and pulled on Giada's arm to get her to stop. "Are you serious? What is this, 1955? Girls can ask boys out and in fact, boys prefer it that way. It lets them off the hook. They're rubbish at asking us out."

"If you're such an expert at this, why don't you go out with him?"

"I don't want to go out with him. He's not my type."

"Ooh! Now I'm interested." Giada nestled in closer to Bronwen, "What is your type?"

"I haven't found him yet. I'm saving myself for Mr. Right…"

Bronwen twirled her dark red hair around her forefinger and fluttered her eyelashes causing Giada to pack up with laughter.

"… And stop trying to change the subject." Bronwen continued.

Giada composed herself with a few deep breaths. "Okay, you've convinced me. I'll go and talk to him"

"And ask him out?"

"And maybe mention the party if it comes up in conversation."

"And ask him out?"

"And maybe sort of suggest, very casually, that we could go together."

Bronwen rolled her eyes and put her hands on her hips as she looked at Giada. "You're not going to do one of those things where you make it seem like you're friendzoning him are you? You know that's romantic suicide."

Giada frowned. Had she already friendzoned him?

Bronwen pulled her in closer and lowered her voice as they came closer to Luke. "So, here's what we're going to do. Just as we pass him, I'll remember that I have a pressing commitment elsewhere and leave you to talk to him."

Before Giada even had a chance to agree, Bronwen slapped her hand to her forehead in a comically hammed up fashion. "Oh shoot! I have to go, I forgot I said I'd help the archangels with… cleaning the bells." Her voice was classically-trained-actor loud and Giada felt her face flush. Was this too obvious? She shot a discreet glance at Luke, but he didn't seem to have noticed: Bronwen's performance had been wasted. Oblivious, Bronwen sped off, leaving Giada to shuffle past Luke, feeling beyond awkward.

Get a grip and talk to him Giada.

At that moment Luke called out to her. "Hey Giada!" he waved.

She breathed a sigh of relief, smiling brightly as she went over to him.

"Hey Luke, I didn't see you there." *Lies*

"Are you up for another practice later?" Luke asked.

Oh no! Even if I haven't friendzoned him, he's definitely friendzoned me.

How could she rectify this situation? If she said she was busy later, he might think she didn't like him. If she agreed to meet him later, it might put her more firmly in the friendzone. A change of conversation was the only way out.

"Are you going to the newly-redeemed welcoming party on Wednesday night?" She blurted out in one breath. *Smooth, Giada - real smooth.*

Luke looked slightly baffled at the sledgehammered conversation break but he nevertheless smiled. "I wasn't planning on it. Why? Are you going?"

"I thought I might. My friend Bronwen's going and she wants someone to go with."

You idiot! Now he's going to think you're going with Bronwen!

Giada backtracked, "um, what I mean is. She wants to know that there'll be someone else she knows there. I'm not going with her."

Luke's smile widened. "What you're saying is, you're going alone."

"Yes…no… sort of". *Oh Hell!* This was going terribly badly.

Luke stood up and took a step closer to her. He lowered his voice and looked into her eyes. His gaze had the same effect as shaking an etch-a-sketch, erasing all thoughts from her mind. "Would you like to go with me, Giada?"

Giada awoke from her reverie as she blinked her eyes at him in disbelief. "I thought you just said you weren't going?"

"I am now" he said. He held her gaze, his expression a mixture of amusement and yearning. Then his eyes roamed down her face, then down her body, drinking in each of her features and curves. His eyes settled on parts of her body as if they were hands, caressing her. She melted as she recognised the longing in his gaze. Did he have any idea how he made her feel? Was he just playing her, or did he feel the same way too? A warm breeze coursed over her skin as he continued to stare at her, causing her to shiver. How could he be so cool and distant in one minute and so full of fire and desire the next?

"So?" he cleared his throat and straightened himself up. Giada became very aware of how broad his chest was.

"Will you go with me?"

The question was more decisive, and Giada felt reassured. She wouldn't have wanted to say 'yes' if she had any suspicion that he was asking her out of pity - just to keep her company because she'd said she was going alone. Now he seemed more assertive, more certain that he actually wanted to go with her. This she could accept.

"Yes Luke. I will go with you."

15

NALEDI

When Naledi entered the community building she saw a table filled with food. There was stewed meat, roasted meat, palechee, chakalaka, samp and beans, fried morogo and steamed bread. She helped herself to a plate and then poured herself a glass of home-made ginger beer. She took the food outside and sat on one of the chairs arranged around the fire. Tau and Kabelo got their food and then came and sat next to her. She looked at Kabelo. He was picking at his food slowly with a pensive expression. He looked up at her and they shared a smile of sympathy.

"Don't worry, we'll get her back," Kabelo said.

Naledi sighed, "we have to." She refused to imagine any alternative.

Kabelo stared into space, "I keep thinking..." He looked down. "Never mind, I'm being ridiculous."

"No, go on. What were you going to say?"

"I can't help wondering if this is some kind of punishment for... you know."

Naledi scrunched her face up. "For you and Lerato being together? That's crazy talk."

"Is it? I know that relationships between angels and humans are frowned upon."

"But God isn't vindictive like that. I'm sure He has good reasons for not approving of your relationship. I mean sooner or later you'll have to go back to Heaven, and it'll break Lerato's heart. But he wouldn't punish you with a demon kidnapping! He doesn't even have any power over the denizens of Hell."

"You're right. I told you I was being ridiculous." He sighed. "It's just that, Lerato being abducted is affecting me deeply. It's made me realise just how much I care about her. It's not easy for me you know, being inside a human body. I'm not used to dealing with all these emotions."

"Hey, most humans aren't even able to deal with their emotions, so you're in good company."

Naledi looked at Tau. He was shovelling food into his mouth like someone who'd just broken a ten-day hunger strike. Clearly too focused on his dinner to listen to what they'd been saying, he suddenly noticed her looking and piped up. "Mmm, they sure know how to put on a spread here. Have you tasted the stew? It's delicious. I haven't tasted food this good since Mama died."

Naledi chuckled. "There's no quelling your appetite, is there?"

"What?" Tau mumbled, his cheeks bulging. "Try it, I'm telling you. It's so good."

They ate in silence for a few moments. The party wasn't in full swing yet and guests were still turning up. Each new arrival went over to congratulate the bride and groom and then their relatives, before going to get food and drink. Before long there was quite a crowd. Some people had finished their plate and were helping themselves to more drinks. Others started dancing. By now the sun had set and the large fire cast an orange glow over everyone's faces.

A merry-looking man walked over to them. Alcohol had lowered his inhibitions and he wasted no time in getting straight to the point. "You're not from around here, are you?"

"No, we're travellers, on our way to Joang. We got a couple of flat tyres a while back which delayed our journey, so we were forced to stop here for the night." Naledi relayed the same story which Tau had given to Ntate Dino earlier.

"What business do you have in Joang?" the man asked. "It's such an unpleasant place, I wouldn't want to go there."

Naledi wasn't sure how to answer this so she turned the interrogation back on the man. "Why? What's so bad about it?"

The man looked surprised. "You mean you don't know? It has a terrible reputation. Rumour is that it's a twilight zone - a place where both dark and light beings can dwell, in physical form, for indefinite periods of time. As far as I'm concerned that makes Joang a no-go area. Who knows what kind of demonic spirits could possess you just by going there?"

Naledi raised her eyebrows as if ignorant and cynical. "Well, that is certainly quite a colourful rumour. What else have you heard?"

"That's about it but I wouldn't go there without acquiring the protection of a sangoma. Do you know of a sangoma who could sell you a protection talisman?"

Tau spat out his drink. "Excuse me," he said as he mopped the spillage off his top.

The man looked at him strangely, "What's wrong with him?"

"Oh, he ... suffers from acid reflux."

"He should get a sangoma to fix that too."

"Indeed." Naledi nodded. She noted the man's pierced ears with small pieces of cotton thread inserted in each. These were signs that he had visited a sangoma recently. "So, you're traditionalists around here? You still follow the old ways?"

"Of course. Why wouldn't we? We get more help from our sangoma than from white doctors."

"I'd love to meet her... or him."

"Sure, I'll introduce you. I'm Nelson by the way."

"Naledi" she extended her hand and he shook it.

Nelson looked around. "She's over there, give me one minute." He walked off and started talking to a middle-aged woman on the other side of the fire.

Tau leaned into Naledi. "Are you insane? If the woman is authentic, she'll immediately identify you as being a sangoma."

"What's wrong with that? It might force them to reveal something. These people seem to completely believe and trust in the old ways. If they know I'm a powerful sangoma, they are more likely to tell us whatever we want to know."

"They're hardly going to admit to kidnapping Lerato, are they?"

"Probably not, but we'll get a steer from their body language if they're hiding something. It's better than asking them outright without them knowing I'm a woman of power."

"I thought the idea was that we ask questions without telling them our true purpose or who we really are?"

Kabelo interjected, "That also might work but we equally might come away with nothing. Naledi's plan is daring. If this sangoma is the jealous type, we might end up getting ordered out of the village. But it's also got more chance of being effective."

Tau raised his eyebrows, "I hadn't pegged you as a gambling woman before."

"I'm not, but needs must," Naledi replied.

Tau and Kabelo went inside to get another drink, leaving Naledi to talk to the sangoma alone.

Nelson returned with the woman he'd been talking to. "This is Ma Monono. Ma, this is Naledi"

Naledi met the warm, kind eyes of Ma Monono as she stood up and extended her hand. She had a buxom frame, round face and long braids, laden with white beads which rattled as her head moved. "Dumela Ma. It's an honour to meet you."

Ma Monono shook Naledi's hand, not taking her eyes off Naledi's for even a second. Naledi felt a crackle of power that only two sangomas shaking hands would ever feel. Ma Monono's eyes narrowed and she half smiled as she cocked her head to the side. "Likewise," she replied.

Naledi felt an unspoken understanding pass between them and waited for the other sangoma to say something but she didn't. Instead she dropped Naledi's hand, asking. "Have you travelled from far?"

"Marula, it's close to the Maloti mountain range."

"Yes, I know it well. I hear there is a powerful sangoma who lives there." Ma Monono's eyes twinkled with conspiracy.

"You're very well informed." Naledi replied as she smiled briefly.

Nelson had evidently grown bored of the conversation and mumbled something about going to get another beer before ambling off. This left Naledi and Ma Monono to talk freely.

The older woman's eyes travelled up and down Naledi's body, scrutinising her thoroughly. "Tell me. What does the most powerful woman in Marula want with Lehlaka? You can cut the crap about the flat tyres. You mean to be here. Why?"

Naledi pursed her lips. "Alright, I'll level with you. We have heard rumours that you engage in devil worship here."

Ma Monono rolled her eyes and shook her head. "Not that again. That one never dies, does it."

"Some people would say there's no smoke without fire."

"It's malicious lies. Plain and simple."

"What reason would people have to spread hurtful lies about you?"

"Jealousy. You see how prosperous we are here. The epidemic has barely touched us. Those rumour mongers from other villages can't stand to see our success."

"Why should we believe you?"

Ma Monono frowned. "You're still not being honest with me. Why should you care enough about devil worshipping that you travel so far? What's the purpose of your trip?"

Naledi stared at the sangoma for several moments as she weighed her up. The woman had the gift of sight alright. She could see deception; she could see truth. The problem was that Naledi could also see these things and she likewise saw that the woman was hiding something. However, she couldn't detect any dark energy here such as there would be if they were demonic acolytes. She decided to trust her instincts and tell the truth.

"Three people from our village have gone missing over the past couple of days. One of them is my best friend. A demon took her whilst I was in the house. I fought to stop it but failed. We believe the other two villagers have been abducted by the same demon group."

Ma Monono's eyes widened. "All young women?"

"No, that's the weird part. One of them is a grandmother. One is a child and my friend is fifteen."

The sangoma's eyes opened wide. "Demons you say?! But how are they getting to Earth in physical form? Somebody must have agreed to host a demon. How could anyone be so wicked. These demon worshippers are a scourge upon Lesotho. And mark you, the demons they serve won't only be taking people from your village. None of us are safe whilst they roam the land, looking for their next victims to slice and dice for their own perverse pleasure."

Naledi raised her eyebrows. "You seem to know a lot about the nature of demons Ma."

"And this is raising your suspicions again, isn't it?"

"Well..."

"I may not have your breaching abilities, but I have travelled the multiverse in my astral form just as you have. I have been to Hell; I have witnessed the depravity of demons and their addiction to pain and torture."

Naledi studied Ma Monono. She seemed to be genuine in her condemnation of demonic worship and if she was not a practitioner, it was unlikely that anyone else in the village was. What was she hiding then?

"That explains your business in Joang. I would offer to give you a talisman, but I think you can look after yourself." She threw her head back to deliver a deep, throaty laugh which ended in a spluttering cough.

Other than the undiscovered secret, there was something else that Naledi was curious about. "Ma Monono, I hope this isn't too indelicate a question, but I feel that as we are talking openly, I must ask. How have you kept the epidemic away from your village? I see plenty of healthy adults walking around. Sadly, it's not the same in Marula. Are you just extraordinarily lucky, or what?"

"You are right. We haven't been badly afflicted, but it has nothing to do with luck and everything to do with discipline. Our village has an acting Chief - Chief Kweda and a group of elders who enforce his laws. Chief Kweda has always come down hard on infidelity. If he hears even a whisper of it, he expels the perpetrators from the village - even the innocent wife, if her husband has been cheating."

"Wow, that's harsh."

"Harsh but effective. Most people have relatives in other districts who they can go to if they get banished. Look around you - the results speak for themselves. When the villagers started seeing people in other villages dying, they started enforcing the laws just as stringently themselves."

Naledi couldn't deny the results and probably the threat of social ostracization had kept more people honest than would otherwise have been the case. She thought with a heavy heart about all the people they'd lost in Marula and wished they could've had a similar system there. She'd been a young child when people had started getting sick and dying but the memories would haunt her forever. She breathed out deeply, looking around the party to lighten her mood. Motsumi had once told her, it was useless to dwell on the past. At least she was healthy and safe, as were her sisters. Now all she had to do was rescue Lerato and she would have no complaints.

"Where are you staying tonight?"

"We're not sure yet. Ntate Dino said he would ask around to see who has space for us."

"I'd be honoured if you would stay with me. I'm afraid I don't have space for the boys too, but you can sleep on my sofa."

"Thank you Ma Monono, that is so kind of you. I am humbled by your generosity."

"Please don't mention it. Us women of power have to look after each other. Come and find me later when you're ready for bed and I'll make sure you have everything you need." She looked in the direction of the community building. "Now, if you'll excuse me, I haven't yet had anything to eat." Naledi saw the sangoma hesitate as another thought crossed her mind. "After I've eaten, I would like to read your bones - if you are willing?"

Naledi smiled at Ma Monono, "Do the ancestors demand it?"

"They do. They are being very insistent on the matter."

"Then of course I accept."

Ma Monono clasped Naledi's hand in both of hers. The corners of her eyes wrinkled as she smiled "Good. I will come and find you once I have eaten."

Naledi nodded and Ma Monono walked off to get some food.

Tau and Kabelo returned and Tau handed her another ginger beer.

"How did it go?" he asked.

"Well she wants to read my bones - the ancestors insisted."

"Interesting," Kabelo replied, rubbing his chin thoughtfully.

Naledi continued "She also offered to put me up for the night at her place so one of us is sorted."

"That's great! Now we just need somewhere for me and Kabelo." Tau replied. "What else did you learn?"

"She was hiding something, but I can't work out what. I don't think they're demon worshippers."

Kabelo looked around, "Perhaps we should talk to some more people and see if we can pick anything up?"

Naledi scrunched her nose up. "We could but to be honest, I'm not sure we'll get the truth out of anyone. This is a tight-knit community, still rooted in the old ways. They still have a Chief and a circle of elders. Chief Kweda is very strict. He prevented the spread of AIDS by banishing anyone who was caught having relations out of wedlock. If we go around asking questions, they will tell us whatever they've been told they can tell us."

"We need a plan B," Tau said, keeping his voice low.

"What do you suggest?"

"I suggest we wait until everyone's asleep and then go snooping around."

"What if you get caught?" Kabelo asked

Tau shrugged, "I'll make some excuse about having left something in the truck. The worst they can do is throw us out of the village, but at least we'll have got what we came here for - the truth."

Naledi held her hands up. "Tau, you can't break into their houses."

Tau looked at her like she'd gone mad. "I know that! I'll just look through some windows and stuff. Don't worry. I'll be discreet."

Naledi tapped her lip. "There is another option. I can astral travel to do the snooping."

"Perfect, why didn't I think of that." Tau said.

Naledi continued, "The only problem with that is that if this secret is linked to the sangoma, she may have put a spell of psychic protection around whatever it is. That would block me from seeing anything in astral form."

Kabelo shifted his eyes from side to side as he pursed his lips. "Then we should stick with Tau's idea. He should investigate. There's nothing to stop you astral travelling too. Let's do both."

"Okay, that makes sense." Naledi nodded. She looked at Tau and he nodded too.

Tau clapped his hands, "If we're all agreed, let's enjoy the rest of the party. I don't know about you but I'm about ready to get my dance on." He raised both hands up into the air and started clicking his fingers as he swayed from side to side. Naledi grinned at him and came closer, soaking up the music and the atmosphere, as she relaxed to enjoy the first party she'd been to in months.

16

NALEDI

Beads of sweat rolled down Naledi's neck and back as she danced. She closed her eyes and threw her head back, letting the guitar melody float over her like a cool breeze on a hot day. Opening her eyes, she smiled at Tau dancing in front of her. The smell of wood smoke was so strong, she could taste it. As she danced, she saw Ma Monono making her way through the crowd.

"I am ready, let us go," she simply said and beckoned for Naledi to follow her.

The other sangoma led Naledi to a house which was both her home and her clinic. She opened the turquoise painted front door. Naledi heard a soft tinkling and looked at the open windows. Rows of wind charms, made from bottle caps, hung from each window and they moved in the breeze, glinting in the soft moonlight. On the floor was a zebra skin rug, behind which, was a sofa and two wooden chairs. The simple whitewashed clay walls were decorated with pictures of relatives, hung at intermittent intervals. Ma Monono gestured for Naledi to sit on one of the chairs.

"No, thank you," Naledi answered, "I prefer to sit on the floor."

Ma Monono raised one eyebrow, "I didn't make you out as a traditionalist."

"I'm not but... I suppose I like to feel contact with the earth when we're invoking the ancestors."

"Yes, I agree," the sangoma replied. With a certain amount of effort, she lowered her weight onto one knee first whilst resting her hand on one of the chairs. Then she winced as she folded the other knee beneath her.

"Are you okay?" Naledi asked, starting forward.

"Arthritis. My knees are not what they used to be."

Naledi nodded sympathetically. Chronic illnesses such as arthritis were beyond the abilities of sangomas to treat. Pain management was the best the older sangoma could do for her own condition.

Ma Monono took a cloth bag from underneath the chair. Inside the bag was an imphepho smudge stick. The imphepho herb, similar to sage, was burnt by sangomas to invoke the ancestors. She also took out a metal bowl, a lighter and another bag. The sangoma lit the smudge stick and waved it around in the air before placing it inside the metal bowl. Plumes of greyish green smoke whirled around them, casting a rich herbal aroma into the air.

"Your surname is Makwetla, is it not?" Ma Monono asked.

Naledi was impressed at the woman's knowledge. "You really are well informed, aren't you?"

Ma Monono gave a smile of satisfaction before she closed her eyes and started reciting Naledi's praise name. This name honoured her ancestral lineage and called them to give their blessings and wisdom for the reading to follow. As the sangoma chanted, Naledi closed her eyes and concentrated on the words. She'd always felt closer to the spirit world whenever imphepho was burnt, and today was no exception. As she closed her eyes, her ithwasa nudged her consciousness. Naledi saw the words of the chant, drift across the backs of her eyelids. The smoke from the imphepho took on a musical quality, dreamy and peaceful like a love ballad. Naledi swayed and felt warmth spread throughout her body. She felt the presence of the spirits begin to draw near. First a feeling of love, security and comfort, like a child whose mother has just walked in through the door. Then her ancestors took on shadowy forms, dark shapes that she only saw when her eyes were closed.

Ma Monono finished chanting and Naledi opened her eyes. The sangoma picked up her cattle tail stick and swished it around to disperse the smoke and any residual negative energy. Then she picked up the smaller bag and emptied it onto the floor. Animal bones fell out and rolled in different directions. Naledi knew how to read bones but she was interested to see what the ancestors would tell Ma Monono.

The old woman gave a deep, gravelly "Mmm," sound as she looked at them.

"Your lineage is ancient and powerful," she began. "But you still don't understand your powers. You were very sick when you were a young child. The illness took you over the other side but then you came back."

"Yes, that's right. I had measles. I died for a few minutes, but my Mom and Dad prayed desperately, and God brought me back. It's one of the reasons why I'm such a devout Christian."

Ma Monono narrowed her eyes and explained, "This is when you were given your powers as a breacher. You see breaching is a type of realm walking. Once you have died, you become part of the spirit world. After that you can enter Heaven or Hell in a way that other humans can't while alive. With realm walkers, the ability stops there but you were granted the more advanced type of realm walking - the ability to not just enter other realms but also to create a portal to them."

Naledi was hanging on the sangoma's words with such deep concentration that she had forgotten to breath. She exhaled loudly and looked down at the bones. Ma Monono followed her gaze and then frowned.

"Your future is split into two paths. Which one you take depends upon the choices you make now. One path leads to peace and safety, but great loss. The other path leads to excitement and power, but great danger."

Oh no! The loss doesn't mean Lerato, does it? Naledi knew she couldn't ask this. The ancestors didn't deal in direct questions, especially those involving someone's death. They worked in metaphors and symbols. Any wisdom gleaned from the bones had to be interpreted in the same manner as a dream.

"Which path should I choose?" Naledi asked.

"I cannot tell you. Nobody can. The choice is yours alone to make."

"I see" Naledi replied. She was glad she'd come to get her bones read. She'd learnt more about her powers and the reasons why she'd been gifted them, but what Ma Monono said about her future was troubling. Naledi was tired of loss. Hadn't she already grieved enough? As Naledi mused on this, the sangoma had one final piece of knowledge to impart. She looked directly into Naledi's eyes, her brown eyes steely and sharp as a crow's.

"You will always be able to cross into other realms. Once a person has been into the spirit realm, they will forever walk between worlds."

There was a weight to her words that made Naledi shiver. The ancestors clearly thought this was the most important thing of all which she had to know but why? Naledi wouldn't get any more answers tonight but she felt herself slipping into an ocean of foreboding. Whatever trials she was due to face, she couldn't shake the suspicion that they would yet again force her to travel to other realms. Either Heaven... or Hell.

17

NALEDI

Towards the end of the party, Ntate Dino came and told Tau and Kabelo that they could stay with his sister for the night. Naledi retired to Ma Monono's home and settled down into the sofa, covering herself with her Sotho blanket which she'd brought with her. The sounds of the last few stragglers making their way home, permeated the night air. Naledi found it hard to get to sleep. Thoughts whirled around her head. Would Tau be able to creep out undetected and what would he discover? What could Ma Monono be hiding? Considering Naledi was also a sangoma, there was very little that should be kept secret between them unless it was something nefarious. And this weighed on her mind. Was she sleeping in the house of someone who was unsafe? Ma Monono didn't feel unsafe, quite the opposite but Naledi had been wrong about people before. Were they involved somehow in Lerato's disappearance?

Naledi knew it was wrong for her to focus more on her friend than on the other missing villagers, but she couldn't help it. She thought of her small, pretty friend, possibly alone, definitely scared and being held against her will. Tears started to form at Naledi's eyes.

Since she'd come fully into her sangoma powers, she was no longer used to feeling vulnerable but she now realised that her weakness was those she loved. Was Lerato even still alive? There was one-way Naledi could find out for certain and that was to astral travel to Lerato. It wouldn't necessarily tell Naledi what Lerato's physical location was, but it would tell her whether or not she was still alive. She could astral travel to Lerato and then take a sweep of Lehlaka and see what she could find out.

She closed her eyes and focused on her breathing, relaxing her body totally. As she was now an accomplished sangoma, astral travelling came quickly and easily to her. In a few moments, she was out of her body. She concentrated on locating Lerato. She searched within the astral realm and found what felt like her friend's soul but when she tried to lock onto it and follow it to Lerato's body, she felt the thick fog of a shrouding spell.

Damnit!

She tried harder and eventually managed to see the hazy outline of Lerato's form. She was lying on a stone floor. She looked a little dirty but otherwise unharmed. Her eyelids fluttered slightly, and her eyes moved rapidly from side to side behind her closed lids. She was dreaming. Even in her astral form, Naledi felt white hot anger burn within her belly.

Don't worry Lerato. The demons who took you will regret the day they decided to mess with my friend.

Naledi tried to move further away from Lerato's body, to get more details about her location, but she couldn't make out anything through the shrouding spell. She had been lucky to even see Lerato at all. She gave up and thought of her physicality, causing herself to instantly snap back to where her own body lay in Lehlaka.

Naledi didn't enter her body again though. Instead, she flew out of the window, circling the village. It was completely quiet but then she heard a noise. Whipping her head in the direction of the snapping twig, she saw Tau's dark form, hurrying out of a house. Naledi flew above him and watched as he stopped and shivered then looked above him.

He senses me.

On some subtle level that he probably wasn't aware of, he knew she was there. He shook his head as if discounting his suspicion and then crept quickly through the undergrowth. He kept off the main pathways so as not to disturb the gravel. Naledi watched him peeking through various windows. One window still had a paraffin lamp on. Tau peered through it and then ducked down quickly. Naledi flew over to see what had spooked him. She saw Ntate Dino busy making out with one of the older women from the party. Naledi instantly looked away, embarrassed to have intruded on such a private moment. As she looked through different windows something struck her as strange. Some of the houses were empty. Did nobody live there or were the inhabitants out or away? How could one small village have so many people out or away at the same time? Equally, how could one small village have so many empty houses at one time?

Naledi soon found out the answer to her question. She heard the faint sound of chanting and drumming towards the top end of the village. This could be what they were looking for: demon worship. She flew towards the sound. Down below, Tau crept not far behind her. As she came closer, she saw a circle of villagers, dancing and chanting to the beat of a drum. The drummer was Nelson, the man she'd met at the party. He had a bandana tied around his forehead and a cigarette hung from his lips. His eyes were closed in deep devotion and a smile of sweet joy was on his face. The dancers' faces equally held expressions of rapturous bliss. Their bodies glistened with beads of sweat.

As Naledi watched, one of the dancers, a woman, dropped to the floor and started convulsing then speaking in some type of gibberish language. Naledi had seen this type of thing before when people were seized by the spirit at church and started speaking in tongues. But which spirit was seizing the dancer? Whatever they were doing clearly wasn't Christian so was this person allowing a demonic entity into her body? Naledi found herself fascinated by what she saw. Some of those present, who weren't dancing, wore masks. The masks were carved from wood and all featured the same grinning abstract face. Was this a representation of the demon which they were worshipping?

Naledi was so enthralled by what she was seeing that she had totally lost track of where Tau was. There was a break in the drumming and simultaneously a twig snapped nearby. Naledi's attention jumped instantly to the noise and she saw Tau crouching behind a bush. He silently cursed his clumsiness. Whipping her head back she saw a look of fear in Nelson's eyes. He gestured with his hands to the rest of the group to be quiet and stay put. Then he stood up and stretched.

"I'm going to take a quick piss." He said loudly. He walked in Tau's direction and made as if to start unzipping his trousers but instead he crouched down and grabbed Tau's wrist. "Well, what do we have here?" he asked, a menacing expression on his face.

Naledi felt her heart rate instantly increase as adrenaline coursed through her. She went rushing back into her physical body and sat bolt upright, opening her eyes wide.

Tau is in trouble!

She flew out of the house, barely caring if Ma Monono heard her or not. She'd seen the house that Tau had come out of. Kabelo was probably inside too. She used telepathy to reach out to him.

Kabelo, come out of the house now. Tau is in trouble. He needs us.

Naledi didn't wait for Kabelo to appear. She ran in the direction of the grove of trees and was there within minutes. Tau was kneeling in the centre of the demon worshippers. Nelson had a large machete which he was holding to Tau's neck.

"I was just curious. I won't tell anyone what I saw, I swear." Tau said, waving his hands in front of his terrified face.

"And what did you see?" Nelson challenged him.

"Nothing" Tau replied quickly. "Nothing at all."

Nelson laughed. "You're a terrible liar."

Naledi ran towards them. "Drop the machete, Nelson."

"Or what?"

She called upon her powers. Controlling the elements, electricity crackled between her hands. "Or we'll see how well you can stab someone with a bolt of lightning coursing through your body."

Nelson instantly dropped the knife and held his hands up. "Whoa!" He dipped his head in respect. "I'm sorry Sis Naledi. I had no idea you were a woman of power. Why didn't you tell me?"

Naledi smiled and dropped her hands but kept on her guard. "You didn't need to know."

She heard pounding footsteps behind her and turned to see Kabelo running up to them.

"What's going on?" he asked.

"These villagers were engaging in demonic worship." Naledi replied.

Nelson burst out laughing. "Hah! Now I see why you're so riled up. Is that what you think this is? Demon worshipping?" He shook his head as if the idea was ridiculous.

Naledi, Tau and Kabelo exchanged puzzled glances.

"Well if it looks like a lion and smells like a lion?..." Kabelo started but Nelson cut him off.

"We worship the old God, Khukwan. We have worshipped him for centuries, since before the white man came. None of us are Christians and we never will be. We reject the white man's religion and his God. We are loyal to Khukwan."

Naledi couldn't believe what she was hearing. She'd heard rumours of small sects of people, throughout Lesotho, who still worshipped the old Basotho gods, but she hadn't believed it was true. She'd never actually met anyone who admitted to it, so she'd thought it was just a rumour. But now here she was, standing right in the centre of a group of Khukwan devotees. As she looked around at the masks, she had a dim recollection of her grandmother, Nkhono, explaining the various Basotho gods to her. Khukwan was a trickster God, a shapeshifter who had come from the stars and given the Basotho people knowledge of the constellations and agriculture.

"How do we know you're telling the truth?" Kabelo challenged them.

Nelson looked at Naledi. "You are a woman of power, with the gift of sight. Look into your heart and you will see that we are aligned with light and not dark. You will find no evidence of evil here, no human sacrifices, no unhappiness and barely any sickness. It is Khukwan who has given us such prosperity. Other villages think we are lucky - maybe we are. They think we are disciplined - maybe we are. But more than any of those things, we are anointed by the grace of our beloved Khukwan. He favours us as we are his most loyal devotees."

Naledi looked around the group. It was true that they didn't carry the aura of evil. She even saw one or two children and one woman held a sleeping baby in her arms. These didn't look like demon acolytes. They were too full of joy and reverence.

"Why don't you join us?"

Naledi balked. "I couldn't possibly. I am a committed Christian."

"A Christian and a sangoma?!" Nelson shook his head in disbelief. "What a waste."

He's certainly not shy to hide his scorn for Christianity.

Naledi felt her cheeks glow with anger at the insult to her Lord and Saviour. If she hadn't been the guest of these villagers she would've given them a piece of her mind, but she held her tongue.

"You don't have to join in. Just sit on the outside and watch us as we worship. We don't expect you to give your allegiance to Khukwan or anything."

Kabelo leaned into Naledi and said under his breath. "It's a good idea. We'll get a better sense of if this is genuine or a front for devil worshipping."

"Alright, I suppose it won't do any harm to just watch." Naledi agreed.

Naledi, Tau and Kabelo sat on the ground, to the side of the circle, and watched. Nelson lit another cigarette, re-adjusted his headband then sat down on a tree stump in front of the large, wooden drum. When he hit it, the loud bass vibrated through the earth, stirring Naledi's heart and uplifting her soul. The dancers began moving around again, gyrating their bodies in time to the drumbeats. Some people started singing softly, others were chanting words that Naledi didn't understand. She reflected that it was possibly in some old, forgotten language, a precursor to Sesotho.

As they danced, the air began to shift. Naledi felt the atmosphere get heavy, like it was infused with power. But what power could it be? Surely this God was just a figment of their imaginations. Not real like her God. As she thought this, a gust of wind began to form at the side of the fire, whipping up a cloud of yellow dust. The dancers moved more feverishly and the excitement in the group was palpable. The wind felt full of substance, with a thickness that seemed tangible. Then Naledi thought she could make out an apparition in the centre of the wind. Could everyone else see that or was this a moment of ithwasa? Perhaps brought on by worry over Lerato? She looked around the group. Some people had tears of joy in their eyes.

"He is with us!" one woman cried out. She fell to her knees, prostrating herself before the apparition. As she did this, the figure seemed to take on more physicality. The wind started to settle down and with it the dust. In its place stood a man. A real life, flesh and blood man who had not stood there before. He was young, dark, tightly muscled and devastatingly handsome. His face cracked into a smile and he gave, a loud, deep, inviting laugh. Power crackled around him and Naledi couldn't take her eyes off him. She blushed as he looked at her and smiled. His eyes roved languidly over her body as if she was naked and in his gaze, she felt like she was, but she didn't mind. She liked it. Forcing herself away from the strong connection she felt they shared, Naledi flicked her eyes to Tau. He glowered at the man as his face flitted between disbelief and rage. Naledi studied the man's eyes - they weren't red, so he definitely wasn't a demon.

Nelson rushed in front of the man and threw himself to the ground.

"Great Khukwan. We are your devoted servants. Thank you for visiting us in human form. Tell us what you want of us."

No way! This is Khukwan - trickster God of the Basotho. Naledi thought. She felt her entire belief system unravel. Everything she'd always thought about Basotho gods being a load of rubbish was wrong. One was standing right before her, as real as any other human here and she'd never seen anyone more attractive in her life.

18

GIADA

It was early morning. Giada was back inside Michael's office at the Hall of Creation, studying the file containing information on Domenico's last movements. She was sitting in the meeting room he'd brought her into on her first day there. Staring at the photos, she racked her brain for any clues she'd missed that would help her with working out what had happened. Deep in concentration, she was startled as the door handle clicked. Giada hastily swept the photos into the file just as a familiar face poked his head around the door.

"Working hard I see?" Luke said

"Trying to" Giada bit her lip sheepishly.

"I'm about to head off. Would you like to walk to class together?"

Would I?!

"Sure" she answered with a slight shrug. Since spending more time with Luke, she'd found she was getting better and better at acting casual around him. Gathering up her file, she followed him out. She handed the file to Michael on the way.

"Did you make any progress?" he asked.

"A little," she replied. In truth she'd made no progress. She felt like she was taking two steps backwards for every step forward. It didn't help that she couldn't discuss this with anyone - not even Luke. It meant she couldn't ask questions. The best she could do was follow people around, hoping someone would give something up in a conversation. It was impossible! She chewed her lip and sighed, reflecting on the unfairness of her life. She was willing to bet good money that nobody else had a mission as difficult as hers. Rika's mission was most definitely something a trained monkey could do. Why had they given Giada one that seemed designed to make her fail? Was this some sick kind of joke? Didn't God want her here? Perhaps this was all just another Hell dimension - an elaborate one where the demons got off on playing poor minions for a fool?

"Penny for your thoughts?" Luke roused her from her ruminations.

She relaxed her shoulders and exhaled. "Sorry, I was miles away."

"Clearly. Do you wanna talk about it?"

Giada looked at him. Did she want to talk about it? With him? She narrowed her eyes at him and was dazzled by his beauty, in the same way that she always was. Giada looked away quickly, not wanting her thoughts to start short circuiting. She did want to talk about it with someone but not with him. Even if she could think clearly around him (which she couldn't), she didn't fully trust him. "Nah, it's not important. How was your morning anyway? Did you make good progress on your mission?" Giada turned the focus on him, and half listened as they walked the rest of the way to school. She knew exactly the person she needed to talk to about this. The person who had become her confidante and mentor since she'd arrived in Heaven: Roberto.

AFTER HER EARLY START, Giada left school mid-morning. Trudging home, she was still brooding on the unfairness of her mission. When she got home she slumped down on the sofa, kicking her legs in front of her and letting her head flop backwards onto the cushions.

Roberto came out of his room and watched her with his doe-like brown eyes. "How was your morning?"

"Eurgh!" Giada slumped down further as she covered her hands with her face.

"That bad, huh?"

She sat up straighter. "I've been given my mission. I can't talk about it but it's way harder than everyone else's."

"How do you know it's way harder than everyone else's?"

"It has to be - my task is impossible. I don't know how they expect anyone to be able to complete it." She threw her arms up into the air in exasperation.

Roberto padded over and sat next to her. His little legs dangled over the edge without touching the floor. "God never puts challenges in our path that he doesn't know we're strong enough to achieve. If the archangels have given you this mission, it's because they know you can do it."

"That's sort of what Gabi said but it's just... I don't really believe her."

Roberto looked at her. "You don't have faith in yourself. That's your biggest problem. The archangels believe in you. God believes in you. Now you have to believe in yourself."

Giada looked at him and felt herself soften as his words soothed her jagged mood. She'd got used to his ways by now, but she still found it strange sometimes, hearing such wisdom coming out of the mouth of a young boy. His voice had the tone of a child, but his thoughts had the depth and profundity of a Zen Buddhist monk - not that she'd ever met a Zen Buddhist monk but if she did, Roberto is how she imagined one would sound.

"Thanks, little brother. You always make me feel better."

"You're welcome big sister." He reached forward and hugged her, and Giada felt all her cares momentarily melt away.

Then he looked at her and his eyes widened with excitement. "Hey, I'm going back out to check on the kittens. Wanna come?"

Giada shook her head, "Some other time, I need to be alone for a while."

Roberto nodded and skipped off. He'd gone from ageless sage to little kid again.

Her mother walked in, removing her gardening gloves. Her cheeks had the same pink, rosy glow they usually did when she'd been gardening. It was a mixture of exertion and joy.

"Are you alright, mi amore?" she asked Giada.

"Oh Mama... I've just had a rough morning, that's all."

Her mother sat down on the chair opposite her. "Do you want to talk about it?"

Giada would've loved to talk about it, but she couldn't. Her gargantuan mission wasn't the only thing on her mind though.

"It's just that... I don't feel I have any friends here really."

"That's not true, what about that nice Bronwen girl you've recently started hanging around with?"

"Sure, Bronwen is nice but I'm not sure if I can really talk to her about everything."

"Friendship takes time to deepen. You have to be patient."

Giada thought for a moment. There was something else about Bronwen, something she couldn't put her finger on and hadn't even really acknowledged to herself yet.

"I'm not sure why but I feel like I don't trust her completely."

Her mother smiled kindly. "That's hardly surprising. You've just spent a few months living amongst the most deceitful beings in the universe. In Hell, you had to constantly be on your guard in order to survive. It's only natural that you struggle to trust people now."

Giada half smiled, "I suppose you're right." But inside she still felt like there was something off about Bronwen. "I dunno, it's like she's too good to be true. She's too eager to be my friend."

Her mother raised her eyebrows and folded her arms. "You have got to learn to accept happiness. You've spent years pushing people away. Even when you were still alive you pushed away all those lovely friends you had in Rome. I think you're still trying to adjust to a life free from pain and disappointment." She brushed some stray hairs out of Giada's face. "It's normal, every newly-redeemed soul goes through this. Just give it time and you'll soon settle in and realise that no one is out to hurt you. You deserve nice friends. Give Bronwen a chance."

Giada reached forward and squeezed her tight. "Thanks Mama. I needed this." She sat back and looked into her mother's eyes. "You're right. I should just relax and stop worrying."

"Why don't you go to the newly-redeemed welcoming party on Wednesday night? You've never been to one and I think it would do you good to get out and meet more people."

"Yeah, actually Mama, I was already planning on going."

"Good! Is Bronwen going too?"

"Yes, I'm meeting her there."

Her mama looked puzzled, "You're not going together?"

Giada tried to keep her manner casual, but her eyebrows rose slightly as did her voice. "No, I'm going with someone else."

It was enough to arouse her mother's interest. Her mama's eyes narrowed then widened as her mouth opened in realisation. "Who is he? What's his name?"

"He's just a friend."

"Then you won't mind telling me his name. Is it a boy from your class? Come on tell me."

Giada felt her cheeks glowing bright red which only added ammunition to her mother's suspicions. "His name's Luke. He's a boy from class."

"What does he look like? Is he handsome? I bet he's handsome. Is he coming to collect you here? Ooh, I'll get to meet him." She clapped her hands together and giggled like a teenager.

"Mama, stop. Please don't give him a hard time. Like I said, we're just friends."

"Friends. Right. Of course." Her mother still studied her with a razor-sharp gaze as her lips twitched with the effort of stifling a smile. It was excruciating.

Giada could stand it no more. "I'm going to lie down for a bit."

"Alright bambina, you do that. Naps are essential - beauty sleep and all that."

Giada lay on her bed, staring at the white high ceiling. The window was open, and a perfect, warm breeze coursed over her arms. The scent of honeydew melons drifted through the window. Everything in Heaven had been designed to delight the senses. But Giada found herself thinking that the one thing God couldn't control was souls. No matter whether they were angels or people, they were what made heaven challenging. She was no closer to finding out what had happened to Domenico.

At least she had the date on Wednesday to look forward to. Was it a date? It had certainly felt more like Luke was asking her out properly this time. Not like when he'd asked her to practice levitation with him. She decided that this *was* actually a date and she allowed herself to get a little excited. Ah, who was she kidding? She was *very* excited. Her stomach filled with butterflies just thinking about it. Her mind flitted over the various wardrobe choices she'd been discussing with Bronwen. She still hadn't come up with a definitive style plan for the evening, but she was close. It was definitely an up hair-do and drop-stone earrings affair, but the main sticking point was the shoes. Heels made her look taller and complemented her figure but if there was dancing, she'd be more comfortable in flats. She'd never been one to favour comfort over style though. Flats were out of the question. Perhaps an in between choice? Kitten or block mid-heels?

As she mused, she felt herself begin to drop off when she was startled awake by a knocking sound at the window. The next moment, a piece of paper fluttered onto her nose. Picking it up, she unfolded it. It was a note and it said.

Meet me by the fountain of eternity at midday. Come alone. I know something that may help you complete your mission.

Giada sat bolt upright. She scrambled to kneel on the bed as she looked out of the window. She whipped her head from left to right but there was no one there. Whoever had given this note knew what her mission was. Was this some kind of joke or was she really about to get some secret piece of the puzzle? There was only one way to find out. She had to go to the fountain of eternity at midday.

19

NALEDI

Khukwan stretched, flexing his neck muscles as he moved his head from side to side, in a way that made them click. His smooth jet-black skin shone in the moonlight. Naledi had never seen a man exude more testosterone. She could almost smell it coming out of his breath. Next to him, Tau looked like a boy. She pushed the thought away and focused on the sound of a bull frog croaking nearby.

"So, this is the breacher I have heard so much about." Khukwan strode forward. Beneath his bare chest, he wore an animal hide which flapped against his muscular thighs as he walked. Standing in front of Naledi with his arms crossed, he looked her up and down as if appraising a prize cow. Naledi closed her eyes and gulped as she felt waves of power radiate from him. The magnitude of his aura made her shiver with a mixture of delight and fear.

"You have heard of me, Kgosi?" She used the polite Sotho term for 'Sir' as she didn't know how else to address a god.

"Everyone has heard of you. My devotees up and down the country whisper of the breacher of Marula, who vanquished two demons whilst still a trainee." He reached forward and brushed a braid out of her face. Tau took a step forward, his fists clenching but Kabelo held him back.

Naledi felt herself blush. She wanted to look away but found she could not. His eyes, trained on hers, had a strange mesmerising quality. It was like she could see the entire universe within those dark, golden-flecked irises.

"What is your business in Lehlaka?"

Unable to lie in the presence of the trickster god, Naledi replied. "We heard reports of demon worshipping here."

Khukwan threw his head back and delivered a hearty baritone laugh. "And how about now? Do you still believe my people are devil worshippers?"

Naledi shook her head.

"And what would it matter to you, even if they were?"

"We are searching for three villagers who have been abducted - two women and a girl. We believe they have been taken for use in demonic sacrifices. We were on our way to Joang when we heard that it may be worth our while to investigate Lehlaka too. It was on the way so..." She finally broke his gaze and looked at her feet.

Khukwan still stared at her but he narrowed his eyes and rubbed his chin. "Hmm. Demon sacrifices you say?" He gestured towards Tau and Kabelo. "Are these your companions?"

"Yes. This is my boyfriend, Tau, and this is my friend, Kabelo."

Khukwan walked over to inspect the young men in the same manner as he had done with Naledi. He barely acknowledged Tau and Naledi saw her boyfriend's lips set as he clenched his jaw. When he got to Kabelo, he cocked his head to one side as his eyes moved up and down. "This one is not what he appears to be," he simply said.

Kabelo instantly let out a high-pitched laugh which turned into a cough. "Excuse me," he said as he thumped his chest. Kabelo gave Naledi a look of desperate pleading. She took the hint and asked a question to divert the attention from him. "Kgosi, may I ask, to what do we owe the honour of your presence among us tonight?"

Khukwan turned back towards her. "Please, call me Khukwan."

Naledi caught Nelson's eye and the man looked as if he was about to have a seizure. His mouth opened and closed like a fish as his face was turning red. Suffice to say that Nelson clearly thought the idea of Naledi using the god's first name was outrageous.

"I'd feel more comfortable calling you Kgos…"

His eyes flashed, "I insist. You are a woman of immense power. We are equals. Call me Khukwan." He licked his lips, then smiled slightly, and Naledi felt herself swoon. It wasn't just his power which excited her. A thorough and full-bodied masculinity emanated from every pore of his being. His body was composed of tight muscles and raw strength. When he moved, Naledi was reminded of a cheetah in full chase; an animal perfectly designed to snag its prey.

Naledi blinked, "Alright, Khukwan. Why are you here?" She flicked her gaze to Nelson and again she saw him flinch.

"I wanted to meet you." He looked up at the stars then added. "And now that I have, I see that my presence is needed. I do love a good demon thrashing, don't you?" He started laughing again.

Naledi laughed along, nervously. She couldn't quite work this guy out. He was a god. Why would he waste his time on helping them? Was it just for fun, like he implied? Or did he have some other agenda? She looked at Tau. He stood glowering at the god. Kabelo still held his forearm, stopping him from doing anything stupid.

Honestly thought Naledi. *Men are so predictable; the tiniest things make them jealous*. Khukwan hadn't even done anything concrete: he'd barely flirted. Okay, he'd touched her braid. So what? It was probably the fact that Khukwan was so undeniably attractive. She looked around at the other women in the circle. Every single one of them was undressing him with her eyes. They didn't even bother to hide it. Is that how she'd looked at him? She looked down, suddenly feeling ashamed. No wonder Tau looked so angry.

Khukwan rubbed his hands together. "When do we leave?"

"We?!" Tau spat

"Yes of course. I'm coming with you."

"We don't need…" Tau started but then Kabelo interrupted him

"Thank you for your kind offer Kgosi but we are more than capable of finding the women ourselves."

"I'm sure you are but an extra pair of hands." Khukwan lifted his hands and wiggled his fingers. As he did so sparks of blue energy crackled around them. "An extra pair of magical, power-imbued hands, is always welcome, is it not?"

Naledi thought quickly. She didn't want to offend the god but nor did she want to start a fight with Tau. "We are overwhelmed by your generosity Khukwan, but I have magical powers myself - as you know."

"Can you do this?" Khukwan asked.

Naledi watched as the air changed around him. He started transforming. First his body hunched over and he went onto all fours. Then he grew more hair. The hair got more mottled and then his face changed. A muzzle grew out of his face and he made an unearthly yelping noise. Naledi squinted, she couldn't believe her eyes. When the transformation was complete, he had changed into a leopard. She'd known Khukwan was supposed to be a shapeshifter, but she hadn't taken it literally. She'd assumed all these stories were metaphors for something else. How wrong she'd been. The leopard padded over to her and licked her calf. His tongue felt as rough as sandpaper. Naledi's insides dissolved like butter on hot toast. She cast her eyes upwards and gulped. When she looked down again, the leopard was changing back into the god. Tau's face - ordinarily brown, had taken on a tinge of puce. Naledi saw his chest rise and fall as he took deep breaths.

When Khukwan was back in human form he asked. "Well? Can you do that?"

"No, I can't but what good is it against demons? Sorry, I don't mean to sound impertinent. It's an honest question."

"I can transform into any animal I wish." His eyes twinkled at her.

Tau could stand it no more. "Kgosi, if you are coming with us, I'd appreciate it if you didn't lick my girlfriend's leg."

Nelson stepped forward, clenching his fists, "How dare you speak to him like that?"

"No, it's okay," Khukwan waved his hand as if Tau was an insignificant fly. "He's protecting the honour of his woman. I can respect that.

I apologise - Tau?" his voice inflected upwards as if he'd forgotten Tau's name. "I'm unable to fully control the animal impulses of the creatures I transform into. Clearly my leopard found her worth licking."

"Say that again and I'll knock your teeth out." Tau replied, a vein pulsing in his neck.

"Hah! The boy is fearless! I like your spirit, Tau."

Naledi suspected he would've gone and ruffled Tau's head if Tau hadn't been so close to rage. Thankfully, Khukwan restrained himself. He was sexy but by God he was arrogant. He loved himself as much as any women present.

Kabelo coughed. "Um, it's getting late now, and we have a long journey ahead of us. I suggest we go to bed."

Khukwan looked at him. "That's a good idea. I'll come and find you in the morning." The god walked off through the bushes into the night.

THE NEXT MORNING Naledi found the boys after a quick breakfast and they checked the truck was roadworthy. Then they went to say their goodbyes and thanks to Ntate Dino and some of the other villagers. Naledi wondered if what they'd experienced the night before had been some kind of shared hallucination. Perhaps the drinks they'd had at the wedding had gone off or been laced with psychedelic plants. Just as she was thinking this she felt the hairs on the back of her neck stand up. She turned around and Khukwan stood behind her. Had he crept up on her or had he just appeared out of nowhere?

"Good morning Naledi." He nodded at the boys, "Good morning Tau, morning Kabelo."

At least this morning he's being a bit more respectful to Tau.

She looked, pointedly, at Tau and he mumbled a grumpy greeting in reply.

A couple of children who had been playing nearby raced over.

"Monghadi Khukwan! Please give us a blessing. Do you have any sweets?"

They both talked at once, and at one hundred miles per hour.

Khukwan smiled indulgently at them. He clicked his fingers in the way that parlour magicians do and two sweets appeared in his hands. He gave one to each of the children.

Naledi noticed something in one of the children's hands which he dropped as he took the sweet. When it floated to the floor she gasped and put her hands up to her mouth.

"What is it?" Tau looked at her

"It's Lerato's scarf!" Naledi crouched down to pick it up. She immediately dropped it again, her lip curling. "It's got blood on it!" Tears sprang instantly to her eyes and she sniffed.

"Are you sure it's hers?" Tau asked.

"Yes, I'd recognise that scarf anywhere."

"But isn't it possible that someone else has the same scarf as her?" Kabelo asked.

"No. That scarf was a gift from her mother. She made it out of an old dress that she bought in the nineties. The chance that someone else would have the same scarf…it's just too much of a coincidence. It has to be hers."

Khukwan's face became serious as he looked at the children. "Where did you find this scarf?"

"We were playing by the main road. We found it there. Did we do something wrong?" The boy looked at Khukwan with large, watery eyes.

Khukwan's features softened. "No, Ngoana, you didn't do anything wrong." He ruffled the boy's hair affectionately and the boy smiled and relaxed his shoulders.

"You can have the scarf if you want?" The boy offered.

"Thank you, my friend would like it, I'll give it to her, but I tell you what," he leaned closer and whispered.

"What?"

"I'll trade you for a whole bag of sweets, how about that?" He clicked his fingers again and a bag of sweets materialised in his hands. The children squealed with joy and grabbed the bag, jumping up and down in circles before running off. They'd forgotten all about the scarf as they shouted for their friends to come and share the sweets.

"Good kids," Khukwan commented as he smiled warmly.

Naledi looked at Kabelo. She could almost see the cogs of his mind turning. "That road leads to Joang. That means Lerato was brought past here on her way there. It's as close as we'll get to a confirmation that she's there."

They got into the truck. Naledi sat between Tau and Kabelo in the front cab and Khukwan jumped onto the back-load bed to sit among their rucksacks and blanket bundles. Pins and needles ran up and down her body as her mind ran wild with all the possible scenarios of how Lerato's scarf had been bloodied. As she sat she said a silent prayer.

Please God, please protect Lerato, Amen..... We're coming for you Lerato, I promise.

Then she had another thought. *Giada, are you there?*

Yes. How can I help?

We're now pretty sure that Lerato and the abducted villagers are at Joang. I'll pray to you when we get there so you can help us. I don't know how many demons there are, but it could be a lot.

Okay, I'll be on standby. Great work, Naledi!

∽

20

GIADA

It was midday. Giada waited by the fountain of eternity. She watched a couple stroll past, arm in arm. The woman giggled as the man whispered something in her ear. Giada felt a pang of jealousy: would she ever have that kind of easy relationship with someone? She thought of Luke. He was hot one minute and cold the next. He'd asked her out, but then had hardly spoken to her since then. Why had he even asked her out? Perhaps he was just busy working on his mission, but she couldn't shake the feeling that he was playing her. Maybe the date on Wednesday would give her more certainty of his intentions towards her.

On her way here, she'd answered Naledi's prayers about the missing villagers and it weighed on her mind. Was it cowardly for her to be waiting for Naledi and her friends to arrive in Joang instead of going to attack the demons herself? If she was really serious about becoming an angel on Michael's team, she'd have to get used to fighting demons. She just didn't feel ready. She'd never killed a demon before and her time in Hell had scarred her. It had taught her just how dangerous demons were. If a demon killed her on Earth, she would be killed forever, with no chance of rebirth. She'd only just got to Heaven and she didn't want to throw away eternal bliss on foolishness disguised as bravery.

She looked up at the cloudless blue sky and brilliant yellow orb of sun. It was one of the best things about Heaven. She'd missed the sky so much in Hell and even on Earth the sky had never been this beautiful.

Giada's body instantly tensed as she felt warm breath on the back of her neck.

"Don't turn around," a female voice whispered. "And don't talk. If you understand what I'm saying, nod."

Giada nodded.

"Good, now meet me at the remembrance crypt. You leave first, I'll follow in ten minutes. Walk slowly, as if you're not heading anywhere in particular. Does that make sense?"

Giada nodded again and started walking. The remembrance crypt was an underground room that had been built to remember angels who had fallen in various battles with Hell over the centuries. Sometimes people went there to pray but it was empty most of the time. As instructed, she kept her pace at a slow saunter, looking from side to side occasionally as if she was just out enjoying the midday air.

The crypt wasn't far from the fountain and after a fifteen-minute stroll, she arrived. Walking down the narrow stone steps, she seated herself on one of the prayer pews. It looked like catholic crypts she'd visited in villages and towns all over Italy. Rome was packed with such places and a wave of nostalgia washed over her. She closed her eyes and could almost hear the sounds of her human home: taxi drivers swearing at passing scooters; and vendors shouting out 'gelato' to passing tourists. She heard footsteps approaching. The footsteps descended the steps. Giada kept her head forward. The person came and sat in one of the pews behind her.

A woman's voice said. "We can talk freely here but keep your face to the front."

Giada replied, "you have some information for me?"

"Yes." She paused. "I know about your mission - you've been asked to find out what has happened to Domenico and some missing humans. You don't have to confirm it. I already know. I came to tell you that there is a plot to overthrow the leaders of Heaven and allow demons to live side by side with us. It started as just a small group of rebels and free-thinkers but now it's spread. It goes all the way to the top."

"How do you know this?"

"I'm part of it but I want to get out. I'm desperate to but I can't without risking my life - I know too much. I figure the best way to stop it is to start talking."

"Why don't you just take this straight to Michael?"

"I can't. I'm an archangel. If Michael finds out I was involved in this I'll get sent to Hell."

That explains how she knows about my mission

"So how is this linked to Domenico?"

"Domenico is involved. I've never seen his face as we all wear masks but I'd recognise his voice anywhere. When he first joined the movement, it was just an exchange of ideas - that's the point at which I joined. But when he saw that it was moving beyond ideas and becoming treason, he started trying to get folks to change their minds. He's been openly critical of the plot for a while and then he disappeared. I think he's been taken out to protect the conspiracy and the conspirators. That's why I'm so scared."

Giada's head bounced with questions. "Do you have any concrete evidence that he's dead?"

"No. I think people have started excluding me more and more because they sense that I'm not a true believer in the cause."

Giada tried something else. "Can you give me any more details about the plot? How exactly do they plan to takeover? And when will it take place?"

The archangel sniffed. "I'm afraid not. Everyone involved in the coup is only given access to small bits of information. That way, if anyone is caught and sent to Earth for telepathic extraction, we can only give away parts of the plan."

"Why do demons want to come here? I thought most of them

were happy in Hell."

"This isn't about living somewhere lovely. This is about revenge. Demons want what angels have and they want to hurt angels in the process."

"Why would any angels go along with this plan? Why did you go along with it?"

She sighed, "I've always been an idealist. I felt it wasn't fair that some of God's creatures didn't get to share in the bounty of his kingdom. I thought I was a freedom-fighter, fighting for equal rights and justice but really I was just on the wrong side. Now I'm in way over my head."

"Do you know anything more about the technology involved in getting demons here? How advanced are their plans?"

"I don't know. I wish I did."

"Hmm, that means there's no way of knowing the timescales. If this could take weeks or months or if it's happening right now."

"Exactly."

"What about the other conspirators. Are you able to give me any names?"

"No. I have my suspicions about who else is involved but nothing solid."

"Is there anything else you can tell me that might help?"

"I've told you as much as I know."

"What if I need to speak to you again? How can I contact you?"

"Put a light in your bedroom window and I will meet you by the fountain at midnight on that night. Now, we must leave before we are seen together. You leave first."

Giada dipped her head and crossed herself as if finishing her prayers. "Thank you. This means a lot to me."

The archangel didn't reply, and Giada walked out. As she passed, she saw that the woman was wearing a mask and hooded robe.

She walked home in the same slow, ambling manner as before, except now she was deep in thought. Should she just tell Michael what she'd found out so far? No. If she told him and his team went into overdrive, questioning angels and rounding up suspects, it might cause the conspirators to go deeper underground or accelerate their plans. She had to keep it quiet.

Giada was so deep in thought that she didn't notice Bronwen approaching her in the other direction.

"Hey Giada, what are you up to?" Bronwen asked.

Giada looked up, startled. "Oh, I'm just taking a walk." Lies still came easily to Giada. She felt a knot of guilt at deceiving her friend, but she had no choice. "How about you? Where are you off to?"

Bronwen's eyes sparkled, "I'm on my way back from top secret business. I've been given my mission. I can't talk about it. Have you been given yours yet?"

"Yes. I also can't talk about it."

Bronwen leant forward and tapped her nose in a comically camp fashion. Giada reflected that, had Bronwen made it to adulthood, she would've been an ideal candidate for a job as a rep in a holiday camp. She had the right mix of bubbly personality and grandiose entertainment style.

"Let's walk back together." Bronwen grabbed Giada's arm and pulled her along. Giada mutely obeyed.

Bronwen lived by herself in a flat near Giada's house. It meant that many mornings they walked to school together and home again at the end of the day. Although Bronwen was the kind of person who wore her heart on her sleeve, there was still a lot Giada didn't know about her. One topic in particular she'd been avoiding asking as she thought it might be a traumatic memory. But now that they had grown closer, the time felt right to ask it.

"Bronwen, I remember you said you were soul snatched – how did that happen exactly?

Bronwen stiffened and Giada immediately regretted her question. "If you don't want to talk about it, I understand," Giada offered.

"No, that's okay, we can talk about it." Bronwen's eyes took on a faraway expression as she relived her death. "It was winter. I was walking across railway tracks on my way home when I was hit by a train. I remember a blinding pain in my head but then I got up again. When I looked down I was confused because I saw someone who looked exactly like me lying at my feet. She even had the same clothes as me. Then I saw blood pooling out of her head and into the snow. That's when I realised that it *was* me."

"Oh Bronwen, I'm sorry," Giada touched her shoulder lightly.

"I was so shocked, I kind of went into a daze. I heard singing and saw a tunnel of light, but I was still in denial I guess. That's when I saw her. A hooded figure standing to one side. She told me that she was my guardian angel, come to lead me to the afterlife. I followed her and... well, you know the rest."

"That's awful." Giada replied. "At least I went to Hell because I'd done something terrible. You didn't deserve it at all."

Giada looked up at the sky. "I've always wondered why people who are soul snatched don't get redeemed straight away."

"I wondered that too, for many years." Bronwyn looked down at her feet. "But I think it's because there are reasons why we get soul snatched - weaknesses in our character that need to be resolved in Hell first before we can get to Heaven."

"And is that what happened to you, when you were redeemed? You resolved your weaknesses?"

"I think so, to tell you the truth it's all a bit of a blur. It happened so fast." Her voice rose at the end and she laughed nervously. Giada felt bad about having brought it up. It was obviously a traumatic memory that Bronwen felt uncomfortable talking about.

Her friend's face brightened as she took a deep breath and swiftly changed the topic. "Anyway, let's not think about the past. We're here now and that's the main thing. What have you decided on as your outfit for Wednesday night?"

"Why don't you come over after school tomorrow and I'll show you?"

"Sure, great idea." Bronwen linked her arm through Giada's and continued chatting about inconsequential school stuff. Giada was only half listening. She felt like she had the weight of the world on her shoulders. Perhaps she was looking at her mission from the wrong angle. Perhaps she should be spying on Hell? She couldn't go to Hell herself of course, but she knew someone who could: Naledi.

21

NALEDI

As they drove, Naledi could feel Tau simmering next to her so she tried to lighten the mood with pleasant chit-chat. "It was nice of Khukwan to offer to come with us, wasn't it?" She kept her voice low so that Khukwan, sitting in the bin of the truck, wouldn't hear her.

"Nice, sure, yeah." Tau kept his eyes on the road.

Kabelo agreed. "Indeed. I'm sure there are a lot of other people he could be helping, not to mention that he lives in a heavenly realm. I understand what a hardship it is for him to constrict himself to life on Earth." His mouth turned downwards at the corners and Naledi wondered how long it had been since he had been in Heaven.

When she looked back at Tau she saw that his fingers were clenching the steering wheel so tightly that they were turning pale. She exchanged a look with Kabelo. He too had noticed and they both cut the conversation short. Naledi stared out of the window to avoid the atmosphere in the truck cabbie which was now thick enough to cut with a knife. After a few moments of silence Tau finally broke.

"What I don't understand is, what's in it for him?" he asked.

Naledi suddenly became aware of how dry her mouth felt. "Nothing's in it for him which is why it's such a nice gesture. Selfless."

"No, I don't believe it. I've never met anyone so conceited. He is coming to get adoration from you. He's got a messiah complex. He thinks he can save us." His voice was getting louder and louder.

"Keep your voice down, he'll hear you," Naledi hissed.

"What do I care?"

"Tau!"

He lowered his voice. "All I'm saying is. We don't need him. I don't trust him. I don't trust his motives. For all we know, he's somehow involved in the abduction."

"How can you say that? We know it's demons. I was there when the demon took Lerato."

"These demons could be working for him."

Naledi rolled her eyes, "Tau, that's ridiculous. What possible reason would he have to abduct a few villagers? If he wanted to do that, he could do it himself."

"It's a bit too much of a coincidence don't you think. He materialises out of thin air and then a day later we find Lerato's bloody scarf nearby? ... No, no, no. As far as I'm concerned, he could've orchestrated this entire thing, just as an excuse to meet you."

Naledi's chest heaved as a burst of laughter erupted from her lips.

"What's so funny?" Tau looked at her and the truck swerved.

"Hey, keep your eyes on the road, brother." Kabelo warned.

"Sorry," Tau straightened the steering wheel.

Naledi composed herself. "It's a bit far-fetched. If he wanted to meet me, why couldn't he just materialise in Marula?"

"Well, I don't know, do I? I'm just trying to make sense of all this. I can't accept that someone like him is coming with us purely to be kind and helpful."

Naledi felt herself getting angry. She wanted to defend Khukwan, but she didn't understand why. She knew if she pushed the issue any further, it would turn into a massive fight, and she didn't want that. Instead she sat with her arms crossed, thoughts crackling in her head like a stir-fry.

∽

They had been on the road for half an hour when the truck suddenly started making a strange noise and slowing down.

"What are you doing?" Naledi asked Tau.

"Nothing, it's not me. There's something wrong with it."

"Pull over, I'll take a look," said Kabelo.

Tau parked at the side of the road and Kabelo popped the engine lid and stuck his head inside.

Khukwan jumped down from the back of the truck. "What's the problem?"

"I don't know yet, I'm still looking," Kabelo called out from beneath the hood.

Naledi got some bottles of water out from behind the front seats in the cab and handed one to each of them. She lifted her head and gulped a few sips down. When she lowered her head, she caught Tau giving Khukwan a dirty look. Thankfully the god hadn't noticed.

He feels threatened by him.

"So, Khukwan, how does it work - the whole, changing into human form thing?" Tau asked, a hint of derision in his voice.

Khukwan's voice had the gravitas of someone telling a story to a bunch of enthralled people by the side of a campfire. "Changing is not the hard part. The hard part is staying in human form. My life force gets depleted the longer I stay on Earth. I have to go back to the heavenly realm frequently or I become vulnerable."

"Vulnerable?" Tau asked with a little too much interest.

"I'm vulnerable to attacks from demonic entities just as any other heavenly creature is - just as you are. Normally I can protect myself very well, using my powers. The longer I stay, the more my powers wane."

Tau's interest was growing by the second. "What would happen if you stayed here indefinitely?"

"I never would, but, in theory, I would die."

"So, you're not immortal then?"

"It depends on what you mean by immortal. Can I live forever? Yes. Can I be killed? Yes."

"Interesting…" Tau's voice trailed off, a guilty look on his face.

Naledi brushed a braid out of her face. "How long do we have your help for then?"

"If I don't have to use my powers, I have about twenty-four hours. If I do have to use my powers then I'll have to go back quicker."

"What other powers do you have?"

"In addition to shape shifting, I can control the elements. I can manifest too, but I prefer to use that only as a last resort. It disturbs the fabric of reality too much."

Naledi smiled. "Yes, I know what you mean."

Tau's eyes narrowed and she saw a vein stand out on his neck.

Kabelo came around from under the trunk. "It's not good I'm afraid. It needs a new fuel pump. I can change it, but we need to find somewhere we can buy one."

"The nearest garage isn't for miles around," Tau replied. "If we have to walk there first, it'll be at least another day before we get to Lerato and the others. We can't afford any more time delays." He looked at Naledi. "Could you manifest a fuel pump?"

Naledi scratched her head. "Hmm, I could but manifestation uses a lot of energy. I'd need time to recover. Then if we encountered any problems along the way, I might not be able to do anymore magic."

Khukwan didn't seem at all fazed. "Not a problem. I can fly us there and you can ride on my back."

Tau looked as if he'd just swallowed a cactus. "What?! I am not riding on your back like some kind of pervert."

Khukwan looked at him like he was an idiot. "I won't look like this. I'll shapeshift into a dragon... or a phoenix... or a giant flying elephant, whatever you want, take your pick."

Naledi opened and closed her mouth a few times. "That's.... I mean, that sounds... awesome, but don't you think it's a little conspicuous? Even light aircraft draws attention around here."

"You could perform a cloaking spell, couldn't you?" Khukwan asked.

"True, I could do that."

"Then it's settled. I will shape shift and you will ride on my back."

"Wait just a minute. Nothing is *settled*." Tau set his mouth.

"Why not? You humans are so sensitive. It's no big deal. I do this kind of thing all the time."

"I do not want my girlfriend wrapping her legs around your back, no matter what form you're in."

"Oh.. Oh! I see what this is about. You think I'm interested in Naledi, in that way?"

"I know you are. I saw the way you were looking at her last night and then you went and licked her leg."

Khukwan held his finger up in protest. "My leopard licked her leg."

"Same thing."

"Not really."

Naledi rolled her eyes. "Tau, can you just drop this. It's…"

Tau interrupted, "You stay out of this. If you hadn't been flirting with him in the first place, we wouldn't be in this mess."

"This mess?!" Naledi was aware she was raising her voice, but she didn't care. "If Khukwan wasn't here, we'd be stuck with a broken-down truck and no way to rescue Lerato. It's not his fault the truck broke down."

"Oh, you would defend him, wouldn't you?"

"Would you listen to yourself. You sound like a jealous husband."

"So, I'm not allowed to be protective of my girlfriend?"

"Protective? Yes. Controlling? No."

"I'm not being controlling."

"Yes, you are and, frankly, it's not an attractive quality."

"Guys… guys…" Kabelo came between them and wafted his hands up and down as if cooling down a hot loaf of bread. "Can you two save your lovers' tiff for another time please? A time when we are not rushing to rescue someone we all love… and a couple of other villagers," he added guiltily, as an afterthought.

Tau huffed and crossed his arms, turning his face away from Naledi.

Naledi had to get one more word in. "And for the record, I *was not* flirting."

"That's enough!" Kabelo shouted. He sighed at Khukwan. "Humans! They're so ruled by their emotions."

"How long have you lived among them Kabelo? I sense your aura is angelic, am I correct?"

"Yes, I've been here almost a year now, six months of which I've lived in Marula."

"How do you manage being away from heaven for so long?"

"I incarnated into the body of a boy when he was at the point of death. His soul departed and mine entered."

So that answers that question, thought Naledi.

Khukwan looked at him like he was crazy. "Was this your choice?"

"I offered myself. I came as part of a mission to spy on Hell and then I was instructed to stay longer. I didn't know why at the time, but now I think it may have been so I can help with this."

"You must miss Heaven very much."

Kabelo shrugged. "I do but I've grown to like it here too." His eyes suddenly looked forlorn and Naledi could tell he was thinking about Lerato. "It's complicated."

"Well, it's good to meet a fellow celestial being on Earth. Surprising, but good." Khukwan clapped his hands together. "Now, as much as I enjoy standing around chatting, which creature shall I shape shift into so we can get this show on the road?" He had a mischievous grin on his face as he looked at Naledi.

She couldn't help herself; a sense of childlike glee took over and she jumped up and down. "A giant, flying elephant!"

Tau interrupted, apparently forgetting his dislike of Khukwan, in his enthusiasm. "Oh, come on! It's got to be a dragon."

"What? No, elephants are so cool!"

"Dragons breath fire, that might come in handy if we have to fight demons."

"We don't need fire. I can shoot fire out of my hands."

Tau scowled again, remembering his quarrel as he folded his arms. "In any case, I don't know why I'm arguing because I am not going on his back."

Naledi glowered at him. "You are so stubborn!"

Kabelo's head flipped between her and Tau. "Alright, I have an idea. Why doesn't Khukwan just give us a ride to the nearest garage, we pick up the fuel pump and come back then drive the rest of the way."

Khukwan chimed in. "Flying all the way there would be much quicker."

"I don't care." Tau said.

"You would rather see Lerato die than swallow your pride and ride on his back?"

Tau looked down guiltily.

Naledi emitted a low growl of frustration. "I have had it with this nonsense. I'm riding on his back and rescuing my friend. If that makes you uncomfortable or jealous or whatever that's too bad!"

"Fine! Go off with him then, see if I care." Tau shouted as Naledi stormed off

"Fine!" she shouted back.

Khukwan hastily followed her and Kabelo rushed off after Tau.

22

NALEDI

Naledi strode through the long grass, thrashing it back with her hands. Just what gave Tau permission to act as if he owned her? He was her boyfriend, that was all. If Khukwan wanted to offer his help with getting Lerato and the others back. And if she wanted to accept that help, then how dare he try and stop her? As she fumed, she'd forgotten all about Khukwan, walking behind her.

He now reminded her as he commented. "You know you're inviting a snake bite by walking through long grass like that?"

Naledi stopped and exhaled forcefully. "What are you still doing here? Can't you see I'm trying to think."

"If demons have Lerato, they won't wait around whilst you sort out your squabbles with your boyfriend. I offered to help, and I still intend to. What you said back there - is that your final decision? Do we go onto Joang now, with you riding on my back?"

Naledi thought for a moment. The offer to go to get the fuel pump had really just been to appease Tau - something she was no longer in the mood to do. "Yes. Let's go to Joang now. I agree with you that we can't afford any more delays."

"What about Tau and Kabelo?"

Naledi put one hand to her forehead and rubbed it. At this moment, she'd love to just leave Tau here, but she knew she'd regret it later. He was acting like an idiot, but she still loved him.

"Let's go back and get them."

They walked back to find Tau and Kabelo walking towards them. Naledi suspected that Kabelo had talked some sense into Tau as his expression looked far more conciliatory than it had done previously. He walked up to Khukwan. "Look man, I'm sorry about the way I was acting. I know you're only here to help us…"

"…and to bump some demon heads together," he interrupted with a glint in his eye.

"…right, and for that. Anyway, what I mean to say is. We're all on the same side so I'd like us to be friends." He extended his hand. Khukwan looked at it, with a slightly bemused expression on his face but he took it and shook it.

"Sorry Naledi. You're right, it makes sense to go on Khukwan's back and we don't have to go and get the fuel pump first, that's just wasting valuable time."

Naledi raised her eyebrows and looked from Tau to Kabelo. "What did you do, brainwash him or something?"

"I simply talked logic."

Naledi frowned, "logic… right, I'll remember that next time."

Tau continued. "At least let me have the dragon though."

Naledi stifled a chuckle. "Okay then. You can have your dragon." Then she looked at Khukwan. "Dragon it is, please."

Khukwan's expression grew serious. His face started turning red, as though he was very angry. Beads of sweat broke out and his veins stood out. His body started shaking and as it did so, a gust of unnatural wind blew around them forming a whirlwind. Sandy dust swirled up around them. A growl came deep from within Khukwan's chest and he threw his head back before crouching to the floor. The dust became so thick that Naledi struggled to still see him. She put a hand up to shield her eyes as she squinted. Dust bombarded her nostrils and she coughed and spluttered. The air crackled with power and Naledi felt her body responding as adrenaline coursed through her. The wind began to die down and she heard another growl, this one more animalistic than the last. As the dust settled, she lowered her hand from her eyes. She staggered backwards as an involuntary fight-or-flight response took over and she quivered with fear.

In place of where Khukwan had stood, there was now a ginormous red dragon. It towered over her, casting a shadow over the hillside as it blew steam from its nostrils. Flapping its large wings a few times, it shook them out, whilst flexing its neck, as if stretching after a long sleep. A large forked, black tongue flicked out of its mouth and licked its nostril. Naledi looked at Tau and Kabelo. They looked as terrified as she felt.

"Do you think he can still understand us?" she asked the boys.

Kabelo answered. "He lacks human vocal chords but can communicate with us telepathically as long as I am here to translate his thoughts."

Tau's expression of terror had morphed into one of wonder. "Incredible. I never thought I'd ever see a dragon in real life. It's a creature of myth and legend - this is beyond my wildest dreams."

"You and me both." Naledi looked the beast up and down. "How are we supposed to get on? It's colossal."

"I'll ask him," Kabelo answered. He looked at Khukwan and Naledi sensed a whisper of communication pass between them. Then she watched as a large saddle, big enough to fit all of them, materialised on Khukwan's back. Descending from the saddle was a rope ladder long enough for them to climb on.

"Cool!" Naledi grinned, "Come on," she beckoned as she walked forward and climbed up the ladder. Once on top, she looked down and watched as Tau eagerly hoisted himself up. Kabelo came up last.

"Does he know where to go?" Naledi asked Kabelo.

"Yes, he knows the whole of Lesotho well. I'll tell him we're ready."

In the next moment, Naledi felt Khukwan shift beneath her as he got to his feet. Then he flapped his gigantic wings and effortlessly took to the sky. He rose slowly at first, probably for their benefit. Naledi immediately felt uneasy. Her advanced sangoma powers enabled her to fly by herself when the occasion warranted it, but she'd never been up so high before. Now she clutched the handles of the saddle tightly, her arm muscles taut, as they rose higher and higher. She looked down and felt nauseous as she saw the ground get further and further away. Soon they could see for miles around. She saw tiny cattle on a nearby field and a miniature man, walking on another field. Khukwan increased his speed steadily and soon they were soaring through the air. The wind rushed past and Naledi wished she'd thought to take her blanket from the truck. She shivered and Tau sat closer to her, wrapping warm arms around her as he drew her into his chest.

"Naledi - the cloaking spell." Kabelo reminded her.

"Oh yeah, I almost forgot." She closed her eyes and uttered an incantation. The cloaking spell wouldn't last long but it would be long enough to get them to where they needed to be and give them the advantage of surprise if there were demons there. The spell complete, she opened her eyes and sat back into Tau's chest. She'd loosened her grip on the saddle as she started to feel a bit more at ease.

"It's not so bad once you get used to it, is it?" Tau commented, kissing her on top of her head as she nestled into his neck.

"Yeah, I could get used to this." Kabelo grinned. He didn't seem scared at all, but then Naledi had often noticed that he was less afraid of death than humans were.

As she got used to the height, the rhythmic beating of wings, coupled with Tau's warm chest, made her feel drowsy. She was just drifting off to sleep when she heard Giada's voice calling to her.

Naledi. I need your help.

Naledi's eyes flew open and then she closed them again. *You're not going to ask me to spy on Hell to stop a demon resurrection are you?*

Not quite Giada giggled. *I need information. I've had a tip off that there's a plot from within Heaven to overthrow the current rulers and allow demons and angels to live side by side.*

You're joking?

Deadly serious.

And angels are going along with this?
Yep.
What do you need from me?
I want you to go to Hell and see what you can find out.
Whoa there - I can't go to Hell. Not right now. As I told you earlier, I'm fully tied up in rescuing Lerato and the other villagers: we're on our way to Joang right now. I was going to pray for you to join us when we arrived.
How long is the journey?
I don't know, we're flying on the back of a dragon...
A what?
...Long story. Not important. Anyway, we'll probably be there soon.
Could you connect with Motsumi and ask him to find out whatever he can instead?

Naledi thought for a moment. *Yes, I'd have time to do that. He might not know anything though.*

Motsumi has his fingers in lots of different pies. I'm sure he knows something that can help. Ask him if he knows anything about the disappearance of an archangel by the name of Domenico too. He was involved in the conspiracy.

Alright, I'll ask him. Naledi nodded.
Okay, I'll let you get on with it. Prey to me when you reach Joang.
Will do.

As Naledi had been at the point of sleep, she didn't need to calm her body further. She mentally reached out into the astral realm, searching for the soul of Motsumi. Once she'd located him, she drew him into a space and time bubble. Opening her eyes in her astral form, she got a slight shock as she saw that her old teacher's eyes were now deep red. She steadied herself and greeted him. "Dumela Molume." She smiled, surprised at how pleased she was to see him. She had missed him.

"Dumela Naledi," Motsumi smiled warmly. "I didn't think I would see you again so soon. To what do I owe the pleasure of your company?"

"I need your help. Giada has contacted me from Heaven. She says there is a plot to overthrow Heaven's leaders and allow demons and angels to live side by side."

"I am aware of the plan. My status as demon has made me privy to information I never would've been given before."

"Then you know what is going on?"

"No. I'm not directly involved. I know some details, mostly what I've heard on the demon gossip mill."

"Do you know how to stop it and when it will happen?"

"No. All I've heard is that this coup is based around some type of new, demonic technology. I don't know what exactly, but everyone is very excited about it down here."

Naledi tapped her lip, thinking quickly. She had to cram in as many questions as she could before they reached Joang. "Have you heard anything about an archangel by the name of Domenico? He was involved in the conspiracy."

Motsumi looked at her, his red eyes serious. "I fear Domenico may be dead."

"What makes you think that?"

"This demonic technology needs angelic essence to work. And lots of it. If he's disappeared, and he was one of the conspirators, I believe he may have been killed for his essence."

"What is angelic essence?"

"It's the astral equivalent of blood but if it gets fully depleted, the angel dies."

Naledi put a had to her mouth. "That is awful."

"Are you close to him?" Motsumi asked.

"No, I don't know him, but I still feel compassion for a servant of God - as should you." Naledi reflected that perhaps Motsumi was starting to lose his humanity now that he was a demon. But then again, he always had been a little detached, emotionally. "Are you still attending Sinners Anonymous meetings?" she asked.

"Of course. I will be redeemed one day. Perhaps, by the time you get to Heaven, I will already be there."

Naledi smiled as a wave of affection passed over her. "I hope so." She felt the pull of her physical body as her ears popped. The altitude of their flight was changing. They must be nearing Joang. "I have to go. But please contact me if you hear anything else."

Motsumi bowed slightly. "I'll do everything within my power - after all, this could be my ticket to redemption."

Naledi rolled her eyes at his self-interest. He hadn't changed a bit.

As Naledi opened her eyes she saw the town come into view in the distance. She had never been there before but she immediately recognised it from her vision. It was a small town with one road containing shops and another couple of roads containing agricultural stores and workshops. She spotted the prison building on the outskirts of the town. "It's that building there." She reached forward and nudged Kabelo as she pointed towards the prison.

"I will tell him." Kabelo answered.

Khukwan turned in the direction of the prison and they started their descent.

Naledi braced herself for a thud but Khukwan landed with surprising grace and lightness in a field a few hundred metres away from the prison. Naledi felt a cloud of oppressive darkness sweep over her and she shivered. She reasoned that it was the effect of so many years of demonic activity in the region. It had imbued it with the sadness and anger of Hell. It also felt familiar. Where had she felt this before? Of course! Uhuru valley. Perhaps this was what all twilight regions felt like. She looked at the boys. Did they feel it too or was she especially sensitive? If they felt the negativity, they didn't show it and she didn't share her feelings. It was hard to put into words what she felt.

Naledi climbed down the ladder and Tau and Kabelo followed after her. "Right, what next?" she said.

"You tell us, you're the one who had the vision about this place," Tau replied.

Naledi rubbed her temples. She hadn't really thought this far ahead. Should they just go in 'guns blazing' as Tau liked to say? Or should they use stealth to try and creep in? The latter seemed to make the most sense.

The air started shifting around them. Dust and wind stirred and

Naledi saw the dragon start to change. In the next few moments, Khukwan stood before them in human form once more.

"How did you enjoy the ride?" He looked at Naledi and she flicked her gaze away. She didn't want Tau thinking that she was flirting with him again.

"It was great thanks."

He clapped his hands together, his eyes glittering. "Now, let's go and kill some demons."

"Wait just one second," said Naledi. "There's one more member of our team." She closed her eyes *Giada, we're here and we're ready for you.*

I'm on my way.

Naledi looked up and saw the familiar orb of light descend from the sky. Inside she saw Giada. Her friend had changed. She looked happier and more peaceful. In her hands, she held a golden bow and arrow.

"Heaven suits you!" Naledi said when Giada had reached the ground. Her feet didn't touch the earth, she floated an inch or two above, with ankles that disappeared into light.

"Thanks." Giada smiled. "What's the plan then?"

Naledi looked around at each of them. "I'll perform a cloaking spell. Then we can sneak in. Khukwan - could you find a quiet way to destroy the locks please? With any luck, we'll find and release not only the villagers but all the other people they're holding too."

Khukwan looked about as excited as a child on his birthday. "Marvellous!"

Naledi performed the cloaking spell and they began walking towards the prison, with Giada floating slightly above. Naledi didn't share Khukwan's optimism or his enthusiasm. Every encounter she'd had with demons had almost been deadly. She only hoped that this time, for once, it would be easy.

23

NALEDI

The prison was a square, grey brick building, enclosed by a tall red brick wall with razor wire on top. There was nobody about and as the mountain wind whistled past her ears, a ball of dry grass rolled past, tickling her ankles. They reached the grey iron front door without any issue. A notice was plastered onto the door saying that the prison was scheduled for demolition. It was dated several months back. Naledi wondered if demons had somehow had a hand in getting the demolition stayed.

Khukwan reached his hand forward and waved it over the door. There was a clicking noise. "After you," he said as he opened it and gestured for them to proceed. Inside the prison walls it was just as quiet as outside. The yellow grass had grown to knee height and the sound of grasshoppers and birds was all that filled the air.

Kabelo transmitted his thoughts to her telepathically. *We'll have to encounter demons or guards or both sooner or later, surely?*

I hope not, but if we do, I'm ready.

They walked up a gravel path leading to the grey, iron front door. Again, Khukwan popped the lock and they walked inside. There was not a soul around. Naledi looked from left to right as her heart pounded in her chest. A fly buzzed loudly at the sweat on her temples and she swatted it away in irritation. They walked through what looked like a reception area and then two more locked iron doors before coming to a communal area. The lunch hall maybe? At this point they had a decision to make. Several doors led off from the canteen. Naledi made eye contact with each of them and pointed towards a random door. She thought it best that they stay together and try each door in turn.

They walked towards the door and when they were about a metre away, the door opened. Naledi gasped and reared back. The large, blonde buzz-cut demon who had abducted Lerato stood before her. He was flanked by another burly, black demon and two more behind him. Buzz-cut cracked his knuckles as his red eyes flashed with violent intent. The demon next to him flexed his neck muscles, as he twisted his head from side to side. Then a fifth demon stepped forward. Naledi hadn't noticed him at first as he'd been behind the other goliaths. Emerging between his entourage, Naledi's blood went cold as she recognised him immediately. It was Ratu: The Chief Scientist in charge of the realm teleporter in Vassago's hell dimension. She'd killed him when she'd defeated the Countess - at least, she'd killed him in Hell. He would've been reborn and now, here he was, standing before her. His red eyes locked onto them.

He can see us she thought. Was her cloaking spell not working? She kept quiet just in case she was wrong.

Ratu leaned forward on his heels, his hands behind his back. "We can see you. We've been watching you since you entered the prison."

"How?" Naledi asked.

"We've put a magic blocking spell on this prison. Your powers are useless here, which makes you our prisoners." His eyes glittered with triumph. "And before you think about trying to contact angelic assistance, we've also performed a psychic protection spell. Angels cannot hear your prayers here."

He looked at Giada. "But I see that you already have angelic assistance." His lip curled as he tutted a few times. "Does archangel Michael really think he can send a trainee angel to defeat us? He's more arrogant than I thought." He turned to his demon henchmen. "Seize her!"

Giada screamed and flew upwards, aiming the bow and arrow at the blonde demon who had fixed her in his gaze. But the demon was too quick for her. He leapt into the air with unbelievable agility and speed. Grabbing Giada with one massive hand, he wrenched the golden bow away from her with his other hand. He then snapped it across his thighs and threw it to the ground. Giada went pale and started trembling, as she looked at the demon. He licked his lips and grinned at her, his red eyes glinting.

Khukwan had a look of glee in his eyes. "Naledi's magic may be useless here, but mine is not."

He shot rapid fire bolts out of his hands, at the blonde demon. Buzz-cut batted them off like mosquitos. Khukwan flew into the air, growing into a huge tyrannosaurus rex as he went. Any bigger and he wouldn't fit inside the room. He picked up demons, one by one and flung them hard against the walls. They were dazed, but unhurt. Shifting back into a man's body, he manifested a large sword made of pure diamond - the hardest substance on Earth. Swinging it around his head, he charged at a dark-haired demon, successfully decapitating him. The demon's body disintegrated with a satisfying sizzling sound. Next, he sprinted towards buzz-cut, but the demon dropped and rolled out of the way.

A short, stocky demon advanced on Naledi. Her stomach clenched. Without her powers she was just a teenage girl. The demon effortlessly grabbed her. She kicked, punched, clawed, spat, whatever she could do to get away. But it was no use, he was much stronger than her. Khukwan came to her aid, pummeling into the demon with the force of a bomb. The demon crashed into the wall and lay on the floor groaning.

Naledi flicked her gaze around her. Each of her friends was locked in battle with a different demon. Tau was on the ground, wrestling a bald demon. Kabelo had picked up a chair and was using it to beat another demon. She looked back to see Ratu delivering a demon death stare to Khukwan. The god turned his face away, but the demon lurched forward and touched Khukwan's bare chest. The god's body snapped upright as he cried out in pain. He retaliated by hurling a bolt of lightning at Ratu.

Just as it seemed they were gaining the upper hand, Naledi watched in horror as scores more demons poured into the room. There must've been about fifty of them. All big, brawny men. They covered the floor of the room like an avalanche. Naledi and her friends were quickly overcome. She instinctively tried to use her powers but of course, they didn't work. She looked at Khukwan and watched in disbelief as he gave her an apologetic shrug and then disappeared.

That flaky, bastard!

She could not believe that the god had abandoned them when they needed him the most. Tau had been right about him. She shouldn't have trusted him. Now they were in deep trouble with no way out.

Naledi watched mutely as each of her friends were put in handcuffs. A sparkly kind of net was put over Giada. Naledi recognised it as an etheric net, made specifically to trap spiritual beings.

Buzz-cut's gaze met Naledi's. An expression of intense hatred shone out of his red eyes. She looked away but it was too late. The devastating effects of the demon death stare were immediate. Naledi's entire body twisted with pain. It felt like every nerve tip was on fire and acid coursed through the cells of her body. The sensation was all consuming, cutting off her mental capacity so that her only awareness was the agony flooding through her. She dimly registered Tau and Kabelo screaming and writhing nearby. Naledi had a distant recollection that she should be fighting but she was too far gone. She'd never experienced pain like it and sweat drenched her face. Her vision started blurring then darkness closed in from the outside of her eyes. Reality dimmed to a tiny pinprick of light before disappearing completely. The last thing she felt was her body slumping to the floor as her consciousness gave in to oblivion.

NALEDI WAS by the side of a swamp, late at night. She heard Lerato calling out for her and rushed towards the sound of her friend's voice. In the dim light she saw the back of Lerato's head. She was submerged in the swamp and sinking fast. Naledi had to save her! She ran towards her but the closer she got, the further away Lerato seemed. Lerato's voice became more and more desperate. She pleaded with Naledi to help her. Naledi tried but she couldn't get close to her, no matter how hard she tried. Suddenly, Naledi felt herself start to sink. She looked down and saw that she was standing in the swamp and she was sinking. She looked around frantically to see if there was a tree branch she could grab hold of, but she couldn't see anything. She sank faster and faster, until the water came up to her nose. She was wet and cold and terrified. As the water entered her nose, she woke up coughing and spluttering.

For a second, she had no memory of what had happened, and confusion clouded her thoughts as she looked around at her unfamiliar surroundings. Water was dripping on her face from somewhere above and she blinked, trying to keep it out of her mouth. She sat up and tried to rub her forehead. Her hand stopped with a clank and she looked down and saw that she was shackled at the hands and ankles. Then the memory came rushing back to her. They'd been attacked by demons. She remembered a brutish-looking, blonde haired demon looking at her then feeling an intense pain like she'd never felt before. The demon death stare. She was lucky to still be alive.

She looked around what she now realised was her cell. It was a simple brick-walled room with no window and bars in place of doors.

She was still in the prison in Joang. Questions flooded her mind. Why had they taken her prisoner? They could've just killed her. Why hadn't they? Were Tau and Kabelo still alive? Were they being kept in the same prison?

She called out. "Hey." Her voice echoed around the bare walls, but she heard no voice in reply. She tried again, "Hello, is anyone there?"

She waited and listened. No answer.

She looked down and inspected her shackles. They were bolted to the walls. She pulled on the bolts. They were secure and new: there was no way she could pull them out of the walls. But then with dismay, she remembered that she couldn't use her magic here. She tried anyway just in case. Nothing. Ratu had been telling the truth.

Without her magic she was as vulnerable as any other human. She wouldn't even be able to use her breacher powers. Ratu had said that she couldn't contact angels, but she tried anyway. She closed her eyes and inwardly called out to them. *Michael, Gabi, are you there? I need you.* There was no response. *Giada - are you there?* Again, there was no response. *Kabelo?* Nothing. She cursed.

With a deep sigh, she slumped down and rested her head against the wall. She checked her restraints again to see if there was any way she could slip her wrists through. They were on tight, even with her slender wrists, there was no way she could get them off. It was no use. Surely they must have guards or someone here? What happened if she needed the toilet? She called out again.

"Hey, is anyone there? I need the toilet."

She listened and heard movement. First the sound of clanking metal. The sound of a key being put in another metal door perhaps. Then the sound of crisp footsteps echoing along the passageway outside her cell door.

The footsteps drew closer and soon a man appeared on the other side of the bars. He was of average height, with a big belly and a bald patch right on top of his head. A few days' worth of coiled stubble adorned his chin. In his hands, he held a bucket and a bunch of keys was clipped to his belt. She looked at his eyes. They were brown.

He's human!

"Where am I?" Naledi asked him. He ignored her. She tried again. "How long have I been here?" No answer. "Can you at least tell me if my friends are here too?" He didn't even look at her. He opened the door and placed the bucket close enough for her to reach but kept his distance from her. His body language was as if he was a zookeeper, dealing with a carnivorous animal. That meant he'd been told how powerful she was. She couldn't decide if this was a good thing or not.

But it did make her wonder. Why were they being so cautious if her magic was useless here? Was there some power she had which she was overlooking?

The man let himself out, locking the door behind him before walking off. "Thank you!" Naledi called out after him in a tone that was anything but thankful. Frustration and shame at her failure flooded her body as she accepted that she was well and truly trapped here.

After a while the guard reappeared with a plate of food.

Hmm, they're feeding me, so they don't intend to kill me.

He slid the food through the door. There were no knives and forks, so she had to eat it with her hands. As she was eating, she looked around her cell again. In one corner there was a metal pipe stretching from floor to ceiling. This was probably a water pipe. It was too far away for her to reach but if she threw her plate at it, the sound would carry through the building. Maybe she'd get a sound back in response. At least it would tell her that someone else was here. She ate quickly. She didn't want the guard to come back before she'd had time to enact her plan. As soon as she had finished, she took careful aim and hurled her plate at the pipes. It hit and smashed into pieces, making a satisfyingly loud clank. Naledi held her breath and waited, her eyes moving from left to right in hopeful expectation. Silence. She couldn't deny her disappointment. She was all alone. Sinking against the wall, she closed her eyes and gave into despair.

However, ten minutes later she heard a loud clank, mirroring her earlier clank. Someone was answering her! They must have got their dinner a bit later than her. The thrill of shared rebellion bubbled through her chest and she giggled with joy. She now knew there was at least one other person being held somewhere else in the building. But it didn't change her situation. She was still trapped here, with no way out.

24

NALEDI

As darkness descended on Naledi's cell, she began to feel more and more despairing. She was desperate to know why she had been imprisoned. What did Ratu want with her? Sure, he must have a vendetta against her after she'd killed him in Hell, but why didn't he just kill her and get it over with? He must want to use her for something, and her mind went wild with all the sick and twisted possibilities of what this could be.

Waves of pain pulsed through her heart and belly as she thought of Lerato. Who would rescue her now? Naledi thought of the bloodied headscarf and fear clutched her throat. Was this entire trip a fool's errand? Was Lerato already dead? A large tear rolled down her cheek. The grief of losing Lerato would be unbearable. Her best friend had become like a sister to her. It was difficult to stay positive when she couldn't see a way out and as time wore on, her thoughts became darker and darker. She should just give up and accept that she'd lost. That single tear opened the floodgates for more and they now rolled freely down her face as she wept bitterly.

Eventually her eyes began to close, as her head lolled against the brick wall. Naledi drifted, her awareness halfway between dreaming and wakefulness. The start of her dream was peppered with images of Lerato. Memories of sharing juicy gossip and collapsing on the mountain grass as they laughed together. Her friend comforting her after the loss of her parents. Lerato's tuneless singing as she swept the floor. The off-key singing went on and on. It sounded so real, as if she was singing nearby. Naledi smiled. Dreams could sometimes seem so lifelike.

She jerked her head upright. *Wait a minute, that's not a dream. That's real!*

Lerato was singing, somewhere in the building. It was faint but unmissable. Carried by the wind through the echoing corridors of the prison. Naledi had often reflected on how ironic it was that those with the worst voices could often sing the loudest. It was a phenomena that she now praised God for. She straightened herself up. Now she had something to fight for. She reviewed her options again. Her best chance was the guard. He was human. When he came to bring her meals, if she could somehow find a way to attack him and get his keys, she could escape. But how would she do this with her wrists shackled?

There was nothing for it. Naledi was going to have to try and slip her hands through the shackles. Her wrists would certainly get bloody. She might even have to break her thumb to do it, but it was her only option. She started working on it, inching the iron bands, bit by bit. She winced as the iron cut into her skin and became slippery with her own blood. She breathed away the pain, telling herself it was a good thing. If the manacles were slippery they'd come off easier. Working at this through the night, she could be ready to jump the guard when he came to bring her breakfast in the morning.

Sweat poured down Naledi's face and pain lanced her wrists as she continued to try and free herself. Then she heard footsteps and froze. Someone was coming. She looked down at her wrists, the blood would be impossible to hide, and she was nowhere near to getting them off. She did her best to wipe the blood on her top, then tried to hide her hands as best she could. A few people were approaching. The footsteps got closer and closer and then three men appeared at her cell door. One of them carried a torch and as he shone it into her cell she made out the face of the guard. Naledi squinted in the dim light and saw behind him were two other men. One of them was Ratu. He blinked at her, rubbing his ruddy complexioned face in the semi-darkness.

"Good evening Naledi" Ratu began, adjusting his glasses on his nose. He looked at her with his eyes wide open. His demonic eyes had no problem with seeing her in the darkness.

Naledi glared at him. "Why am I here? What do you want with me and why have you kidnapped my friend?"

Ratu stood with his hands behind his back, his expression placid. "Kidnapping your friend was the best way to get you to come to us. As you'll recall, we tried to take you in Marula but when my associate failed, he took the next best thing." He smiled deviously. "You came right to us."

"Who is 'we'?" Naledi asked.

"That doesn't concern you. I'm in another hell dimension now and continuing the work that I was doing before. Now however, I have added another element to my experiments. You will be one of the study participants."

What did he mean by 'study'? Naledi shuddered. She knew this man was capable of using minions for ghastly experiments. She didn't doubt that he'd use humans in the same way. "If it's me you want, let my friend Lerato go."

"Ah but it's not just you I want. I need humans of all types for my work. Old. Young. Female. Male. Magical. Non-magical...." He paused and looked at her, "...Angels. Realm walkers."

Naledi bucked at her restraints. "Tau, Kabelo and Giada!"

Ratu ignored her and continued his explanation. "It's important that I have enough test subjects, or the results won't be valid."

Naledi tried again. "Please. Just let them go! What do you need them for?"

"You'll find out soon enough," Ratu wearily replied.

Naledi's eyes moved from left to right. She tried another question. "What work? What tests?"

Ratu's eyes flashed. "I'm glad you asked." He adjusted his spectacles again. "I am working on a pioneering scientific method to transfer magical powers from one subject to another. If I succeed, this will make me the greatest scientist in the universe. This has never even been tried before and I'm so close to success. It's very exciting."

Yeah, I'm thrilled for you.

Naledi continued her interrogation. "Who else do you have here? Do you have another two from my village? A girl and an old woman?"

Again, Ratu ignored her and it became clear that he would only tell her what he wanted to and no more.

He looked down at her bloodied wrists then removed his spectacles. He took a handkerchief from his pocket and started cleaning them. "Even if you were able to get your hands out of the shackles, the guard would quickly and easily disable you before you reached your friends." He put his spectacles back on his face. "Without your powers, you are merely a puny teenage girl."

"You expect me to just give up and go along with your crazy plans?"

He simply looked at her. Naledi looked away as her mind briefly recalled Ratu's look of horror just before he had been torn apart by the hell hounds she had summoned. She looked back at him. "I didn't set out to kill you, you know. You were just in the wrong place, at the wrong time. I don't deserve your vengeance."

Ratu half smiled. "You misunderstand. This isn't about vengeance."

"What's it about then?"

"Science, pure and simple. You and your group of friends are the best subjects for my experiments."

"So, they're still alive?"

Ratu didn't answer but he'd as good as confirmed it. A mixture of conflicting emotions swirled within Naledi's belly. Elation that her friends were alive and that she wasn't here alone. Despair that her friends were here, and she was powerless to save them. Guilt that if it hadn't been for her actions in Hell, none of this would have happened.

THERE WAS no question of getting back to sleep after Ratu left. Naledi had to figure out a way to escape before morning. She wracked her brain. Her thoughts flitted from one dreadful scenario to another and after a while she realised she was far too anxious to come up with a solution. She decided to meditate to calm her mind. Crossing her legs, she did a body scan, relaxing each part of her body before finally relaxing her face, forehead and jaw. Then she focused on the breath coming in and out of her body. She was so stressed that at first, her thoughts continued to intrude every couple of seconds. But after a while she felt herself sink deeper into stillness. It was in these quiet moments that Naledi sometimes heard the call of spirits or even noises from other realms. A familiar smell of sulphur tickled her nose. Her awareness of Hell often came to her the most quickly, having spent so much time there.

It was at that moment that a lightbulb went off in her brain.

Motsumi! Of course!

Ratu had said that there was a psychic protection spell on the prison and that angels wouldn't be able to hear their prayers. But what about demons? She was willing to bet they hadn't bothered adding a psychic protection spell against Hell. Why would they?

She reached out into the astral realm, seeing if she could sense Motsumi's soul. She found it and quickly directed it to a space and time bubble. He knelt in front of her, in the all-white domain. She knelt before him, in her astral body.

"Well Naledi," he half smiled. "I don't hear from you in months and then you contact me twice in one day."

"It's an emergency Molume. I need your help again. I've been captured by demons. They're led by Ratu - do you remember him? He was the lead scientist in charge of Vassago's realm teleportation technology."

Motsumi shuddered. "How could I forget."

Naledi continued. "They're holding me inside a prison in the twilight region of Joang."

Motsumi frowned. "How did they manage to capture a woman of your power?"

Naledi shifted awkwardly as she looked at her feet. "They tricked me. They kidnapped Lerato and brought her here. I came here willingly, trying to rescue her. Then once inside they grabbed me. They've put a magic blocking spell on the entire prison, so my powers didn't protect me. It's not just me. They have Tau, Kabelo, some other villagers and Giada."

"And what do they intend to do with you?"

"Ratu is working on a way to transfer magical abilities from one being to another. That's why he wants different types of beings - humans, angels, realm walkers, breachers. He plans to use us as lab rats."

Motsumi pursed his lips. "I assume if you're contacting me, it's because they have also performed a psychic protection spell on the prison, cutting you off from angelic communication?"

"You assume right."

Motsumi silently stared into the middle distance before speaking. "Demons can exist in twilight regions, in physical form. But they have to have a way of getting from Hell to Earth. Ratu must have successfully completed his realm teleporter technology. Either that or he's working with a breacher."

Naledi felt they were going off topic. "What does it matter how they got here? I need you to think of a way to rescue us."

Motsumi clicked his tongue. "I *am* thinking of a way to rescue you. Don't you see. However, they got there, I can use the same method to get there. I have allies here now, lots of them. We can take out Ratu and his henchmen."

"Well it's not as if we have loads of time for you to research it. Ratu is going to start performing his experiments on us in the morning."

Motsumi's eye twitched. "That's why I wish you had contacted me sooner."

"I didn't think of it until now."

"Naledi - just because I've released you from bondage, it doesn't mean that I'm no longer here for you. You should always come to me, whenever you're in danger. I may not have all the powers you have but I have significant resources at my disposal, especially now that I'm a demon."

"Does that mean you'll help?"

"I'll try but I can't promise. As time is of the essence, I will leave you now." He narrowed his eyes. "Don't leave it until the last-minute next time."

Hopefully there won't be a next time.

25

NALEDI

After a fitful night of barely any sleep, Naledi awoke. She immediately started trying to get her shackles off again. She'd heard no news from Motsumi so she had to do whatever she could to escape, without his help. Even if Ratu had said she'd have no chance against the guard, she had to at least try. Her efforts were short-lived, however. Ratu soon turned up flanked by a couple of burly men, one of which was the guard. Ratu's eyes flashed at her as the guard opened her cell.

"Now for the moment we've all been waiting for."

He offered no further explanation and Naledi's heart thumped in her chest as the icy hand of fear reached into her stomach. The guard walked over to her and unlocked her shackles. As soon as she was free she clawed at him, punching, kicking, scratching, whatever she could do to get free. She knew it was futile, as underlined by the patronising chuckles of the other men. The guard easily restrained her and locked her wrists into handcuffs.

"Come along," Ratu instructed, in a tone reminiscent of an owner talking to his dog.

Naledi glared at him. "Where are you taking me?"

They ignored her and she bit her lip. The taste of blood filled her mouth.

As they walked through the prison, Naledi's eyes darted from left to right. She was desperately trying to find any means of escape. The windows all had bars on them, welded into iron window frames. She tried a quick prayer to the angels to see if the psychic protection spell had been placed around the whole prison. Her heart sank as she got no answer. Next she tried summoning her powers. But again, she got nothing.

After walking through a series of corridors, they arrived back at the canteen. The room looked different from before. It was now filled with strange looking bits of machinery and other people in chains, being guarded by more thick-set, large men. Naledi scanned the room and her eyes lit up when she saw Lerato. She made eye contact with her friend and Lerato smiled weakly back at her. Nearby her was Esther Mothopeng and old Ma Mutsi. Naledi smiled at them but her heart broke as she saw that their eyes were full of hope. They thought that now she was here, she'd be able to rescue them. How wrong they were. To the people of Marula, she'd become a kind of celebrity superhero. Rage and nausea twisted her insides at the thought that she was just as powerless as them. She'd set off to rescue them but only succeeded in putting herself in danger too. The sting of failure was crushing.

Naledi was chained next to Lerato, with her handcuffs still on.

"Do you know what's going on?" Naledi whispered.

Lerato's eyes widened and she shook her head slightly as if warning Naledi not to speak but it was too late. The guard who had brought her over slapped her hard across the face. Pain blossomed on her cheek. She brought her hand up to rub it away. She turned her head to look at the man, but he kept his eyes forward. Lerato gave her a look of commiseration but kept silent.

A door at the other side of the room opened and Naledi felt her heart leap out of her chest as she saw Tau step through. He was also in chains and was followed by Kabelo. Tau's face was ashen. Naledi looked at Lerato and saw the look of joy on her face at seeing Kabelo. Naledi knew she shouldn't feel so thankful that Tau and Kabelo were here. She should prefer them to be spared from whatever horrible things Ratu planned to do to them. But she couldn't help feeling comforted by their presence. Together, their odds of survival and escape were greater.

Where is Giada?

Her question was answered as another door opened and a heavyset guard walked through it, dragging the etheric net with Giada trapped inside. He set the net in the corner of the room and stood beside it with his hands on his hips.

At the front of the room was a blackboard, filled with equations. Ratu stood in front of it, scratching his head. He feverishly rubbed out parts of the blackboard and scribbled other parts in. The noise of the chalk scratching on the blackboard was the only sound. It echoed throughout the large room making Ma Mutsi flinch. Naledi felt a wave of pity at the thought of what this dear old woman had already endured. Naledi looked over at little Esther Mothopeng. She looked terrified and even though Naledi knew she risked another slap, she had to try whatever she could for the girl.

"Ratu, please, let Esther and the other children go."

"Silence whilst I work," he said.

Naledi heard a menacing growl from the guard behind her. She turned and saw that his eye was twitching, and his fist clenched. He seemed to be a hair's breadth from hitting her again. Goosebumps appeared on her flesh as she trembled.

Ratu finished scribbling and stood back. He muttered to himself under his breath and eventually turned around triumphantly.

"Yes. YES!" his eyes shone. "We are ready. You and you first." He pointed to Lerato and Naledi. A couple of guards strong-armed them up to standing and led them over to two of the machines. They looked like images Naledi had seen in books of electric chairs and her stomach turned to liquid as the primal fear of death pooled inside her. Her legs seemed to suddenly stop working. It was like she was rooted to the spot. The guard impatiently slapped her on the back of her head, causing a burst of pain which broke her fear-induced reverie. She put one trembling foot in front of the other. Time seemed to slow down. Sounds became muted and she was acutely aware of the beating of her own heart. Beads of sweat rolled down the sides of her face. She walked as if in a trance and sat on the chair. The guard secured her hands and feet using metal straps which he locked shut. Then he removed her handcuffs and her other chains.

Lerato sat opposite. Her bright, pretty face was now a death mask: stiff and haunting. Her large eyes were pools of ink submerged in purple shadows. She sniffed and Naledi realised she was holding back tears. Even at this moment, a moment which could be their last on Earth, her friend was thinking of everyone else's feelings. She was trying to pretend she was strong for their benefit. Lerato was really the most incredible person Naledi had ever known. Naledi gave her what she hoped was a sympathetic, reassuring smile but it could just as easily have looked like a grimace of terror.

"Switch on the machine" Ratu ordered.

The guard standing by the side of Lerato's chair flipped a switch and a whirring noise began. Then the guard by Naledi did the same thing. Nothing happened at first and Naledi wondered if it needed time to warm up. Although she was grateful for the temporary reprieve, as the seconds ticked by her fear increased and she felt she might lose control of her bladder.

She flicked her eyes from Kabelo, to Giada, to Tau and then finally to Lerato. Each of her friends had a wild look of fear and desolation. They all believed that Naledi and Lerato were about to die. What had happened to Motsumi? Had he made any progress at all? He must've not had enough time.

Come on Molume.

She began to pray. She knew that nobody in Heaven could hear her, but she was so scared she didn't know what else to do. Suddenly the whirring of the machine stopped and some kind of blast of energy entered her. She screamed as her entire body was lanced with pain. Writhing in agony, she gasped as every other waking thought was overtaken by the extremity of the sensation. Dimly, she heard Ratu's voice saying.

"Yes! It's working, I knew it would."

Whether Motsumi was coming or not now made no difference.

It was already too late for Lerato and Naledi.

26

NALEDI

Pain seared through every nerve ending of Naledi's body. She twisted and screamed, trying desperately to escape the agony. She felt something intangible but important detach itself from her body. The stress made her ithwasa return with a vengeance. Reality wavered, the colours of the room dripping down like wet paint. Then all at once she felt a popping sensation and her soul left her body. Her consciousness floated above the room, observing from within the astral plane. Meanwhile, her body was an empty shell, slumped in the chair with eyes closed, as if sleeping.

Am I dead?

No, if she was dead, she would hear the chorus of angels and see a tunnel beckoning her to Heaven. She wasn't dead, merely unconscious. Lerato was also knocked out. Naledi became aware of a presence at her left shoulder: her friend had also left her body. Naledi racked her brain for a way to make use of the astral plane to attack Ratu and rescue herself and everyone else. Alas, she couldn't think of anything. She was in spirit form and unable to use her powers or to effect any change on the physical world.

Just as it seemed that all hope was lost, Naledi heard an unearthly loud roaring sound. The shock sent Naledi rushing back into her physical body. A shadow fell across the room as all the windows darkened. The guards looked up nervously and in the next moment there was a crash and part of the ceiling caved in. Dust and debris flew everywhere. A large reptilian body swooped down from the sky and opened its mouth. A stream of fire blasted from its lips and hit Ratu. Naledi fist pumped the air. It was Khukwan! He'd come back for them. Ratu was consumed by fire. A high-pitched scream escaped his lips and he felt to the floor, rolling around in flames. One of the guards rushed over and threw a Sotho blanket over him. The flames were extinguished but his body was badly burnt and smoking. The smell of cooked flesh filled the room and Naledi gagged.

She looked at Ma Mutsi. The old lady was covering Esther's innocent eyes as she cradled the child's head into her bosom.

Khukwan circled round, flapping his great wings as he huffed plumes of steam at the guards. Some of them started running for the door. Khukwan gave another roar. His reptilian eyes spotted Giada in the corner and swooped down, picking up the net in his teeth whilst simultaneously tearing it open. As soon as the she was free of the net, Giada flew into the air, free of the prison boundary and the psychic protection spell.

In the next moment the entire room flooded with light. Supernaturally bright rays cast a sunshine haze over the room. Through the hole in the ceiling, Naledi saw large, brilliant orbs of light descend from the heavens.

Still suffering ithwasa, Naledi doubted what she saw and wondered if everyone else saw the same thing. She looked down and saw Esther and Ma Mutsi staring with their eyes wide and mouths agape. Yes, they saw it too. As this was a major celestial event, it must have pierced the earthly veil that normally kept angels hidden from human eyes.

Michael was accompanied by a heavenly host of warrior angels. Some of them swarmed down and attacked Ratu, striking him down with angelic arrows. He screamed and started swatting his hands in the air as if being attacked by a swarm of hornets. As the angels attacked, the demon, a strong stench of sulphur filled the room and his scream was like fingernails scratching on a blackboard. Naledi covered her ears and winced. As all this was happening, Michael swooped down and broke the chains on Naledi's chair with one stroke of his sword. He pulled Naledi off the chair as another angel switched off the machine. Then he released Lerato in the same way. Naledi slumped to the floor. She felt as if her body had been put through a meat grinder. She turned her head to see Lerato trembling next to her. Her friend looked to be in just as bad shape as she was.

The battle continued to rage around them. Ratu was being savaged by archangels. They tore at him, obliterating every fibre of his being until he disintegrated to nothing. Khukwan circled above them, blowing fire at groups of demons. Everywhere she looked angels were killing demons. As each one died, it turned to dust on the floor, before being blown away by the mountain breeze which now blew freely through the open ceiling. The demon acolyte guards meanwhile cowered under tables. Some ran for the exit. Michael waved his hand and all the doors locked, trapping everyone inside. Then he waved his hand again and what felt like a pulse of energy radiated throughout the room. Naledi felt overwhelmed by love and peace. Pins and needles ran up and down her body and as she looked around the room, it seemed that she had never seen a more perfect, beautiful group of humans.

She felt like crying tears of joy. The depth of feeling was beyond description. She knew, without a shadow of doubt, that she was in the presence of God. Something she'd searched for and yearned for her entire life, had finally arrived. She was home. The quality of the light changed, and everything was surrounded in a fuzzy white brilliance which reminded her of something. Where had she seen that light before? Yes, of course. It was the light of Heaven. And the feeling was how she'd felt when she'd gone there. Michael must have grace-bombed the room.

Naledi looked around and saw that some of the demon acolytes had tears streaming down their faces. Others were on their knees, bitterly praying for forgiveness. One or two just sat with eyes closed and beatific smiles on their faces.

Esther looked at Naledi and said, "What is happening?"

Naledi smiled at her, "We're taking you home."

The little girl smiled warmly at Naledi and then started half laughing and half crying. The poor child had been through a lot.

Michael floated above Naledi. "Are you alright?"

Naledi patted herself down as if checking she was still in one piece. "Yes, I think so. How about you Lerato?"

"I feel fine. Eish! But it was painful though. What do you think he was trying to do to us?"

"Some kind of power exchange but he failed. We're still alive anyway!"

Lerato shakily got up to her feet. "Thank you for coming for us Naledi."

"Of course, Lerato! I wouldn't leave you. You know I would have kept searching for as long as it took to find you. You're my soul-sister!" She forced herself to her feet and staggered towards Lerato's open arms to share a much-needed hug.

Naledi released herself from Lerato's embrace. Tau came over and enclosed Naledi in his warm arms. "I was so scared. At one point I thought I would lose you."

Naledi breathed in his rich, sweet aroma, nuzzling her forehead into his shoulder. "Turns out I'm pretty tough to kill."

"You're not wrong," he chuckled.

Tau let go of Naledi and walked over to Khukwan, who was now back in human form. Tau held out his hand and Khukwan took it. "Thank you brother, you saved our lives."

"I only wish I could've got here sooner."

"Why did you leave in the first place?" Naledi asked.

"I had no choice. I could feel my powers draining away. As I explained before, I can only spend a limited amount of time on Earth before I have to replenish my life force in the heavenly realm. I pushed myself as far as possible. But I was at a point of such weakness that, had I attacked, I would not have been successful - or worse, I could've been captured too. I returned as soon as I could."

"And just in time," Kabelo commented, raising his eyebrows.

"Khukwan, I owe you my life. If there's ever anyway I can repay you..." Naledi said.

Khukwan waved his hand in dismissal. "I am a god, it's my job to protect humans against the forces of evil. You don't owe me anything." He looked around sniffing. "As much as I've enjoyed this bit of demon bashing, it's time for me to go home. Farewell everyone." Then leaning forward he added, "Naledi, let's keep in touch." He waved and then dematerialised in a cloud of hazy light.

Archangel Michael came over to her.

"Thank you Michael."

"It is an honour to serve."

She looked around at the guards. Some sat forlornly. Others still seemed bathed in bliss. "What should we do about them?" She asked.

Michael raised his eyebrows. "Nothing. They won't return to their demon worshipping ways now that they've been grace bombed."

Tau added. "We could ask them to drive everyone home?"

This was a good idea. There was no way Naledi would be able to breach a portal in her current condition. Even if she could, the other humans wouldn't be able to travel through it.

The guards agreed to take them all home and the group divided into various trucks. All the villagers from Marula got into the back of the same truck except for Ma Mutsi who got into the front. Naledi's own truck was still out of action at the side of a lonely road but she didn't want to go and get it now. She was so exhausted, all she wanted to do was go home and sleep. She could always breach a portal back to the truck with Tau later and they could drive it home.

She tested her powers, reaching for the threads of reality. As she reached for the familiar, thick soupy texture she frowned. That was odd. She couldn't feel anything. She tried again with the same result. She sat up abruptly.

Lerato, sitting next to her, felt her body language and looked at her. "What is it?"

Naledi didn't answer. She was still thinking. Perhaps she was too tired? But she'd never not been able to feel anything at all. Even when she was really tired, the power still kindled faintly at her fingertips. This was different. Her powers were entirely absent. She opened her mouth, her eyes moving from side to side as she looked at Lerato.

"I think I've lost my powers," she said.

27

NALEDI

Lerato looked at Naledi, her forehead creased with worry. "What do you mean, you've lost your powers?"

"I mean exactly that. I just tried to breach a portal and it didn't work."

Lerato cocked her head to the side and raised one eyebrow. "But I thought you said it didn't work when you were tired?"

"It doesn't but this is different. Normally, even when I'm tired, I can feel something. Now I don't feel anything."

Tau, who was sitting on the other side of Naledi, joined in. "Naledi, you've been through a lot. Maybe you're more tired than you've ever been? I think we should just go home; you get some quality sleep and then I'm sure you'll be fine."

Naledi sighed. "I'm sure you're right," she mumbled. But she was just making him feel better. She didn't believe she was fine. Far from it. It was impossible to describe this to Tau or Lerato. They didn't know what it was like to have her powers. Her powers were gone. She felt it with every fibre of her being and the truth of it penetrated her consciousness like a white-hot lance. Grief gushed over her. She was surprised at the desolation she felt. It was as if somebody had chopped off one of her limbs. She hadn't wanted these powers and had resisted them for so long. Yet, now that they were gone, she desperately wanted them back. It was beyond logic. All that having powers had ever done for her was drag her into grand battles of good versus evil. If she yearned for a quiet life, then why did she feel such pain at this loss? She should be celebrating.

As her thoughts went around and around, Lerato looked at her. "You're still thinking about it, aren't you?"

"Yep."

"Just try and forget about it. There's no use worrying about it now. You're very tired. You'll think better when you've had some sleep."

"I guess you're right." Naledi said quietly. She doubted she would be able to sleep. Not with the loss of her powers weighing heavily on her mind. But she was wrong. Soon her eyelids felt droopy and she succumbed to sleep, as the rumble of the truck carried her body home to Marula.

NALEDI WAS WOKEN by the sound of the cock crowing in the neighbouring village. There was a knock at her bedroom door and Tau poked his head around.

"Morning beautiful." He walked over to sit on her bed and stroked the side of her face.

Naledi rubbed her eyes. They felt like someone had poured sand over them. "How long have I been asleep?"

"About thirty-six hours."

"Thirty-six hours?! Wait a minute - what day is it today?"

Tau laughed. "Wednesday. I've never seen someone who isn't a newborn baby sleep so soundly."

Naledi rubbed her temples. They'd all missed two days of school already and it was already too late for them to go today.

Tau walked towards the kitchen. "I'm starving, you must be too. There's no food in the house so I'm going to the shop in the next village to get a few things."

"Thanks" Naledi's stomach growled at the suggestion and she sat up, gathering her knees to her chest. Her mind instantly returned to what had been bothering her just before she fell asleep. Her powers had gone. She closed her eyes and tried reaching out for the threads once more, just in case it had been tiredness. Nothing. She could no longer breach portals.

Lying back in bed, her thoughts whirred. She had to get a definite answer on what had happened to her. This time she wasted no time in contacting Motsumi. She quieted her mind and created a space and time bubble, locating Motsumi within the astral realm.

Her old teacher sat in front of her looking flustered. "I'll need a bit more time to rescue you from the demons…"

"What?" Naledi interrupted him then remembered that the last he'd heard; she was being held by demons. She flicked her wrist. "Oh, that's all over. We got rescued by someone else."

"Oh!" Motsumi looked a bit dejected. "Who?"

"Khukwan, the Basotho trickster God."

Motsumi's eyes opened wide. "You really do have friends in high places. How did you manage to ally yourself with him?"

"We met him on the way to Joang. Look, it's not important. I need to ask you something else."

"Go on."

"My powers are gone."

"Your powers are not gone. This is a sangoma spiritual practice. It's one of your non-magical powers. Be more specific."

Naledi rolled her eyes. "My magical powers are gone."

Motsumi pursed his lips and raised his eyebrows. "Impossible. You attained your powers at the Pool of Vitality. That means they can never be taken away from you." He looked down at her, his thoughts clicking into gear. "Unless you're talking about your breacher power?"

"Yes, my breacher power. I can no longer do that."

"I see." He touched the fingertips of his hands together. "And when did you discover this unfortunate truth."

"Just now, I mean, before I went to sleep. I tried to breach a portal home. I was very tired, but I felt nothing, no threads at all."

"That's not good." Motsumi replied.

Naledi knew she had been right to talk to him. Being a former breacher, he understood immediately that this meant her powers were gone.

Motsumi stood up and began pacing with his arms behind his back. "Is this related to what you told me about Ratu's experiments to transfer powers from one being to another? Did he use you as a lab rat?"

Naledi's heart sank. She'd been avoiding admitting it, but she couldn't hold the truth back from Motsumi. "Yes. He strapped me and Lerato into a machine. I felt immense pain and I blacked out. Then I left my body. We thought that whatever it was didn't work but maybe it did."

Motsumi stopped pacing and looked at her. "If what you're saying is true, then it means Lerato is now a breacher."

"Possibly. We haven't tested it yet."

"But you still have your other magical powers." Motsumi continued.

"Do I?"

"Yes of course. As I said, it is impossible to lose those as you gained them by completing the trial to beat your adversary at the pool of vitality."

Naledi felt herself relax slightly. If she still had her other powers, at least she wouldn't have to let all her students go. She could still practice as a sangoma. She'd just be a regular sangoma instead of one who also had breaching abilities.

Motsumi looked at her with a furrowed brow. "You seem perturbed. Do you mourn the loss of your breaching abilities?"

"Yes! I do actually."

"But I thought they've brought you nothing but hardship."

"They have but they're a part of me. I feel like I've been violated."

Motsumi was silent for a few moments, perhaps reflecting on the loss of his own breacher powers. "I understand," he finally said. "But there is a way to get your powers back you know."

Naledi's head whipped up. "Is there?"

"There has to be, but I don't know the method. You will have to travel to the akashic realm to find out."

"How will I get there now I'm no longer a breacher?"

"You can still astral travel." He tapped his lip with his finger. "You may still be a realm walker but it's a bit of a risk to take if you're not."

Naledi nodded. If she attempted to go into a portal and wasn't a realm walker, she'd be killed by the excessive energy inside.

Motsumi continued. "I think you should spend time thinking about this though. It's still very new and you're tired and in shock. Wait a while and see if you still want your powers back when you've had time to reflect. You have a greater chance of living the quiet life you've always wanted, without the encumbrance of breaching."

Naledi looked down as she pondered what he'd said. She was glad she'd contacted him and already felt a bit better. At least she still had her other magic powers and if she wanted her breacher powers back, it sounded like it was possible. She had no reason to feel so glum.

Motsumi broke her thoughts with a change of topic. "I'm still investigating the angel Domenico and the plans to overthrow Heaven. Please tell Giada, when you next speak to her that I have some important information to aid in her investigations."

"I will do," Naledi replied. She could understand why Motsumi hadn't burdened her with the details. She had too much on her mind and may not have remembered it anyway. As much as she wanted to help Giada, and be a servant of God, this wasn't her fight. In spite of her long sleep, she was exhausted. Not so much physically tired as mentally and emotionally drained. It felt like she'd spent every bit of her reserves in rescuing Lerato. She needed a day of rest to really think things through, as Motsumi had suggested. Just one day to feel normal. Was that too much to ask?

28

GIADA

It was Wednesday night and Giada stood appraising her outfit in the mirror. She smiled at her appearance. She was feeling more confident since her successful mission on Earth. Against her expectation, she'd helped to find the missing villagers of Marula. But then her smile dropped. She still didn't know what had happened to Domenico. Naledi had told her that Motsumi suspected the angel was dead but he didn't know for sure. That meant the investigation was still open. Michael and Gabi had been delighted with her work so far, but there was still more for her to do.

Bringing her attention back to tonight's date, she smoothed her dress down. She'd decided on a fitted red midi dress and mid-heel black sandals. Her long, thick dark hair was swept up into a loose bun with a few wavy strands loose at the front. Delicate, drop stone jet earrings hung from each ear and she had a matching necklace. She'd done light make up, eye liner and mascara to emphasise her large brown eyes and a bit of light blusher and lip gloss. It had been a long time since she'd worn make up and she was shocked at how much older it made her look. Her mother came into the room.

"Very elegant mi amore. I think there is just one thing missing."

She withdrew a bottle of perfume from behind her back and squirted it in the air near Giada.

"Walk through it," she urged.

Giada did so and an exquisite scent of spring flowers and sandalwood filled her nose.

Replacing the cap on the perfume bottle her mother commented. "You're irresistible. If that boy isn't impressed, he's either blind or stupid or both."

Giada blushed and looked down. "Do you think I should take a jacket?" She wondered if her dress was a bit too formal for the party. A denim jacket would make it look a bit more casual.

Her mother, who lived by the maxim *there's no such thing as overdressing,* disagreed. "No. It's never cold here so why should you cover up. You are a beautiful girl, with a beautiful body. Enjoy your femininity." She started walking out of the room and Giada followed. "If I still had your youth and figure, I'd flaunt it every day."

In truth, her mother was still an attractive woman and Giada often noticed her getting looks from some of the older men in Heaven. She was faithful to Giada's father though and waiting for the day when he would join them. He was still alive in Rome and in good health. It would likely be several decades before he died.

"Mama?" Giada began, "how do you know if a boy really likes you?"

Her mother turned around to face her. "I think you can just tell in the way that he looks at you and the way that he treats you. It's hard to explain." Her face softened with compassion, "Why do you ask? Do you worry that Luke doesn't like you?"

Giada frowned. "I don't know. He seems like he does one minute then the next minute he seems frosty. I can't read him."

"He's asked you out tonight. Why would he do that if he didn't like you?"

"I'm not sure, that's what I keep wondering."

Her mother cupped Giada's chin with one hand. "You worry too much. Sometimes the simplest explanation is the right one. He's asked you out - he must like you."

Giada smiled and nodded as her mother kissed her on the cheek, but she couldn't ignore the uneasy feeling that swirled around her insides. Was her mother right? Was she worrying too much? Or was Luke a player who got a kick out of toying with girls? But then surely someone like that wouldn't get to Heaven, would they? She felt so confused. Maybe tonight would help her get answers to these questions. She didn't have any more time to think about it though as there was a knock at the door.

Giada felt a flutter of excitement. "That must be him, I'll see you later Mama." She kissed her mother on the cheek and walked to the door.

Her mother tactfully stayed in the living room, although Giada could see her eagle eyes trained on the door to get a look at the boy who had captured her daughter's heart.

When she opened the door, Giada's breath caught in her throat. Luke was wearing jeans and a white t-shirt which perfectly complemented his tan. He looked at her from under his floppy fringe and smiled.

That smile should come with a warning she thought as a butterfly bomb exploded in her stomach.

"You look beautiful," he said.

Giada felt her shoulders relax as she smiled back at him.

He offered her his arm, "shall we?"

It seemed like quite a formal way for a boy his age to talk and Giada wondered how long he'd been in Hell. He could be from a very different time. In fact, that could explain his stand offish behaviour. Perhaps dating was different in his era? Giada made a mental note to ask him later. She took his arm and they strolled out.

"Have a good time" her mother called out, as they left.

They walked in awkward silence for a few moments before Luke broke it by asking. "Is this your first newly-redeemed welcoming party?"

"Yes. How about you?"

"I've been a couple of times before."

"What are they like?"

"Yeah, they're fun." Luke's voice raised a little in a manner suggesting a lack of enthusiasm.

"Would you have gone tonight if you hadn't been going with me?"

"Probably not." He laughed and Giada joined him.

"So, they're not all that fun then."

Luke shrugged. "What can I say, they're lovely, delightful parties. Good, clean fun."

Now her interest was piqued. "As opposed to?..."

Luke scratched his neck and looked slightly uncomfortable. "I dunno, I remember parties on Earth being a bit wilder than here, that's all."

Giada's head whipped towards him. "Are you serious? You look about fifteen."

"I'm sixteen," Luke corrected her.

"Alright sixteen then. How did you get invited to these 'wild' parties at your age?"

Luke looked at her. "Didn't you go to wild parties?"

"Not really. My parents wouldn't let me. I died young and before that... I had a difficult few years and let's just say that I didn't have the largest circle of friends."

"I find that hard to believe."

"Not everybody finds me as charming as you do." She smiled and fluttered her eyelashes and he laughed. She wasn't about to let him off the hook of answering her question though. "How come your parents were so lenient with you?"

"They weren't lenient with us. They were non-existent. I never knew my parents. Me and my brother were abandoned at a young age. We spent our childhood being shipped from one children's home to another. There aren't many people out there who are willing to adopt two at once and we refused to be separated. We never found out who our birth parents were."

Giada's smile dropped. "Oh... I'm sorry, I didn't know." She felt herself go crimson at having put her foot in her mouth.

"No, that's okay. How would you?" He looked up at the stars. "Anyway, most children's homes don't care about what the kids get up to.

In their view, as long as we were fed and clothed, their duty to us was done."

Giada's mouth felt full of cotton. "Luke, that's terrible." What else could she say. She couldn't offer any words of sympathy that wouldn't sound flippant. She had often *felt* abandoned by her parents whilst growing up, but she hadn't actually *been* abandoned. She couldn't imagine the deep well of pain this must have created inside Luke. It explained a lot about his personality. He must have serious trust issues. No wonder he wanted to be close to her one minute but then became aloof the next. He was probably terrified of being abandoned again. She was suddenly filled with shame at how self-absorbed she'd been. If it was such a struggle for Luke to get close to people, she should give him time and space. Instead, she'd been obsessing about whether or not he liked her as if it was all about her when it clearly wasn't.

Luke must've noticed her sombre expression. "Don't let it get you down, it was a long time ago and I'm over it now."

Giada half smiled at him. She didn't believe he was over it. From what she'd heard, abandoned children didn't ever get over it. Not even when they were adults with their own children. The pain, of having been rejected by the two people who were supposed to love them the most, followed them around like a spectre for the rest of their lives.

It was clear that Luke didn't want to dwell on this though, so Giada perked her expression up and changed the subject. "Where did you live, on Earth?"

"In Ohio in the 1920s."

She'd been right. He *was* from an earlier era. "What was it like then?"

"Very different to how I understand it is now. There was obviously no technology, but also people had less in general. We lived during the great depression, so it was pretty tough."

The great depression! Of course. This was just getting worse and worse. Giada had tried to change the subject to something lighter but had yet again strayed into traumatic-memory territory. It seemed

Luke was now willing to share further though as he continued. "Me and my brother managed to get work digging a railway tunnel. We were lucky because there were so few jobs around. It paid peanuts but we got a hot meal at lunch on the days we worked. That was our one meal of the day. It was grainy soup with stale bread, but it tasted like the most delicious thing in the world - we were always so hungry."

"How did you die?" Giada asked, tentatively.

"We were working inside the tunnel one day and it collapsed on top of us. We didn't die instantly but we were deeply buried. We held out for a few days, getting weaker and weaker, from hunger and thirst. I remember going to sleep one day and waking up in Hell with my brother beside me."

"Do you know why you were damned?"

Luke sighed and his brow furrowed. "We did a lot of things to survive that I'm not proud of. We stole. We lied. We cheated. We murdered people when we were desperate enough." His eyes had a misty quality as he half-smiled. "You know there are areas of town in every major city that are no-go zones? People warn you not to go there because there are criminals hanging around who plan to do you harm. In Cincinnati, we *were* those criminals. I remember walking along streets and people crossing onto the other side to avoid us. I liked it when they did that: it made me feel powerful. If I wasn't going to be loved, at least I'd be feared. My brother permanently had a cigarette hanging out of the side of his mouth. I walked everywhere compulsively swinging a switch blade. It was like my protective armour. But I wouldn't hesitate to use that knife when I needed to, and sometimes even when I didn't need to. I couldn't feel anything other than anger, hate and desperation every single day."

Giada was transfixed. She would never have guessed any of this by looking at the boy who walked next to her now. He looked so clean and wholesome, but he carried around a dark past, filled with misery. She suddenly realised they were cut from similar cloth. She hadn't had it nearly so tough in life, but she understood what it meant to walk around with constant pain and hate. She understood what it meant to carry the weight and guilt of terrible past deeds on her shoulders. As she looked at Luke though, he didn't look guilty. He had a level of detachment as he talked about his past - that was probably how he protected himself from the horrors of his memories. Either that or he'd worked through his issues, before getting redeemed, as she had.

THEY ARRIVED at the party and Giada was met by the sight of thousands of multicoloured bubbles, floating through the air endlessly from some unseen source. Music blasted from a row of massive speakers at either end of the hall and fluorescent lights and lasers beamed up through the night sky. The party was held in the Hall of Creation and there was enough space for thousands of revellers inside. She wondered how she would ever find Bronwen. She didn't have to wonder for long. Her friend was near the entrance and rushed over to them.

"You're here!" she reached forward and crushed Giada in a hug. "Hi Luke" she raised her hand in greeting and Luke mumbled a greeting back. Giada reflected that he was a bit stand-offish towards Bronwen and she couldn't understand why. But then again, he was a bit stand-offish even with her. It was just his way and one of the things she found maddening about him.

Bronwen pulled her in conspiratorially. "Rika and Britney are here too, and you look way prettier than them."

"Thanks, Bronwen...." Giada smiled weakly. She would've preferred that the compliment wasn't laced with an insult toward the other two girls, however unpleasant they were. "You look really nice too," she replied. Bronwen was wearing a cream coloured, chiffon-layered, ankle-length dress which swished when she walked.

"Let's go and dance - Luke, do you mind?"

"Not at all. You go and enjoy yourselves."

"Come with us." Giada urged.

Luke waved his hands in front of his face. "I'm not really much of a dancer."

Giada narrowed her eyes at him, "I'll get you dancing later." She allowed Bronwen to pull her towards the dance floor as she gave one final glance in Luke's direction.

Bronwen danced with the same free abandon that she did everything. Her arms swung from side to side loosely and her head bopped up and down, red hair swirling around her face. She was the very definition of 'dance-like-nobody-is-watching'. Her attitude was infectious and pretty soon Giada was joining in with just as much enthusiasm.

After a couple of songs Giada needed a rest so she went to find Luke. He stood watching her at the side of the room.

"It's pretty hot in here, right?" Giada flapped her hands over her face, hoping it wasn't beetroot red.

"Fancy a walk outside to cool off?" Luke offered.

"Sure, good idea."

Giada followed him to the patio, bordering a large lake outside. Hundreds of tea lights, bobbed up and down, casting droplets of light onto the surface of the water. Other couples sat around or walked, chatting quietly. Luke linked his hand into hers. A rush of electricity ran up and down her body.

"Are you having a good time?" He asked.

"So far so good. How about you?"

"It's nice but what I like the most is spending time with you." He stopped walking and stood facing her. "Giada. I know I'm not the easiest person to get close to, but I want you to know that..." he hesitated, his dark eyes searching hers, "... I really like you."

Giada looked down shyly before lifting her chin to look into his eyes. "I like you too Luke."

He held up a hand to her cheek and touched it lightly. "You're so beautiful."

She felt her breath quicken as he came closer. Warmth radiated from his breath. He smelled like cherries and happiness. Tilting his head, he ever so slowly caressed the back of her neck with his hand.

She closed her eyes and felt her muscles softening as his warm hand stroked her neck. When he brought his lips onto hers, her entire body became weightless. Everything dissolved around them and it was just him and her. He brought his hands around her back and pulled her closer to him. His body pressed against hers and she thought she could stay in this moment with him forever. Then all at once it was over and he pulled away, smiling shyly at her.

Giada felt dizzy. *He does like me!*

But in the next instant she felt him closing down again. Retreating into himself as if nothing had happened between them. Was this real or was it an act? If so, why was he acting? What did he have to gain by being with her? Or was she being silly and overly suspicious? He'd shared his terrible childhood with her - no wonder he held himself back. Should she just relax and take it slow? And trust that he liked her, as her mother had advised her?

As the kiss she'd shared with Luke, already seemed like a distant memory, she sighed. Her time in Hell really had done a number on her. She could no longer trust that a boy liked her, just for her. But then Luke was also suspicious and guarded.

Maybe they were perfect for each other.

29

NALEDI

Naledi stretched and got up. Dineo and Puleng bounded into her as she walked into the living room.

"You're back! We missed you," Dineo beamed, burying her face in Naledi's skirt.

"Was it okay at Grannie Mothopeng's house? Was she kind to you?"

"Yes. She cooked us samp and beans. Better than yours." Puleng replied

"Is that so?" Naledi laughed and pinched her sisters cheek playfully.

Lerato came out of her bedroom. "Morning. How are you feeling after your marathon session of sleep?"

"Much better, I feel like a new person." The deeper truth of what she'd just said hit Naledi in the gut as she suddenly remembered the loss of her breacher powers. "Lerato. We need to talk. In private." Naledi beckoned for her to come as she walked back to her room.

Lerato looked puzzled but she followed her.

Naledi closed the door behind them and stood, facing Lerato as she wrung her hands.

"What's wrong? You're scaring me." Lerato said.

"I've just had a talk with Motsumi."

Lerato sighed. "What's McShifty done to you this time?"

"Nothing! I reached out to him actually. The thing is, I tried to breach a portal this morning and my powers have definitely gone. I've slept really well now so it can't be tiredness." Naledi looked at her, waiting for Lerato to make the same connection she had. Her friend didn't disappoint her.

"You don't think..." Lerato's eyes moved from left to right, "... that machine Ratu put us in actually worked, do you?"

Naledi nodded. "Uh huh, that's exactly what I think. But there's only one way to find out. You need to try breaching a portal."

Lerato looked aghast. "Try? Me! I have no idea how you do what you do."

"Neither did I the first time I did it. It's a spontaneous magical ability. Just try."

Lerato huffed but she closed her eyes. She kept her eyes closed for a few seconds and then opened them. "See, nothing happened."

"You're not trying hard enough."

"But I don't know how to try hard enough. What am I supposed to feel? Just give me a few pointers."

Naledi searched her mind for how best to describe it. How could she put into words something that was beyond human understanding? "It's like you'll feel something gloopy and thick all around you. Like reality has a tangible, stringy feeling. You grab hold of that and then pull - don't pull too much. Just make a small portal, right here inside the room. Then you'll pinch it shut."

Lerato raised her eyebrows. "Okay, I'll try again." She closed her eyes and kept them closed for longer this time. Naledi watched her features. She saw as a slight smile then a look of surprise came onto her friend's face. It looked like she was getting somewhere. Then Lerato moved her hands and a small portal opened in front of them in the room. Lerato opened her eyes and laughed out loud. "I did it! I'm a breacher, how cool is that?" She looked at Naledi and then wiped the smile off her face. "Oh, I mean... how awful."

Naledi half smiled. "No, it's okay Lerato. You don't have to pretend for my benefit. It is cool."

A feeling of grief swept over Naledi's body as her worst fears had been confirmed. She didn't really understand where the grief was coming from. She'd never wanted her breacher powers and indeed had often felt trapped by them. Being a breacher meant that she was always in demand by both Heaven and Hell. It also meant that whenever someone was in trouble, she was forced to go riding to their rescue on her big white, breacher horse. But her powers had started to become entwined with her identity. Losing them was like losing part of herself.

Lerato noticed her confused state. "How do you feel about it?"

Naledi wrestled to control the mixture of emotions which fought for dominance within her. "I'm not sure. Confused I guess. Part of me wants my powers back and Motsumi said it would be possible for me to get them back if I want them. And that's the kicker because another part of me sees this as a blessing - a way to live the quiet life I've always wanted."

Listening to the words she'd just spoken triggered a memory. All at once, the reading of the bones which Ma Monono had done for her in Lehlaka made sense. Naledi's eyes widened at the epiphany. "Ma Monono..."

"Who?" Lerato asked.

"Oh, she was a sangoma we met on the way to rescue you. Anyway, she read my bones and said she saw two possible life paths for me. One which led to peace and safety but great loss. Another which led to excitement and power but great danger." She looked at Lerato. "At the time I was so worried because I thought the loss she was describing was your death but now I understand. She was talking about the loss of my breacher powers."

Lerato raised her eyebrows. "Wow, so she was definitely a talented seer then. What else did she say?"

Naledi closed her eyes and rubbed her temples as she tried to remember. Her eyes flew open and she lifted her forefinger. "Ooh, she also said I'll always be able to walk between worlds. Do you think that means I'm a realm walker now?"

Lerato shrugged. "It must do."

"Motsumi also thought I might be but it's a big risk to take if I'm not. The energy of a portal is enough to kill a regular human."

Lerato looked up at the ceiling. "What about your sangoma powers? Have you lost those too?"

"Thankfully not. I earned those by completing a trial at the pool of vitality so Motsumi says they'll be with me forever."

Lerato seemed to be considering what Naledi had just said. "Forever? What about if you lose your virginity?"

Naledi looked at her, with her mouth open. "I hadn't even thought about that." She squirmed, "I can't ask Motsumi that, it's far too personal."

"Maybe you should go back and ask that Ma Monono? She seems to know what's up."

"Or I could astral travel to the akashic realm."

"Yeah, or that." Lerato raised one eyebrow. "All I'm saying is, you're getting older. We all are. Sooner or later you'll want more and so will Tau. Marriage, maybe even kids some day?"

Lerato was right, as usual. If Naledi was honest with herself, she already wanted more. Now that she was no longer battling poverty every day, she was starting to think about the future. Once she'd finished school, she wanted to go to University. But after that, she wanted the things that every other woman in Marula had. She hadn't dared admit this to herself, because these desires made her feel guilty. She'd been gifted with more power than any other human on Earth and instead of being grateful, she yearned for a simple life. To settle down, marry a nice man and have children with him.

The sound of the front door opening, as Tau came back, broke her reverie.

"Breakfast is here, I've got fresh fruit and warm rolls. Come and get it!"

Lerato rushed out of the door with the eagerness of someone who had just walked ten miles, on an empty stomach. She always did have a big appetite. Naledi trailed behind her, still deep in thought.

Perhaps she's brought the loss of her breacher powers on herself? By the strength of her desires and intentions. Perhaps this was the best thing that had ever happened to her? Perhaps she was getting exactly what she'd secretly always wanted?

30

GIADA

The day after the party Bronwen invited Giada to her flat for a girly gossip session. It was unusual for a girl of Bronwen's age to live alone. Most people had so many dead relatives they could live with in Heaven. Bronwen had told Giada that although she did have some relatives in Heaven, she wasn't close to any of them. She'd said she was happier alone anyway. This didn't make sense to Giada as she seemed like such a sociable type, but she didn't push the issue. Bronwen's bedroom had an en suite dressing room with a mirror facing the double bed. She was getting herself ready, doing her make up in the mirror as Giada sat on the bed. As she absent-mindedly played with one of Bronwen's silk scarves, Giada confided to her friend all that had happened between her and Luke.

"Let me get this straight." Bronwen began, "even though he kissed you, you're still not sure if he likes you or not?"

Giada ran the scarf through her fingers. "I know it sounds like I'm really down on myself but it's difficult to explain. It just lacked the genuine heat and intensity of a real kiss."

"How many real kisses have you had, Cassanova?" Bronwen looked at Giada in the mirror as she pulled her cheek down slightly to apply eye liner to her lower lash line.

Giada half laughed and looked back at Bronwen in the mirror. "Not many, I'll admit but I think most of the passion was coming from me. I get the feeling he's playing me, and I have no idea why."

Bronwen shook her head and looked at Giada. "Why does a smart, beautiful, kind girl seem so convinced that a boy couldn't possibly really be into her? In spite of all evidence screaming in her face that he is interested in her. Huh?"

Giada stopped playing with the scarf as another thought came to her. "He also didn't mention any follow up date. Don't you think that's strange?"

Bronwen opened her mouth and leaned into the mirror as she widened her eyes to apply her mascara. "Not really. Maybe he's going to ask you on another date today?"

"Yeah, maybe..." Giada's voice trailed off as she got an uneasy feeling in her belly.

Why is she always defending him?

She discounted the thought as soon as it arose. Bronwen was just being a good friend; trying to make her feel better. It was normal female friend behaviour. Or was it? Giada struggled to remember. In fact, it had been so long since she'd had a close female friend that she didn't know how boy talk worked. She'd been a child when she'd cut herself off from her friends in Rome.

Suddenly Giada heard a slight noise as Bronwen inhaled sharply.

"What's wrong?" Giada asked.

"Nothing, I just got something in my eye. Mascara is the worst sometimes, isn't it?" Bronwen blinked rapidly and closed her eyes.

"Yes, the worst," Giada agreed. She caught Bronwen's reflection in the mirror just as she opened her eyes and her blood ran cold. One of Bronwen's eyes was red. Not slightly red like she hadn't had enough sleep. It was the deep, pure scarlet eye of a demon. Thinking at lightning speed, Giada flicked her gaze in the opposite direction and pretended that she hadn't seen anything.

"Anyway, enough about me. How was the rest of your night?" Giada asked. She saw Bronwen's face reflected in the window opposite. Bronwen quickly reached onto the counter and put a contact lens back into her eye. Her body relaxed as soon as the contact lens was back in and then she flicked her eyes into the mirror to check Giada hadn't seen. She seemed satisfied that she hadn't been caught and carried on applying the rest of her make up.

"It was really fun. I danced. I met lots of new people. I didn't meet any cute guys but there's still time for that." Bronwen chuckled and Giada joined in, as naturally as she could. Her mind was reeling.

Finishing her make up Bronwen came and sat next to Giada on the bed. Giada tried to act normal, but she felt her body flinch almost imperceptibly. She inwardly swore at herself. She mustn't let on to Bronwen that she knew. At least not until she'd figured out what was going on here. Flicking her gaze at Bronwen, it seemed her friend hadn't noticed. Giada was desperate to get out of Bronwen's house and be alone to think about what she'd discovered. But she couldn't. She had to stay a bit longer, in order to quash any remnants of suspicion Bronwen may still have that she'd been unearthed. Giada would have to wait until a reasonable time to leave and act like nothing at all had changed between them. She inwardly thanked her ability to lie convincingly.

"I'm sure you'll meet someone nice soon. After all, we have the rest of eternity, right?" Giada smiled.

"Right" Bronwen smiled warmly and Giada felt her own smile weaken as a wave of sadness passed over her. She looked away before Bronwen noticed. How could her friend be a demon? She was such a nice person. But then she was obviously just pretending to be a nice person. She must be. It was impossible for demons to be nice. Hang on though, Motsumi was now a demon and he was nice - sort of. She also hadn't minded the Chancellor when she'd worked for him in Hell. So, demons could actually be nice. This was so confusing. What was Bronwen's agenda? More importantly, how had she got into Heaven? None of this made any sense. Giada shook the thoughts away and forced herself back into the room.

Act natural. You can think about this later. And now you've been silent for too long.

Giada blurted out. "I've been thinking. Maybe we could go on a day trip together soon. I haven't explored the caves of humility yet. Do you fancy it?"

Bronwen's eyes lit up. "I'd love to. We could take a camera and get some lovely photos together."

"Good idea. How about tomorrow? I'll come here mid-morning and we can hike there together." Giada didn't really want to come back. Not tomorrow morning, not ever, but she wasn't thinking straight.

"Sure, but you're not leaving already, are you?" Bronwen pouted. "You've only just got here. I've made myself up. I thought we could go and hit the shops. There's a new boutique in the plaza that I really want to check out."

Giada thought quickly. "I'd love to, but I promised I'd help Mama with something."

Bronwen's smile dropped and Giada felt bad. "I tell you what, I'll come back later, and we can go."

"Awesome! You're the best Giada." She squeezed Giada in a side hug and Giada felt like the shittiest soul in the universe.

"See you later" Giada cheerily said, getting up and walking out as calmly as her acting skills would allow.

Once she was a decent distance away from Bronwen's home, Giada sped up her pace to a brisk walk. Thoughts raced through her mind. She barely noticed her surroundings as she made her way home.

Bronwen is a demon.

Is that why Bronwen had wanted to be friends with her - because she recognised a kindred spirit? It added fuel to the fire of Giada's fear that she didn't truly belong in here. How was it possible? There was no way for a demon to enter the heavenly gates but yet, here one was. The evidence was ironclad. Giada knew what she had seen. And Bronwen's follow up body language confirmed it. Her furtive glances at Giada. The slight fear, in her eyes, that she'd been discovered. Giada's blood pumped loudly enough for her to hear it. If Bronwen was a demon, could there be others here? This had to be linked to the plot to overthrow heaven and allow demons to enter. She had to tell the archangels. But could she trust any of them? The person she'd met with who had told her of the plot to overthrow Heaven had been an archangel. The conspiracy went all the way to the top, anyone could be involved. Could she even trust Michael? He seemed honest but then so had Bronwen. Giada felt so overwhelmed, she had no idea what to do.

Arriving home, Giada mumbled a greeting to her mother in the living room, before going straight to her room and flopping on her bed. Staring up at the ceiling, she suddenly felt very alone and lost. She was no closer to finding out what had happened to Domenico and now she had information that could be key, but she had nobody she could trust. Her thoughts turned to her friends in Sinners Anonymous. It was ironic that she'd made friends in Hell, way easier than in Heaven. She missed them, especially Aaron. She even missed Motsumi. Wait a minute! She sat up. Motsumi! She'd asked Naledi to ask Motsumi about the plot to overthrow Heaven and about Domenico. What with everything that had been happening over the past couple of days, she hadn't even found out yet what, if anything, he'd told her. She reached out to connect with Naledi telepathically.

Just then she heard the voice of Bronwen being let into the hallway by her mother.

Shit! She knows I'm onto her. Why else would she be here so soon?

The next moment, Bronwen was at the bedroom door. "Hey, you forgot to take this back." She held up a clutch bag that Giada had lent Bronwen to use on the night of the party.

"Oh, thanks," Giada scrambled off her bed and took the bag from Bronwen.

"Did you finish helping your mother?"

Giada smiled stiffly. "Not yet. I'll come over to yours later okay?"

Bronwen wafted her hand in the air. "Sure, but it's no biggie if you don't. I've got a few errands to run anyway."

Errands to run.

Bronwen had never used that term before in the entire time Giada had known her. Something was off about her body language. She was up to something. Giada made the decision, right then and there, to follow her.

"Bye then." Bronwen's voice went up an octave. The girl was a terrible liar. It was a wonder she'd managed to keep the fact she was a demon from Giada for so long.

"See you later." Giada smiled. She waited until she heard the front door shut then crept to the side of the living room window. Bronwen was striding purposefully away from the house. Giada waited until she was a healthy distance away before taking pursuit, sticking to the shadows as she followed her.

31

GIADA

Giada's time spent following the Countess in Hell had not been wasted. She was now adept at trailing people. However, she still felt nervous as she followed Bronwen. Hell was full of sneaky people doing sneaky things, but it was different in Heaven. Any dodgy behaviour immediately drew attention here as it was so rare. What if someone spotted her and blabbed to Bronwen? She supposed she could always use the 'I'm-doing-my-redemption-school-mission' excuse. But then Bronwen's suspicions would be raised and whatever she was up to, she'd likely put it on hold or stop completely.

Giada put her concerns to one side and tried to stay hidden as best she could whilst at the same time not looking too shifty. Fortunately, Bronwen wasn't the naturally suspicious type and she walked with purpose, cheerfully whistling. Something about Bronwen's demeanour made Giada feel a sudden pang of guilt. Whatever Bronwen was up to, Giada was basically setting her friend up for something unpleasant. At the very least she'd be sent back to Hell. Bronwen had been nothing but kind to her. So, she'd somehow managed to get into Heaven under false pretences. Was that so bad? Giada thought back to how desperate she'd been to get to Heaven when she'd been in Hell. Wouldn't she have done the same as Bronwen if she'd been given the chance? Was it right for her judge Bronwen in that case?

As these thoughts turned around in her head, Giada sharply withdrew her breath as she saw Bronwen hesitate. Giada stepped to the side so that her face was obscured by some bushes and bent down as if she'd dropped something. Bronwen turned around and her eyes scanned the path but then she shrugged and turned back to the front. Giada exhaled and stood up again.

Bronwen walked to the outskirts of Heaven. On her first day, Giada had learnt that the boundary of Heaven was protected by an etheric forcefield which enclosed the entire realm. The only beings which could pass through this barrier were the Almighty, and angels. This included trainee angels like Giada. Breachers could get to the heavenly admittance plane but no further. Deceased souls made their way into Heaven via the gates of Saint Peter, but angels could pass through at any point.

Giada watched as Bronwen walked to the etheric forcefield. She was walking quickly now and had stopped whistling. As Bronwen stopped in front of the barrier, Giada stationed herself behind some trees. She saw Bronwen turn her head from left to right a few times. Then she simply walked through the barrier and vanished. Giada was gobsmacked. How had Bronwen managed to do that when she was a demon? It looked like she had done this before. This demon was just going back and forth between Heaven and.... Where? Hell? Earth? Giada had to find out more.

She strolled towards the barrier but at a point further down. She didn't want to risk messing up the entire operation by coming face to face with Bronwen. Giada emerged onto the ultra-green, lush grass field of the heavenly admittance plane. In the distance she saw the queue of newly deceased souls waiting in front of Saint Peter. The air smelt of honeysuckle and Giada smiled as she was taken back to the memory of when she had first arrived here with her mother. She had been so overjoyed to have finally made it. But she couldn't waste time thinking about that now. She spotted Bronwen further down and saw that she wasn't alone. She was meeting someone.

Giada got as close as she could without being seen and hid behind a group of bushes. She narrowed her eyes, trying to get a good look at who Bronwen was meeting with. It was a black girl, average height, a bit plump, with a round face. It struck Giada that the girl looked very familiar. Yes, she had definitely seen her before. Giada kept watching, trying to work out where she knew her from. Then it hit her like a tonne of bricks: she was one of Naledi's students. She stifled a gasp and sank back further behind the bushes to think for a few moments.

Giada had seen an image of the girl flash through Naledi's mind as she'd discussed her students a few days ago. This didn't make sense. Had Naledi's student died and come to Heaven? It was possible but if that was the case, what was she doing all the way over here instead of lining up with the other new arrivals? If she hadn't recently died, how had she got here? The only way for a human to get to Heaven without dying was if that human was a breacher. Naledi was a breacher but there was no way she'd be involved in getting a demon into Heaven; she was far too devout a Christian for that. In any case, humans couldn't even pass through a breacher portal unless they themselves were breachers or realm walkers. Giada peeked through the bushes at Bronwyn and the girl again. The girl was doing something with her hands. She moved them through the air and the next moment, a portal appeared. Bronwen and the girl disappeared though the portal together.

She's a breacher!

Giada was tempted to rush over and see where they'd gone before the portal closed but she didn't. She couldn't risk Bronwen and the breacher girl discovering she was on their trail. She'd found out a lot today. She should be satisfied with that and quit whilst she was ahead.

But she found she couldn't. So many question swirled around in her head. Motsumi had told Giada that breachers were very rare. He'd thought that he and Naledi were the only breachers in Africa when he was alive. Had he been lying about that or just wrong? Or was it true at the time but since then Naledi's student had emerged as a breacher? Any of these were possible. What niggled at Giada's mind though, was that Naledi hadn't told her the girl was a breacher. Giada was certain that Naledi would've mentioned this if she'd known. The fact that she hadn't mentioned this meant that she didn't know. Why would the student hide this fact from Naledi?

The more Giada thought about this, the more she felt that there was something fishy going on here. Naledi could be in danger and if so, Giada had to help her. She decided to follow the breacher and Bronwen to find out more.

Giada didn't need the portal to find them. She used a technique she'd learnt at Redemption School. She held an image of the breacher girl in her mind's eye. Giada instantly materialised nearby where the girl stood in front of Bronwen, talking. They were in Naledi's home village of Marula. On Earth Giada was usually invisible to all humans except clairvoyants. However, as Bronwen was there and, as she didn't know if the breacher had any clairvoyant skills, she kept herself hidden behind some bushes. Bronwen and the girl talked for a while and then Bronwen went back to Heaven. Giada had a hunch she should stick with the breacher, so she followed her.

The girl walked to Naledi's old house where she met another girl. Giada remembered Naledi telling her that she no longer lived there as she'd moved to Motsumi's old house. She kept the house and used it for teaching and treating clients.

The other girl the breacher met with was shorter, skinny with hair cut very short, large eyes, and a gap between her two front teeth. Giada also recognised this girl as being a student of Naledi's. She cast her mind back to the telepathic conversation she'd had with Naledi, trying to remember the girls' names. In frustration she gave up. She couldn't recall them. Looking again at the skinny, gap-toothed girl, Giada frowned. When she'd been shown the girl in Naledi's mind's eye, she had seemed different. Her body language had been timid and unsure, now she seemed dominant which was odd considering she looked younger than the breacher. Giada positioned herself outside, peeking through the open window.

The smaller girl sat on the sofa with her arms crossed. Her eyes glittered at the older girl as she entered. The older girl then actually knelt in front of the younger girl and dipped her head in respect.

"Well?" the younger girl asked, cocking her eyebrow.

"We are on track master."

"And they still have no idea – even Archangel Michael?"

"None. She has performed her role well. You were right to put your trust in her."

The younger girl's eyes flashed, and her lip curled. She stood up and clenched her fists. A vein pulsated at the side of her forehead. "I don't expect an appraisal from you. I am your master. You'd be nowhere without me. You'd still be an ordinary human, wishing you had magical abilities." Her voice raised until she was shouting, flecks of saliva escaping from her lips. "I gave you everything. I showed you how to find your sangoma teacher. I allowed you to be included in our plans - plans that will change the entire Universe. You owe me everything. Don't ever give me your opinion about my plans again. Is that understood?"

The older girl flinched, "yes master. Sorry master."

Giada looked again at the younger girl. There was something unnatural about her movements, something that didn't add up. She cast her mind back to how the girl had looked when she'd first seen her. It was like she was a different person.

A different person....

Of course! She looked like she was a different person because she *was* a different person. Giada's pulse raced as the sudden realisation of what was going on dawned on her. This younger girl was no longer inside her own body - she was hosting a demon! And this older girl was the demon's acolyte. From what they were saying, it sounded like this relationship had been established before they'd begun training with Naledi.

Giada was shocked. How many of Naledi's other students were being controlled by demons? Did Naledi know about this? Had she been corrupted again? No, Giada refused to believe it. She'd seemed so happy and contented and proud of her students when she'd spoken about them. Giada had detected no hint of lies or shame. It was true that Naledi had almost gone over to the other side in Hell, but she hadn't gone through with it. She'd settled down and now wanted to live a quiet life. Plus, Naledi had just risked her life, rescuing her friend from demons. Could she be lying? Perhaps the entire kidnap and rescue of Lerato was some kind of elaborate demon smokescreen, which Naledi was in on? Giada supposed it was possible, but she trusted her gut. Instinct told her that Naledi was on God's side and therefore ignorant about the dark plans of these two.

What were their plans? Giada hovered, hoping to hear more.

The younger girl lifted her chin, put her hands behind her back and started pacing. "Did you tell her we need another angel as soon as possible?"

"I did, master, but it takes time to gain trust. Bronwen believes she is almost there with a newly-redeemed angel."

"She needs to move on it now before it's too late. The longer we wait, the more we risk discovery. We're so close to Heaven being ours, we can't let it slip through our fingers."

Giada inhaled sharply. They were talking about her! Bronwen was planning to use Giada in some way.

Another angel...

This must be what had happened to Domenico. He was abducted by a demon. But why? What were they using him for? Was he still alive? Surely not, if a demon had got his hands on him. It sounded like this was bound up in the plot to overthrow Heaven. She'd heard enough. Now that she knew for certain that Michael wasn't involved, she had to get back to Heaven immediately and tell him everything she knew.

She floated up, skimming the roof of the house, as she took to the sky. But she only got a few metres higher than the house when she hit some kind of barrier above her. It felt like tentacles of slimy seaweed were wrapped around her and tightening fast. It was a feeling she recognised, having felt it recently when she'd been trapped by Ratu.

Oh no! It's an etheric net. I'm trapped.

She flapped her arms about, struggling wildly as she tried to break through. But the more she thrashed, the tighter the tendrils wrapped. Instead she reached out for help telepathically.

Michael, Gabi, I need help. I'm trapped on Earth.

As she thought this, the demon possessed girl and her acolyte came out of the house. The demon narrowed her eyes and looked directly at Giada.

"If you're praying, you may as well give up. They can't hear you."

Giada spoke aloud, knowing that demons can't hear angels telepathically. "What do you mean? What have you done to me?"

"We've protected this house from angelic influence by putting an etheric net around the entire perimeter. It allows you to come in, but it doesn't allow you to fly out. The net is under a psychic protection spell. Angels can't hear you. And don't bother trying to get anyone else to come and help you. I know you're friends with Naledi. She won't be able to hear you either. She's too far away."

Giada thrashed again. "Let me go!"

The demon girl laughed. "Absolutely not. You're ours now and you're just what we need." Her eyes darkened in a look of pure evil. Giada shuddered. What had they done to Domenico? And what were they going to do to her?

32

GIADA

Giada felt the etheric bonds close tighter around her.

"We can't keep her here, Naledi may return at any moment. She could already be in Marula. We will go to the far end of the village, keeping well away from Naledi's house. If it's deserted, we can perform the procedure there."

"What procedure? What are you going to do to me?" Giada demanded.

The demon cocked her head to the side and narrowed her eyes. She opened her mouth and Giada thought she was about to get an explanation but then her mouth closed again, and she turned her back on her.

"Take her, Bongi."

Giada watched helplessly as the older girl - Bongi, walked towards her. She had a zealous sheen to her eyes. She wrapped chubby fingers around the etheric prison and started pulling. Giada could now see the lines of the net. They wavered, translucent and glittering, every so often, in the light. Giada couldn't believe she hadn't spotted them before her entanglement. She'd been so focused on her desire to get back to Heaven and tell Michael what she'd learnt that she'd been careless. Now she was trapped. She shuddered as her thoughts ran amok with visions of what they could have done to Domenico. And what they planned to do to her.

Bongi pulled Giada down the hill towards a grove of trees on the outskirts of the village. They encountered one or two villagers along the way and Giada desperately called out. But alas, they couldn't hear her. Nor could they see her. Humans only had the subtlest awareness of angelic voices when they were praying or alone and free from distractions. When they went about their day to day lives, they were completely oblivious to her presence. The residents of Marula were no different. Villagers passed by, waving or tipping their head in greeting to the two girls. They were all completely blind to the spiritual reality that these were not ordinary teenagers but a demon and her acolyte.

As they neared the grove, Giada became more and more desperate. They were far enough away from the village that they wouldn't be disturbed and there was nobody else around. Tears pricked at her eyes and her breaths came out in ragged rasps. A faint breeze whistled over the lonely mountains. Giada wondered if the landscape had always looked as desolate as this.

Bongi started chanting and a magical golden chord appeared in her hands. She used this to tie the etheric net to a thick tree branch with Giada trapped inside. When she'd finished, she wiped the sweat from her brow and checked the knots were secure before standing back.

"Shall I get him now?"

Giada wondered who they were talking about.

"Yes. It's time," the demon girl replied.

Bongi closed her eyes and started moving her hands. A look of intense concentration was on her face. The air around them started to shift and change quality. A recognisable smell wafted by. It was honeysuckle, spring flowers and cut grass: the smell of Heaven. As Bongi's hands moved, a portal opened in front of her. Bright light streamed through the portal and Giada squinted. She saw a figure approaching. As her eyes got used to the light she recognised him. It was Luke. A rush of relief spread through her body at the sight of his handsome face.

"Luke!" she smiled and then her smile dropped as she saw his expression. His eyes were full of hate and malice. His lips were set in a thin line of contempt. He looked at her briefly, barely acknowledging her. Giada was taken aback by his brutal coldness. Realisation hit her all at once, like a punch to the gut.

He's not here for me. He's here for them.

"Darius," the demon girl began. *Who the hell is Darius?* Giada thought.

"As you can see, we've captured another angel."

Luke or Darius or whoever he was put his hands on his hips and studied Giada. "She's still a trainee. Her essence won't be as strong as Domenico's was, but it will have to do for now."

Domenico! So, they *were* responsible for his disappearance....and his death? What was her 'essence'? The cold, clammy hand of dread worked its way up Giada's spine and clawed at her throat. She began to hyperventilate. Whatever this was, she doubted she'd come out of it alive. She thought of her little brother, Roberto. She'd only just got to really know him and now she was going to die. Maybe she could still talk some sense into the boy she'd formerly known as Luke?

"Luke, please. Don't do this."

Luke sneered at her. "You still don't get it. Not very bright are you? I am not Luke."

"Who are you then?"

"I'm his twin brother, Darius."

Giada's thoughts whirled, "Darius... his brother in Hell but how?..."

"As you're about to die, I'll allow you the courtesy of the truth. I was there when Luke got redeemed. I wasn't surprised that he got it first. He's always been weak. A regular goodie two shoes." He clenched his jaw and his eyes clouded over. "There was no way I was going to let him get to Heaven without me, so I knocked him out and jumped into the tunnel of light."

Giada's jaw dropped open. "And that worked?"

"Entrance to Heaven is linked to DNA. As we are identical twins, the system couldn't tell the difference."

Giada couldn't believe what she was hearing. If this was true it was a serious weakness in the system. Was this the first time this had happened or had there been other souls who'd had their place in Heaven stolen by their own twin?

Giada's attention was pulled back as Bongi started chanting. Watching in horror, Giada saw golden surgical instruments appear at her feet. Bongi held one of these up and it glinted in the sun. Giada's insides turned to liquid. It was a scalpel. The demon girl registered her fear and her eyes flashed with excitement. With a shock of disgust, Giada realised she was getting off on seeing her so scared. It was like Giada was back in Hell, surrounded by pain-inflicting addicted demons. In addition to the scalpel, there was also a golden bowl with engravings around the outside.

Bongi advanced on Giada but the demon girl held her back. "Allow me," she said simply. A look of manic joy spread across her face. Giada's eyes flicked from Bongi to the demon to Darius. She had to stall for time.

"Didn't you feel bad, stealing your brother's place? Even a demon must have some loyalty towards his own family."

"He would've done the same thing to me if the situation was reversed."

Giada very much doubted this. If that were the case he wouldn't have been redeemed.

Darius continued. "Anyway, if you're so worried about Luke, I'll give you some peace of mind. Your death will allow us to invite more of our comrades to Heaven. Someday soon I might even ask Luke to join us there - once we've taken over and the angels no longer run things."

Giada felt sick. "You're mad. You can't possibly kill enough angels to get all of Hell to Heaven."

"We don't need to. All we need are enough soldiers to stage a decent coup. There are plenty of God's army who are on our side too. Heaven is not as conflict-free as you've been led to believe.

Then once we get our hands on the spark of creation, it'll be game over."

As he spoke, Giada's thoughts raced, trying to think of a way she could get free. What could she lie to him about to get him to let her go or at least buy her some more time?

The demon girl yawned theatrically. "I'm bored. Time to die." She walked towards Giada with the scalpel held in her hand. Her eyes shone with delight.

Giada racked her brains.

Think, Giada. Think!

Then it came to her all at once. "How can you be sure that Luke isn't already in Heaven?"

The demon girl stopped walking and looked at Darius. *They do care about that* Giada thought with satisfaction.

Darius' face flinched slightly before he corrected it. "Nice try. He's in Hell, I saw him there recently."

Giada took a chance. "You're bluffing. I know you are because he's in Heaven."

The demon girl's face crinkled as she looked at Darius. "You lied to us." Her eyes blazed with anger.

"No, I didn't! She's lying, can't you see. She'd do anything to get out of this."

"Angels are terrible liars. If anyone around here is lying. It's you." The demon girl pointed the scalpel at Darius.

Giada felt like she was onto something, so she kept going. "I saw him at the caves of humility. He totally blanked me, I thought it was strange at the time. Now that I think about it. You two don't look exactly the same. I've always thought he has different moods but now I realise it's been two different people."

She was gambling on the assumption that identical twins felt flattered when they were told they looked different.

Everyone wants to believe they are special.

Darius faltered, his dark eyes flickering with confusion. Giada now realised the haunting, glassy quality of his eyes, which she'd previously found so beautiful, was due to the contact lenses he wore.

"The only way for him to be in Heaven would be if I'd been redeemed." A brief look of joy flitted across Darius' face and for a moment, Giada thought she'd got him. But then his features hardened. "Impossible. There is no way I'd be redeemed." He walked over to Giada and slapped her hard across the face. "Do you think we're stupid?" He turned around to the other two. "She's trying to divide and conquer. Trying to manipulate us. It's the oldest trick in the demon book. You picked up a lot in Hell, didn't you? Or perhaps you were always a filthy liar and never lost your skills."

Giada's eyes narrowed and she held her chin up, but inside she couldn't ignore the sting of his words. She'd tried her hardest to become a better person. She *was* better. She knew she was, otherwise, she wouldn't be in Heaven. But there was still a tiny part of her that worried she wasn't good enough. Like most demons, Darius knew how to hit where it hurt.

She snarled at him. "Heaven will never be yours. God will never allow it. You're living a fantasy."

Darius lunged forward and grabbed her by the chin. "God won't have any say in the matter. Once we take over we will cast Him out. We've never been more powerful than we are at this moment."

The demon girl rolled her eyes. "Oh, for the love of Satan! This is like watching the world's most boring production of King Lear. Can we stop talking now and get to the essence extraction?"

Darius dipped his head. "My apologies Asmodeus. You're right, let's get on with it."

Giada gulped as Asmodeus, the demon inhabiting the girl's body, walked towards her, grinning maniacally. She'd tried everything she could but now she was out of options. She was all alone and about to die. Again.

33

GIADA

Asmodeus was by Giada's throat in a second. She held the scalpel to her throat.

"You'll just feel a slight prick..." she laughed, "...just kidding, I'm going to cut your jugular." The tip of the scalpel touched Giada's skin. She felt nauseous. Again, she tried stalling for time.

"How... how can you cut me? I'm not fully physical when on Earth."

Asmodeus wasn't to be distracted. "It's an etheric scalpel, made specially for angels." She made a tiny incision, just breaking the skin on Giada's throat, without piercing the vein. The demon was going slowly, making it as painful as she could.

Searing pain lanced Giada's throat and her vision started to blur. The world spun. Silence descended on the grove and everything receded into the background. Giada's awareness was trained on the sharp blade against her neck. She detached from the world around her as her perception focused intently on her fear and imminent death.

Giada started to whimper. "Please don't kill me. Please, I'll do anything, I'll...." She didn't get to finish her sentence.

A sound like the far-away rumble of thunder from a distant storm punctuated the silence. Asmodeus removed the blade from her throat and turned to see what the noise was. Giada exhaled, relaxing her shoulders as she almost wept with relief. Whatever this was, it had just given her a temporary reprieve. Asmodeus still held the scalpel and Giada was still trapped in the etheric net but for now, she was alive.

A dark grey cloud rapidly approached the horizon. But there was something strange about the cloud. It was much darker than a cloud should be, and it moved in an odd fashion, as if it was comprised of lots of smaller clouds all moving at the same time. Giada narrowed her eyes and in the next instant, the cloud came into greater focus. It was not a cloud at all, but a great flock of black birds.

Within milliseconds, the flock was above them and the sky filled with crows. They came from every direction like a great black ocean, squawking and flapping. Asmodeus blinked and staggered back, rubbing her eye to dislodge the feather that had just got into it. Just as she shook her head and blinked, a large sloppy bird poo landed in her other eye. She cried out and dropped the scalpel.

The noise of the crows was deafening, and the sky darkened as the colossal flock blocked out the sun.

"What's happening? How are you doing this?" Darius snarled, jabbing his finger at Giada.

"I'm not doing anything," she replied.

He opened his mouth to speak again but in the next breath the entire flock of crows swooped down and attacked, as if controlled by an unseen force. They pecked at Darius and he swore and twirled, trying in vain to bat them away. They clawed at his face and neck, making micro tears in every exposed piece of his flesh.

Meanwhile Asmodeus had crouched down towards the floor and was swearing as she covered her head with both hands. Crows pecked at her hands and droplets of blood rolled down her wrists.

"Where did these birds come from?" She asked, in a tone of genuine bewilderment.

Her voice was now high pitched - younger sounding. And the quality of her eyes had changed. She no longer displayed the calculating gaze of an arch demon and Giada realised that the possessing demon, Asmodeus, had fled from her body to escape the attack of the birds.

Bongi had picked up a stick and was thrashing it around in the air to try and keep the crows off her but it was no use. There were too many of them and her flesh was getting just as bloody as the others.

Giada knew she wasn't doing this so who was? There was only one person she knew who could control animals like this: her brother Roberto. She turned her head for signs of him, but she couldn't see him anywhere.

Is he even able to control animals from Heaven?

Surely he couldn't be that powerful? But then her little brother continued to surprise her.

Darius strode over to her and grabbed her by the neck, momentarily ignoring the crows which continued to assault him. "I know you're doing this. Make it stop!" Flecks of spittle flew from his mouth and landed on her nose.

Giada narrowed her eyes and smiled at him. "If you untie me, I'll make it stop."

Darius gave a curt smile of contempt. "Nice try. I am not releasing you." He looked across at Bongi.

"Do a location spell to find out the source of this animal magic."

Bongi was still wildly thrashing with her stick. "I can't. I'm too distracted."

Giada chuckled. "Like I said, let me go and I'll make all this stop so you can go back to...what was it you were doing again? Oh yes, killing me." She flattened her voice and looked him dead in the eye.

Darius raged. "If you think a few birds will stop us, you've got another thing coming." His breathing came out in laboured rasps as he batted away as many crows as he could. For each crow that he swatted, another two or three appeared in its place. His skin was now a mass of torn flesh and the smell of blood filled the air. "Asmodeus!" Darius shouted. He looked over at the girl, but she was trembling and whimpering in a ball on the ground. Darius huffed and rolled his eyes. "Do I have to do everything myself?" Ignoring the birds which still attacked him, he strode over to retrieve the scalpel from the floor. He also picked up the metal bowl from where it had rolled, out of Asmodeus' hands. He walked over to Giada, his expression placid and clinical. "Now" he said as he reached the scalpel forward.

In the next moment a large baboon leapt through the undergrowth and launched itself at Darius, tackling him to the floor. The baboon pawed at him, as it let out a series of gibberish hoots. Then it sank its large canines into Darius' leg, and he cried out in pain, dropping both the scalpel and the bowl.

Giada heard Roberto's voice shout out. "Let her go."

She looked up and saw him standing on a nearby ridge overlooking the valley in which Giada was being held captive. Giada bit her lip and tasted blood. It took every ounce of her self-control to stop herself from calling out her brother's name. She didn't want to put him in more danger than he was already in. If they knew she cared about him, they would hurt him even more when they caught him. What was he doing here? How had he found her?

Go back to Heaven, Roberto. Please!

She knew that he couldn't hear her from under the etheric net, but she prayed anyway.

Darius was being savaged by the baboon. The animal was very strong and very large. They rolled around on the floor, Darius grunting as he tried to get the beast off him. Clouds of dust filled the air and Giada coughed and tasted grit.

"Get him!" Darius demanded in a voice of garbled strangulation. He carried on wrestling with the baboon, but Giada watched in dismay as Bongi opened a portal by her side and reappeared next to Roberto. She grabbed him and lifted him off the floor, with her strong, meaty hands.

Giada couldn't hear what was being said but she saw Bongi's lips moving rapidly as if she was muttering something. Giada gasped as she realised that the sangoma was incanting a spell. Bongi's lips stopped moving and Roberto collapsed by her side. As soon as he was unconscious, the crows stopped their assault. They flew off haphazardly in opposite directions. The baboon jumped off Darius. It shook its head as if waking up then it picked its nose, scratched its head and ran off.

Bongi moved her hands around and Giada saw another etheric net glinting in the sunshine. She picked up Roberto in the net and slung him over her back. Walking over to where Giada was held, she started muttering again. Another golden chord appeared in her hands. Bongi used this to secure Roberto to the same tree as Giada.

"Are you okay boss?" she said, walking over to Darius. "I can heal that." She bent down to lightly touch his leg.

He slapped her hand away, clicking his tongue. "I don't need healing. I'm a demon, you idiot. I regenerate." Giada looked at his leg. The blood was already coagulating. Within the next few minutes the wound would completely disappear. Something about this thought struck Giada. Demons normally couldn't regenerate on Earth. Marula must be a twilight zone now. It made sense; she'd learnt in Redemption School that twilight zones were created when a demon incarnated on Earth. Naledi's student hosting a demon, must have caused a weakening of the etheric boundary between Hell and Earth. It explained how demons had been able to come here and abduct people in the first place. But how had they got between here and Joang? Could they have used magic to travel at super speed, in order to get there before they started to disintegrate? Or perhaps Ratu had devised a technological solution? Or maybe Bongi had breached portals to get them there? Giada looked back at Darius who now stood up and was dusting himself down. She couldn't waste time thinking about this now. She had to focus on freeing herself and Roberto.

Giada studied Bongi's reaction at being scolded by Darius. The girl's eyes flashed, and her jaw moved as if she was gritting her teeth.

She doesn't like taking orders. She'd love to be the one in charge.

Giada stored the information away in her mental rolodex of things she could use against her enemies. If Bongi didn't like being bossed around, what was in this for her? Why was she doing it? Darius' next comment answered the question for her.

"I expect you to pay more attention from now on. Or you can

forget about being the only breacher in Africa. If it wasn't for us, you wouldn't even be a breacher - or a sangoma!"

So Bongi's powers had come from demons! How had this exchange come about? Was it a simple soul transaction, much like how Motsumi had got his sangoma powers? Or was it something else?

Giada looked over at Roberto. He mumbled slightly as he started to stir. "What's going on? Giada?...." He woke up and looked at her, his eyes clouded with confusion. Then he looked from left to right, taking in the scene around them and his expression shifted to anger. He struggled and twisted, trying to get free from his binds. "Let us go. What have you done to us?"

Darius grinned at him. "How kind of you to join us. Now we can extract the essence of two heavenly beings instead of just one."

"What do you mean 'essence'?" Roberto asked.

Darius ignored him. "I'll do it myself this time. I don't want anyone else messing it up."

Roberto looked at Giada and reached for her hand. She took it and gave his hand a squeeze. He half-smiled at her. Even in his last moments, he was still the most amazing kid she'd ever known. So brave. And the way he'd fought for her...yet again she couldn't believe how lucky she was to have a brother like him. Even if they were both about to die here, at least they were together.

"How did you find me?" she asked under her breath.

"I followed you. I know you've been a bit down recently. I could tell there was something going on with you and I guessed that you were in some kind of trouble."

"But you never should've come here. Now we'll both die."

Roberto looked down at the floor and then back at her. "It's okay. Whatever happens, I accept my fate. I've lived a good life on Earth and a good life in Heaven. I trust God's plan for me."

Giada wished she could be as calm about the situation as he was, but she couldn't. She didn't want to die. Not here, not now and certainly not at the hands of demons.

She looked over at Darius and was filled with disgust that she'd ever found him attractive. Where she'd once seen soulful eyes, she now saw eyes full of malice and spite. Where she'd once swooned over floppy brown hair, she now saw the lank, dishevelled tresses of a mass murderer. He'd actually told her who he was, when they'd had their date together. He'd told her he was the type of guy people crossed the street to avoid. Someone who wouldn't hesitate to murder others for his own gain. Why hadn't she listened? She'd been so bowled over by his 'good looks'. He wasn't even that good looking! Now, all of his hot and cold behaviour made sense. He'd been bait, softening her up so that she'd trust him enough to walk straight into his angelic extraction trap. And she'd fallen for it!

Giada looked at Asmodeus. She was standing up and dusting herself off. A moment ago, it had seemed like the human girl had taken back control of her body. Giada felt a glimmer of hope that maybe this was still the case. When Asmodeus raised her head, and looked at her, any hope Giada had felt was extinguished. Where a few moments ago she'd been a quivering wreck, now she folded her arms and cocked her head to one side. Her lips were set in a hard line and her eyes were steelier than a shark's. There could be little doubt that Asmodeus was inhabiting the body once more.

Giada tried her last hope. She looked at the older girl. "Bongi - that's your name isn't it?"

"And what if it is?" Bongi scowled as she looked at her.

"I'm friends with your teacher, Naledi. She's told me all about you." Giada smiled kindly at her. "She's very proud of you. She told me you're her best student."

Bongi's expression momentarily softened but then she clenched her jaw. "So what?" she replied.

"Why are you taking orders from them? You're better than them. You're obviously a natural leader. Why are you letting them push you around?" Giada felt a little sick at the knowledge she was using a classic 'Countess-style' manipulation technique. But she had to get free. Not only for herself and her brother, but also to warn Naledi. Bongi was bad news and who knows how much damage she'd already done to Naledi's students or what else she was planning to do in the future. Maybe the other student had only hosted the demon because of Bongi's influence?

Darius crouched down to pick up the scalpel and bowl again. "Don't answer her Bongi. In fact, ignore her completely. She's trying to manipulate you."

Bongi looked Giada in the eye. She didn't say anything, but Giada saw sadness and regret in her expression. Whatever deal Bongi had made, it was clear to Giada that Naledi's student now wished she hadn't. Giada sensed that this girl was in way over her head and was just as trapped as Giada was.

As she studied Bongi, a thought occurred to her. Asmodeus had said that angels couldn't hear her. She'd also said that Naledi was too far away. Did that mean humans who were closer could hear her? She thought back to her time in Hell. As nightmarish as it had been, she had learnt some valuable skills whilst there. The Countess had told her she was a talented sin-baiter. Could she use this skill now? It was worth a try. Relaxing her thoughts, she concentrated on Bongi's mind. She instantly heard the familiar internal chatter of human ego. She listened for a few moments to get a feel for the way in which Bongi spoke to herself and then she waited until an opportune moment. A moment of doubt. She didn't have to wait long. As she'd suspected, Bongi's mind was a sea of turmoil.

This doesn't feel right. I never should've got involved with this in the first place Bongi told herself. And Giada added,

That angel is right. Why am I taking orders from them?

Then Giada waited and listened for evidence the idea had taken root. She was delighted to hear Bongi follow on with her own thought.

I'm already a breacher, I don't need these idiots anymore. And Giada added,

If I switch sides now and help the angels, they might agree not to tell anyone. I'll be a hero, and nobody will ever know I got my powers from demons.

Again, Giada waited and again she heard Bongi expand upon the idea.

It's the perfect solution. Maybe I won't even have to go to Hell when I die. All I need to do is loosen the etheric bonds a bit. I could pretend to trip nearby and then do it as I'm getting up.

Giada chewed her lip and widened her eyes. It was important that she maintained the illusion of being terrified even though inside she glowed with triumph. She daren't even communicate to Roberto what she had done. She couldn't risk giving the game away. In any case, perhaps she'd left it too late. Darius was advancing towards them with the scalpel in one hand and the bowl in the other. Giada looked at Roberto then back at Darius. She wanted to beg him to do her first. She couldn't bear the thought of losing Roberto again. But if she did that, he might guess that she had an escape plan. So, she kept quiet. Her breathing increased as Darius was almost upon them.

Bongi stepped in front of him. "Let me just check the restraints." She walked to the etheric nets, pulled on the ropes and nodded at Darius. "They're fine."

Giada had to stop her mouth from dropping open. Why hadn't Bongi loosened the bonds as she'd been planning? Had she had a change of heart? Giada could try again but they were out of time now. Darius was seconds away from cutting their throats.

34

GIADA

Darius grinned as he approached Roberto. He'd guessed that he would get extra pleasure from watching the pain Giada experienced at seeing her brother die. She cursed herself. She must not have hidden her feelings for her brother as well as she'd thought. Giada looked at Roberto and felt tears prick at her eyes. She never should've followed Bronwen. She should've gone to tell Michael; the minute she knew Bronwen was a demon. It had been stupid of her to believe that Michael could ever be involved in a demon coup. Now she'd have to watch Roberto die. Again. But this time she was powerless to stop it. She looked down, unable to bear it.

All at once she felt the rushing of wind and heard a familiar baritone African voice call out.

"Cease and desist. Or meet your doom!"

It was Motsumi! And behind him was the Chancellor and her friends from Sinners Anonymous. Giada's jaw dropped open as exhilaration tingled through her body. A familiar eggy smell wafted through the air. It was a smell that used to disgust her but now she'd never felt more relieved at its presence. The sulphurous smell of Hell meant that she was saved! She grinned and waved at Aaron, Susan and Maureen – she'd never been happier to see them.

Darius shouted. "Go back to Hell. This doesn't concern you."

The Chancellor's face went scarlet and steam started pouring out of his ears. "How dare you. You insolent little pipsqueak. It most certainly does concern me. I don't know who you are, but I am the Chancellor, currently governing the Seventh Circle. And I am not about to allow a demon uprising on *my* watch!"

Darius and Asmodeus looked at each other, confusion on their faces. "What are you, some kind of hippy?" Darius asked.

The Chancellor's jaw clenched, and he blinked, his eye twitching as he struggled to stay calm. "What I am, *boy*, is a conservative. Hell is for demons. Heaven is for angels and never the two should meet. What you are attempting here is an *abomination*!" He thundered the last word, spittle shooting out of his mouth. "Stop this at once or we will stop it for you."

Asmodeus looked at Darius, "This is absurd. They don't have the power to stop us."

"Don't we?" Motsumi answered, curling up half his mouth as he raised one eyebrow. Motsumi didn't wait for a response. He strode forward, red eyes blazing with fury. As he walked, Giada saw his lips moving. A whirlwind stirred at her left and as she turned her head, she saw another portal opening. Out of it came Lerato, Tau and Naledi. Naledi rose up into the air, her body becoming huge as she lifted her hands. She pushed one hand forward and a giant lightning bolt shot out of her palm, hitting Darius square in the chest. He flew through the air backwards, landing in the long grass with a thud. He groaned and rolled around on his back, his body smoking slightly.

"That was a warning," Naledi said. "The next one will be a kill shot."

Darius sat up, panting, one hand clutching his chest. Naledi raised her other hand.

A look of fear flashed across his face. "Wait!" He put his hands up. "If you kill me, you'll never find out when the coup will take place. Or who else is involved."

Motsumi and the Chancellor exchanged a look. "Just what I'd

expect from a treacherous worm like you," said Motsumi. "The first sign of any danger to yourself and you offer up your co-conspirators."

Asmodeus rounded on Darius, hands on her hips as her eyes blazed. "I'll kill you myself before I let you divulge our plans." She pounced on him and his chest thudded back to the floor. Straddling him, she pressed both her thumbs into his eyes in an effort to gouge them out. It was a rash move. The diminutive female body Asmodeus was hosting was no match for Darius' superior size and he easily rolled her over. They wrestled for a moment or two on the floor, Asmodeus grunting with the effort.

Naledi flew over to where Giada and Roberto were held and waved her hands over the etheric nets. Immediate relief rushed over Giada's body as her bonds disappeared and she was freed. She gathered Roberto up into a hug and swung him around in the air. Then she put him down and held him back at arm's length, smiling at him. He smiled back at her sweetly.

Meanwhile, Bongi was shuffling sideways, in an effort to be inconspicuous. Giada spotted her. "She's getting away!" she yelled, pointing at her.

Naledi flew up and waved her hands over Bongi. An etheric cage instantly enclosed her, trapping her inside.

Maureen and Susan were watching the fight between Asmodeus and Darius as if it was their afternoon's equivalent of reality TV. Maureen held up her fists, miming the fight, as she ducked and twitched, her double chins wobbling. "Yeah! Knee him in the balls!" She shouted.

Giada strongly suspected that Maureen had been a fan of the WWE when she'd been alive.

"Whose side are you on here?" Susan asked, putting one hand on her hip.

"I'm just hoping they go the distance." Maureen unashamedly replied.

"Are you okay?" Naledi asked, looking from Giada to Roberto.

Giada felt her neck, the incision was still there but angelic beings healed quickly, and she could feel it was already closing up. "I think so. Thank God you came. But how did you know?"

"Motsumi called for us."

"How did he know?"

"I'm not sure. Let's ask him later." Naledi looked back at Darius and Asmodeus. Predictably, Darius had won the fight. He wrenched Asmodeus to standing, holding the girl's wrists, tightly in both hands.

"This is an outrage," she spat. "I'm a centuries old demon and I outrank every single one of you." She looked at the group of damned souls, clustered around Motsumi. "You should be falling on your knees and begging me for mercy, you should be...gaarrgh!" She screamed, crashing to the floor like felled timber, as Naledi shot another lightning bolt from her palm.

The girl lay on the floor, not moving. Her eyes were closed.

"Is she dead?" Giada asked Naledi.

"No. I didn't want to kill her, just damage her body enough that the inhabiting demon would go back to Hell. Thato is one of my best students."

Giada couldn't believe what she was hearing. "But she allowed a demon to take residence in her body?"

Naledi shook her head. "I don't think so. Just before I left for Joang, I had a talk with her. She'd been hanging around with some shady local boys who have a reputation for taking drugs. I think she took drugs before engaging in spiritual practice. I warned her something like this might happen, but she clearly didn't listen."

As they were talking, Darius spotted his opportunity and started sprinting towards the portal, back to Hell.

"Oh no you don't," Motsumi said. His lips moved and a wall of granite sprang up in front of Darius. The demon boy smacked into it at full force, knocking himself unconscious.

Motsumi walked over to Darius and muttered under his breath. An etheric net sparkled in his hands, translucent in the sun. He cast the net over Darius and closed it shut, securing it against the same tree Giada had been held at minutes before. Then he did the same to

Thato. "We can't risk it. Asmodeus could take her body back the minute she's conscious." He said.

"You're right, it's best to be cautious. I'll have to do months of cleansing rituals to free her from this possession completely." Naledi looked at Thato and sighed, her face marked by disappointment.

Giada walked over to her Sinners Anonymous friends. "It's good to see you guys again!"

"Likewise!" Aaron beamed at her. "We didn't contribute much to the fight but when we heard that you were in trouble, we wanted to offer what we could."

Motsumi walked over. "Your presence was important as a backup. We didn't know just how many demons we would find here."

Naledi looked at Motsumi quizzically. "How did you know to come here anyway?"

"You asked me to find out whatever I could about Domenico and the plot to overthrow Heaven, remember?"

"Ah yes."

"As I said before, I'm very well connected in Hell now. My network of spies delivered enough information for me to find a breacher who they had been working with in the Third Circle of Hell."

"Bongi?"

"No, this was an Asian girl. Anyway, after a short torture session, led by Mephistopheles, she was ready to tell us anything we wanted to know. Her and Bongi, in tandem, have been opening portals to allow demons through to Earth and Heaven. They used cloaking spells to move the humans between Marula and Joang, without being seen. They drained Domenico of all his angelic essence and that allowed demons to pass through the heavenly gates, and boundary, undetected. We forced the breacher to open a portal for us to get here."

Giada asked. "So, does that mean that Domenico is dead?"

Motsumi nodded. "I'm afraid so."

Giada looked at Naledi. "You know, Bongi never was a real sangoma. She gained all her powers via her alliance with demons."

Naledi scratched her head, frowning. "But demons can't give her the power to breach." She walked over to Bongi's cage. "How did you get your breaching powers Bongi, tell us or you die."

Giada was impressed. Naledi was considerably less kind-hearted than she had been before. Either that or her lying skills had improved a lot.

Bongi burst into tears. "It wasn't my fault. Asmodeus used me!"

Motsumi was having none of it. "A demon can't make you do something you don't want to do."

Bongi's breath came out in blubbering shudders. "She told me I would be the most powerful sangoma who had ever lived. She lied to me!" She sank down and sobbed, covering her face with her hands.

Motsumi looked like his patience was wearing thin. "You're not answering the question. How did you get your breaching powers?"

"I was an acolyte of Asmodeus. She was in an alliance with Ratu. Once Asmodeus had inhabited Thato's body, the etheric boundary was temporarily weakened enough for Ratu to pass through it. Ratu used his machine to transfer the powers from another breacher. A boy in Durban, who had just come into his powers. After he did it on me, he couldn't get it to work again. It drove him mad, trying to figure out what the glitch could be."

Naledi and Lerato exchanged a strange look that Giada couldn't quite interpret.

What was that about? She wondered, but she didn't say anything or intrude upon their private thoughts.

"What are you going to do to me?" Bongi sniffed.

Motsumi looked at the Chancellor then back at Bongi. "Nothing. You've had a lucky escape. Ratu is dead, Asmodeus will be repelled by Naledi's cleansing practices. If I were you, I'd spend the rest of my life praying fervently and doing good works and with any luck, you may still make it to Heaven when you die."

This didn't sit well with Giada. "But she's still a breacher, and a sangoma? Doesn't that make her dangerous?"

At that moment the sky filled with light as archangel Michael descended from Heaven. Holding his sword of righteousness aloft. It flashed with a brilliance that momentarily hurt Giada's eyes and she blinked rapidly.

Settling to hover, just above the ground, he beamed at them. "What is given with one hand; can be taken away with another."

"Huh?" Giada said.

Michael laughed. "I can take away Bongi's sangoma powers. I can also take away her breacher power and transfer it back to the boy she stole it from."

"Can you?" Naledi and Lerato both said in unison.

"Yes, so I can do the same for you too if you want?" His eyes twinkled. Giada's eyes widened as she guessed what had happened. Ratu's attempt at the transfer of power in Joang had been successful. Naledi was no longer a breacher: Lerato was.

Naledi looked at Lerato, a pensive look on her face, then she looked down at the ground.

Michael looked at Motsumi and the other damned souls. Making eye contact with the Chancellor, he dipped his head, in what looked to be a respectful manner. "Chancellor," he said.

"Michael," the Chancellor replied, smiling politely.

"Wait - you two know each other?" Giada asked.

Michael looked slightly uncomfortable. "There are certain times when it makes sense to cooperate with Hell and in those instances, we go to the Chancellor."

Giada's mouth dropped open. Now it all made sense. Why the Chancellor had books in his collection that hinted at rebellion. Why he'd been so against the Countess' plot to put demons on Earth. He wasn't just a conservative, he was a collaborator! She wondered why he hadn't yet been redeemed. Maybe he liked it in Hell after all. Or maybe he had chosen to stay so that he could help out Heaven from time to time.

Michael walked over to Bongi. He reached his sword through the cage and touched her lightly. She cried out in pain and then sank to the floor, unconscious.

Lerato looked at her. "That looked like it hurt her as much as it had us."

Michael spoke. "When she awakes, she'll be a normal human again. Now - you two next?"

35

NALEDI/GIADA

Michael reached his sword forward but before it touched Naledi, she held her hands up and backed away. "Whoa, wait a minute. I've been giving this a lot of thought and I've decided..." She took a deep breath and turned to Lerato. "Lerato, how would you feel about keeping the breacher powers?"

Lerato's face lit up then dropped again. "Do you really mean that? I mean, are you sure?" Her shoulders were up near her ears.

Naledi nodded.

"I'd like that a lot." Lerato replied, relaxing her body.

"Are you sure?" Naledi asked. "You know what a big commitment it is."

Lerato nodded, her expression serious. "I know."

Naledi still wasn't reassured. "It's just that, I don't want to force it on you and..."

"Naledi stop. I've always envied your abilities. Truth be told, I've always thought they had been given to the wrong person. I'm the adventurous one. I'm the risk-taker, the thrill-seeker, the heart-breaker, the soul-shaker, the money-maker...."

Naledi interrupted. "It's not just about having fun you know!"

"I know it isn't." Lerato exhaled loudly. "I know I'm not explaining myself very well." She looked up at the sky then back at Naledi. "I've always felt I should be with you on all these dangerous missions. Now that you still have your sangoma powers, and I have breacher powers, we can be a team. A dream team - we'll be unstoppable!" Her eyes twinkled.

Naledi smiled at her friend. She was right. The worst thing about Naledi's powers had always been the loneliness. The time that she'd been trapped in Hell, slowly turning into a demon, had been the worst. She'd missed her friends so much. In order to save Giada and Roberto, she'd taken a risk and entered the portal with Lerato. In doing this, she'd learnt that she was now a realm walker, like Tau. That meant she could go with Lerato and help her wherever and whenever she was needed but she didn't have to be the one leading the operation. It was perfect. Perhaps she could even finally settle down with Tau.

He walked over to her now, flashing white teeth, as he delivered a devastating smile. "Are you sure this is what you want?" He said, as he put his arm around her shoulder.

"I've never been more sure." Naledi answered.

Michael spoke. "It doesn't have to be so final. You can change your mind at any time. Just call for me and I'll come."

Naledi nodded. "Alright. But I won't change my mind."

Tau chuckled. "Lerato might change *her* mind when she realises what a tough gig this is."

"Never!" Lerato shouted, joining him in laughter. "Come on, we better get back and rescue Kabelo from Dineo and Puleng." She continued. "I'm sure he's already suffered enough."

Naledi grinned. "You're right." She turned to Michael. "What are you going to do about him?" She cocked her head towards Darius.

"We have a facility at a secret location on Earth where we take demons for telepathic extraction. The procedure is more difficult than it is for angels and sadly it's not without pain."

"Sadly?" Giada echoed incredulously.

"I have compassion for all God's creatures, even those residing in Hell, who harbour malice in their hearts. Darius may still achieve redemption someday, if he wants to." He looked back at Naledi. "Anyway, we'll soon find out who the other conspirators are in the planned coup. We'll stamp it out before it's begun."

Giada looked at Michael. "Who told you about the coup?"

"Naledi prayed for my assistance. Then on my way here I telepathically connected with what was going on. I heard everything."

Giada frowned. "Did you hear what happened to Domenico?"

Michael's expression grew dark. "I did. He is dead." He sighed and rubbed his temples. "But at least we know now. And we never would've found out had it not been for your excellent work, Giada. The fact that you also thwarted a demon coup only makes me more certain that you belong on my team. I knew you would succeed. Come back to my office with me and we'll talk more about the details of your angelic graduation."

Naledi looked at Bongi and Thato sadly before looking back at Motsumi. "It's my fault. I should've been able to sense that Bongi was lying to me."

"No. Don't doubt your skills. Demons use powerful dark magic to cover their tracks. You know that." Motsumi replied.

Naledi sighed. She knew he was right, but she still felt responsible. "I'll take them both home for cleansing. Bongi should be good to go in a day or two but Thato will need a lot longer." She shook her head sadly. "Why didn't the silly girl listen to me? None of this would've happened if she had."

"She's very young and impressionable. I'm sure she will have learnt her lesson after this." Tau said.

"I hope so but it's kind of put me off taking any more students who are that young again."

Motsumi bristled. "Are you suggesting defying the ancestors? That's even more dangerous than risking a drug taking student who gets possessed by a demon."

Naledi sighed. "I guess you're right."

She smiled at him knowingly. "It's not easy, this teaching thing, is it?"

"No. It is not." Motsumi replied, smiling at her warmly.

Giada sat in the sunshine, on a stage in front of an arena of heavenly souls. Her mother and Roberto sat in the front row, beaming at her. Archangel Gabriel was delivering the welcoming speech for the Redemption School graduation ceremony. Giada sat deep in thought. Two weeks had passed since the battle with Asmodeus and Darius. Michael had officially offered her a place on his team, and she'd accepted. When this graduation ceremony was over, she'd be a full angel, on the path to becoming an espionage archangel one day. In spite of all her self-doubts, she belonged here.

She frowned as a wave of guilt washed over her: Bronwen had been sent back to Hell. Even though Giada had learnt that Bronwen had been using her, Giada had still tried to petition on her behalf. She understood how desperate life in Hell could make a soul. But Michael had reminded her that there was a purpose to redemption. No matter how badly Bronwen wanted to be here, she had to work on herself and learn what she needed to learn. She'd get redeemed one day and Giada would still be here. Time passed more quickly in Heaven. Soon, Bronwen would be back and this time, there wouldn't be any secrets between them.

There had been a huge scandal when all the conspirators were unearthed. The biggest news, from Giada's perspective, had been that Rika and her friends were all demons! It totally made sense and Giada was so relieved to see the back of them as they were sent packing.

"Giada Cantinelli," Gabi said, as she turned to look at her. The crowd erupted in applause, bringing Giada's thoughts swiftly back into the arena. She stood up to collect her certificate. Kneeling down at Gabi's feet, the archangel touched her forehead. Giada felt her back itching. She knew what was happening. She'd seen it on the graduates who'd come before her.

Large, feathery, white wings sprouted out of her back, breaking through the fabric of her dress. Giada flexed her rear shoulder muscles and the wings beat, causing a gust of wind to pass over the crowd. She heard whoops and cheers from her mother and Roberto.

"Give them a try!" Her mother shouted out.

Giada looked up at Gabi and the archangel gave her a nod of approval. Giada took to the sky, soaring through the clouds. Her whole body tingled with happiness. She was now a full angel, completely accepted and with a bright future ahead of her.

After a few rounds of the arena, she flew down to the ground, landing lightly back onto the stage. Scooping her certificate up, she walked down the steps at the side of the stage to join the other newly graduated angels.

One of the helper angels handed her a bouquet of flowers. White orchids - her favourite. Music tinkled softly around them and through it, Giada heard a deep voice behind her say. "I hope you'll give me the pleasure of the first dance later?" Giada's smile dropped. Her stomach clenched with fear as she recognised the voice.

It couldn't be?

She spun round, feeling faint. A boy who looked exactly like Darius stood in front of her. Except he didn't look exactly like Darius. Where Darius' eyes had been cold and heartless. This boy's eyes twinkled with warmth and generosity. Like Darius, his hair was dark but unlike Darius, it was cut short all around, defining his sharp cheekbones even more. Giada relaxed slightly.

The boy stuck his hand out. "Hi, I'm Luke. The real Luke."

Giada smiled and took his hand. "Pleased to meet you." Then her smile dropped again. "Wait, you're not actually Darius, pretending to be Luke, are you?" *He could've just had a haircut.*

Luke laughed. "No. Not this time. The Chancellor made an agreement with Michael to keep Darius imprisoned in Mephistopheles dungeon for the next thousand years. That ought to give him enough time to come to his senses."

"I hope so" Giada replied.

"Then I got redeemed - again. Only this time, there was no thieving twin brother, to knock me out and take my place."

Giada fluttered her eyelashes at him, giving him what she hoped was her prettiest smile. "Welcome to Heaven."

"Thanks. It would be great to have someone to show me around, before I start Redemption School. Michael suggested you might have time in between your assignments with him?"

"Oh, he did, did he?" Giada half smiled. Michael was not as all-work-and-no-play as she'd thought. She also suspected Gabi's hand in this. She looked to the stage and caught the archangel's golden eyes twinkling at her knowingly. Gabi must've always known Giada had a crush on Luke. It had probably been obvious to anyone with eyes. Giada didn't care now though. Nothing could ruin this day. She was alive. She was an angel and now she had a handsome boy who actually wanted to spend time with her.

Heaven isn't so bad after all.

~

Did you enjoy this book? If so, please write a review on the store front of your choice and Goodreads now and tell all your friends about it.

If you want to stay updated about my latest book releases, join my VIP list! Visit www.jalihenry.com, enter your email address and you'll be the first to know when the next book is released. I'll also email you with exclusive offers of giveaways and promotional deals.

Please come and join my facebook reader group https://www.facebook.com/groups/3128187757251090
Or follow me on Instagram https://www.instagram.com/jalihenry/
Or on TikTok @jalihenryreadsfantasy
Or on Twitter @jalihenry

ALSO BY JALI HENRY

Cursed Charm, Arcane Witches #1 (New Adult Dark Urban Fantasy)

"He's had centuries to master this game and he is very, very good at it..."

One minute I'm a regular Londoner – overworked, underpaid and living in a flat the size of a shoe box. The next minute I'm doing magic and hunting vampires. You see, it turns out that I'm an arcane witch. Never heard of them? Neither had I until I got attacked by a vampire while trying to make a food delivery. Ok, that wasn't all bad. It did get me through the doors of the sexiest doctor this side of the Thames. The trouble is he's hiding something. I know it's something BIG but I just can't work out what it is...

Now the other arcane witches want me to join their crusade. They say if we don't hunt vampires to extinction, the blood-suckers will take over the world, turning humans into cattle. I tell those crazy witches to get lost, but that's a mistake. The vampires know about me. They know that I'm special and they won't stop until I'm dead.

I soon find myself locked in a battle of wits against the most devious vampire in existence. I'm in way over my head, but the biggest fight may be the one for my own soul...

For fans of Annette Marie, Linsey Hall and BR Kingsolver. If you love sassy heroines, villains you love to hate and unputdownable chapters, you'll love this fast-paced urban fantasy book.

Content: Contains language, violence and mild steam.

Lightning Source UK Ltd.
Milton Keynes UK
UKHW010114031121
393296UK00001B/246